The Farmer Stands Alone

By

Bill E. Schultz

First in the Derry-O Mystery Series

Chapter One

"The End"

New York, New York

The courtroom became suddenly quiet. Oh, it had been quiet before. The white-haired judge had seen to that. He had used a sullen glare directed at the occupants behind the dark-stained mahogany desk. Behind that desk sat the defendant in his three-piece suit, gold watch bob barely visible. The accused sported a pencil thin mustache the ends of which he routinely and with great aplomb twirled. The ends became a twisted curl that framed the white teeth that readily came forth. The teeth shown brightly, not in a smile but, in a smirk. He had been talking, smirking, and putting on an air of confidence that fooled no one. His attitude had changed abruptly when the courtroom became especially quiet and he realized the judge was staring at him.

The new quiet of the courtroom was one that was born not on fear of what the judge would say or do. It was a quiet born of anticipation. Like the quiet just before the 151st drip from a faucet that has been dripping for the last hour when you've been trying to get to sleep, hoping that slumber would come before the next drip, but it never does. Like the quiet in a marriage bed following an argument between husband and wife, when neither dares breathe for fear even a breath will send a signal of repentance or of indifference. Like the quiet immediately after an accident involving two speeding cars, when both engines stop and the air is being gathered up for an explosion.

"Has the jury reached a verdict?"

"We have your honor."

"In the matter of the state of New York versus Joseph P. Titaglio we find the defendant guilty..."

The rest of the 12 counts are read but no one pays attention. Reporters have already left the room; grabbing forbidden cell phones, speed dialing as they go.

Titaglio looks slowly around the room. He ignores the hand of his attorney on his arm, which was silently sending a message to turn and face the judge. Titaglio is searching for his quarry, the traitor that set him up; the gutless one who had to disguise his voice and hide behind a screen. But Titaglio knew who he was.

Titaglio wasn't a smart man. He wasn't much of a planner. He had learned that success came to him when he was able to visualize what success would look like. As he searched the courtroom he had a vision of his next triumph – what he would do with Elvis Anderson.

It was a vision of what was left of Mr. Anderson hanging on a meat hook being stripped of skin. Then with great care, Mr. Anderson would go piece-by-piece into the grinder. Titaglio envisioned a barbecue in his back yard where he would be surrounded by his faithful and they would be enjoying the unique flavor of a Titaglio hamburger. Yes, Joey "Tags" Titaglio vowed he would taste the flesh of that Benedict Arnold. He would eat him rare. He had done it before with his enemies. This one would be no different.

Washington D.C.

"Chief, we can't find E.Z." reported the clean-shaven man dressed in a blue

sports coat and gray slacks.

"What do you mean? He was supposed to report back to Washington yesterday."

"He never showed. Noble and Barnes checked at the hotel he was scheduled to stay at. They manager said he checked in, but there was no sign that his room was even slept in."

"Any sign of a struggle?"

"No. Not that they could see."

"Get on it. If Titaglio gets him, we'll never see him again."

New York, New York.

One of the men, who had been sitting in the gallery the day before, felt the vibration of his phone before he heard the Star Spangled Banner ring tone that told him that his FBI contact was calling.

The man said, "You got him, bookman?"

"No, it wasn't us. When we got there, he was gone."

A raised voice can be heard.

"Hold on, you didn't pay us to do anything more than tell you what room he was in."

The man in New York set down the phone, and turned to the other person sitting in the room.

"He's gone."

"Joey ain't going to be happy about that."

"We'll find him. He ain't that smart."

Chapter Two

"The Days of Their Lives"

Paul Banion – Day One:

The alarm woke me up. I stared at the red, digital numbers and mumbled a prayer of thanksgiving. The *alarm* woke me up.

Not gunfire. Not the breath of a would-be assassin as he strangled me. Not "Tags'" Rottweiler chomping on my face. Not some two-bit hooker sent to pleasure me and then stick a shiv in my back. Not the cold steel of a stiletto, drawn across my throat. Not the filthy liquid of some backwater swamp filling my lungs as I dropped to its murky bottom entombed with cement. Not a knotted rope snapping my neck after a fall of 10 feet.

The *alarm* woke me up. Not the nightmares that had yanked me from slumber every night for the last 6 months.

Maybe this *was* the first day of the rest of my life. Oh, how trite. But trite can be good. Breathing can be good. Life can be good.

I rolled out of bed and headed to the bathroom just down the hall. The ancient wooden floors creaked as I made my way in the dark to the second door on the right. Just inside the wooden frame door was the old style push button light switch. It activated the bare bulb hanging in the middle of the room. The motion of the door opening sent that bulb rocking back and forth, causing shadows in the corners to dance with each other in sensuously. A mouse was startled into hasty flight across the floor and up into the cupboard.

"I'll let you go this time, Mickey, but you better not let me catch you in here again."

I knew all too well what that mouse felt like. I just hoped the cats in my former life would never find me. If they did I was dead meat.

I splashed cold water on my face, and then grabbed the towel I'd bought at the Target in Hawks Hill the day before. It was part of a set and matched the new sheets and the shower curtain purchased in Fargo. Not that I cared that they matched, they just did. I had decided on the plane that the safest thing was to buy no more than one or two items at any one store. No sense in taking chances now.

I headed down the steps to the kitchen below. Still clothed only in my t-shirt and underwear, my feet felt the tread of the rubber stair liner as I descended the steps. It didn't feel quite right walking around with so little clothing, but the one pair of jeans I brought with me had been splattered the night before and had been left in the entryway to dry out.

The automatic coffee maker purchased at the K-Mart in Hawks Hill had obviously started its assigned task, but the half full beaker and the lack of indicator light made me realize it had shut off prematurely. The coffee that was there was strong and pee-water warm. It took only a second to figure out that the plug-in had no power. One more thing that was going to have to be fixed.

"Smelled something when I woke up."

"I hope you're referring to the coffee," I said as I turned slowly to face a slightly distorted reflection of my own brown hair, blue eyes, and six foot two frame. Except this reflection was wearing a washed-out blue shirt, half-tucked into denim jeans with bright red suspenders setting off the various shades of blue denim that colored shirt and pants.

I resisted the urge to give him a hug, knowing that Ox never welcomed physical contact and emotional displays. His outstretched hand grasped mine and squeezed. I squeezed back.

"Ox, you ugly beast, how are you?"

"Fine."

Ox could be on fire and his reply would be "Fine". Ox seldom used sentences longer than five words. His philosophy was that every individual had a limited number of words they could use in a lifetime and there was no sense in wasting a single word when a smile, a handshake, or a stiff poke in the jaw spoke volumes.

"Tell me about the set-up," I squeaked, unsuccessful in my attempts to retrieve my hand from his iron grip.

Now might be the time for me to introduce myself to the occasional reader. For the past thirty-two years my name has been Elvis Zeus Anderson. My pre-baby boomer mother named me for her favorite entertainer and my Greek instructor father had chimed in with my middle name after his favorite mythological character.

"It's a name with character," my mother would tell me at least once a week.

"I don't need character. I need to get home from school without half the neighbor kids laughing at me."

Then Jack Forester moved next door and took a liking to me. We always looked more like brothers than I looked like my own brother, Apollo Everly. The Ox, as we called him, would walk home with us and no one else would even come close.

By the time I got to high school, I had won the battle with my mother and went by the initials E.Z. Not that it was much of an improvement, but by then I had started to catch up to Ox in size and stature, had learned a little Greco-Roman wrestling from my father, and had generally educated myself on manipulation, exploitation, and other skills required for leadership *or* the study of the law. I had arrived.

During those late grade school and junior high school years, Jack, Apollo, and I would spend at least a month to six weeks with my maternal grandparents in Wisconsin. They had a small dairy farm there and the three of us loved being on the farm. So much so that by the time we were in high school, Jack had found a part time job on a dairy farm not far from where we lived. That's where Jack really became Ox; the hard work agreeing with him as did the food the farmer's wife put on his plate three or four times a day.

Ox went to vocational school and became a licensed peace officer for Orange County. Through their education program, he completed his degree in criminal justice and was well on his way to a career in law enforcement.

I completed college in the requisite 4 years, with a 3.989 grade point average, entered law school, where I was less than stellar in my academic performance but more than adequate as a witness for whichever mock trial happened to be going on.

E.Z. Anderson became known as the witness to have on your side. I knew how to help the attorney who was examining me and how to cause shame and embarrassment during the cross-examination.

A recruiter for the Federal Bureau of Investigation observed my talent. Within thirty days of my graduation from law school, I had been enrolled at Quantico. It was much more exciting then spending the summer studying for the bar exam.

The next seven years are a story unto themselves, which I will share at a later date. For now it is enough to know that my name has been changed to Paul Banion.

As of yesterday, I am a dairy farmer in the heart of dairy country in West Central Minnesota and have every intention of living the rest of my life, one day at a time, milking cows, shoveling manure, feeding a few chickens, slopping some hogs, raising some Appaloosa horses, and dying of old age.

Shelley Robison – Day two thousand one hundred ninety-three.

"Six times 365 plus… 2 leap year days… plus today- 2,193 days of being Mrs. Mike Robison. How much more can I take?"

She ciphered the numbers in her mind's eye and projected them onto the ceiling. The number was one more than her calculations of the day before, her sixth anniversary. Married at 18 to her high school sweetheart and the captain of every team at Harmony High School, Shelley had thought life would be so much better by now.

A tear stole its way out of the corner of her eye, trailed a straight path to the little bump on her ear and, when joined by its brother, rolled around and into the ear canal. It was just like Mike to blow off such a special day. Not even a card.

Shelley lay in bed wanting the alarm to go off before Mike woke up. If he woke to the alarm he would be more apt to get out of bed. If he woke up before the alarm, there is no telling what he might want to do. And Shelley was not in the mood. Her recollection of their argument the night before caused the tears to increase their flow to a steady stream. Soon her nose plugged up and starting overflowing as well.

The light coming through the skylight caught her attention. She looked over at the alarm clock and realized that either it had never gone off, or Mike had turned it off. She hesitantly reached her left hand from its perch on her stomach over to the indentation in the mattress where Mike should have been. He wasn't there.

"Horsefeathers," she exploded, using the expletive her father had taught her as a child. She realized that she had overslept and would now be late for work.

A quick splash of lukewarm water, a swishing of her mouth with brush and paste, a cursory trip through her rich, blonde hair with her favorite comb, and she was ready to slip into the flowery dress she'd laid out the night before. The rope sandals were informal, but acceptable in mid-summer.

Shelley scooted down the steps, grabbed a bagel and a bottle of water on her way out to the car. She hoped Mike had fed her horse, let the dog out, and would take care of the chickens, but she didn't have time to worry about any of them right now. She'd have to call him later to remind him.

As she fired up the metallic gray Grand Prix, she was startled by a sharp report, reminiscent of hunting season, but that was three months off.

"Probably some kid shooting off a late fire-cracker," she surmised.

Ellie Carlson – Day 181

"Oh crap!" screeched Ellie.

A host of deputies poked their smiling and laughing faces around various nooks, crannies, and corners in the locker room. Several openly commented on the view, making remarks about the lovely vision facing them.

The sack of clothes Jim Barton had brought in from his daughter's wardrobe of "barn clothes" had obviously not seen a washing machine since the last time Jim and family had rounded up calves to castrate and dehorn them. But it wasn't the style that bothered Ellie or even the stench. It was the fact that the shirt was missing the top two buttons and her black lace bra looked woefully out of place under the plaid shirt.

"Eat your hearts out," teased the twenty-four year old Ellie as she turned her back and deftly slipped the bra off and down the sleeve of the manure stained shirt.

After six months as the rookie on the county sheriff's department, Ellie was used to the kidding and teasing she received. She'd known most of the guys since she was ten or eleven. At about that time her dad had retired from his lucrative private detective agency and returned to his home farm. No more than six months later he had been elected sheriff after the previous sheriff died in a collision with a tractor and hay rack. Sheriff Jimmy Johnson had been in hot pursuit of Oscar Woodly, town drunk of Crystal Lake.

Gregory Oscar Arnold Thomas Carlson had been blessed with three middle names and it had haunted him since his elementary school days when his cousin and classmate had announced that Gregory should henceforth be named GOAT. The nickname stuck and now appeared on the ballot as Gregory (GOAT) Carlson. He was facing election this fall for his 4th and, Ellie hoped, final term. Ellie knew she deserved her position as deputy, but she also knew she had to work twice as hard as anyone else and would have every junk duty there was for the next four years. Her dad was just that way – fair.

"Here, put on this hat," her dad said as he came into the locker room and tossed her his good luck Vikings cap, autographed by Warren Moon. "It'll bring you luck."

"Let's go," he hollered to the rest of the crew.

Ellie walked out the door and climbed into the cab of a 1 and ½ ton dually, Dodge Ram with an 18 foot, fifth wheel stock trailer hooked on behind. The diesel engine rolled to life and Ellie slipped it into gear as she adjusted the mirrors.

Thirty minutes and twenty-two miles later, she reached under her seat to make sure her Glock was in position. The turn signal announced a right turn onto one of the few remaining dirt roads in Maplewood County. She slowed way down so as not to kick up any telltale dust and to keep her cargo from choking on the fine powder left from gravel that was too dry.

As the big rig approached a grove of trees, Ellie slowed even more, then took a wide left hand turn into the driveway of the only farm on the dead end road. Blocking her way was a homemade, plank gate that was over six feet tall and had barbwire strung across the top. A sign warned those approaching that behind this barrier lurked danger in the form of dogs and an owner that was willing to part with bullets.

Ellie's rig slipped slightly off the main path and butted right up to the gate. She made several attempts to back up, but each attempt brought the fifth-wheel closer to the precipice that dropped into a 3-foot ditch. After five minutes, she climbed out of the cab, walked around the rig as far as she could, then back around the other way, kicking rocks in anger over the predicament she found herself in.

Three short blasts on the horn brought two large, barking dogs and a 14 or 15-year-old kid.

"What do you want?"

"I'm stuck and can't back up."

"So?"

"Well, if you opened the gate and let me pull forward I think I could get out of here."

"Can't do that."

"You've got to be kidding."

"Nope. Dad says nobody comes through the gate."

Ellie walked up to the young man, put on her best smile, threw her shoulders back and realized the advantage of missing the top two buttons of her shirt, when the adolescent's hormones drove his eyes directly to the gentle swelling sitting interestingly six inches below her chin.

"My face is up here."

"Just how bad do you want the gate open?"

"How old are you?"

"Old enough to open your gate," he said with a smirk.

"OK, let me turn around and I'll give you the ride of your life."

Ellie mounted the cab and inched forward as the youth slowly opened the gate. It was obvious he wasn't going to open the access anymore then necessary for her to get through.

"I'm going to have to go up to the yard and turn around," Ellie chirped through the window. "You want to ride with me."

"Sure I'll ride you," misquoted the grinning adolescent.

Mike Robison – the last day:

The urge woke Mike from a fitful sleep. For nearly six years that early morning urge was to reach over to Shelley and "get lucky." But this urge was more intense, becoming rapidly familiar and much more desirable than others. In addition, he knew that his stash was getting surprisingly low.

Mike slipped out of bed, picked up his jeans off of the chair next to Shelley's makeup table and quietly opened the door whose hinges he had oiled just the night before. The door opened with nothing but a near silent "whoosh" over the carpet. Mike waited until he was on the second to last step before slipping on his pants then sitting down to lace up his boots.

"Damn. Nothing," he swore to himself as he glanced down into the pocket of his plaid shirt, hoping there would be at least the remnant of a smoke. He hoped it hadn't slipped out when he'd taken the shirt off. Shelley could only be fooled so long.

Mike hushed the dog, then put him down the stairs to the basement. He hiked over to the shed and grabbed his metal shears. A simple sewing scissors would work for the task he had in mind, but Shelley might wonder where her good Fiskars had gone. A plastic grocery bag was stuck into his back pocket and a pair of once white leather gloves stuck into the opposite pocket. Mike was ready.

The hike down the dirt cow path was beautiful this time of morning, especially in late summer. There were some wild flowers that, in happier times, he and Shelley had planted next to a fencerow. He spooked up a deer and then spied two fawns hiding about ten feet into the alfalfa field. Mike reminded himself to take it a little slow along the edge of the fence when he cut the field later that day.

There is nothing worse than running a fawn or two through the haybine.

"I'll have to call out the local "Joined Deer" dealer to clean that mess up," he joked to himself.

"Shelley wouldn't have appreciated that joke," he said out loud. "Hell, she wouldn't even get it."

Mike became increasingly tenser as he approached the end of the cow path and came to the edge of his property. He had marveled at the luck he had when his new neighbor had completely redone the fence along Mike's pasture. The old fence had been falling down and been kept operational only because Mike had strung some electric fence in front of the dilapidated barbed wire fence put up by Shelley's dad 40 years ago. The electric fence kept the cattle from leaning over the barbed wire to reach the proverbial green grass on the other side of the fence.

Mike crawled under the electric fence, then stood up briefly in between that and the barbed wire. He pushed down the top two strands and threw his leg over, hopping off of one leg onto the other and in the process catching the inseam of his pants on the barbed wire. The sharp point bit into the sensitive skin of his inner thigh and Mike let out a yelp. A flock of blackbirds burst forth from the cornfield in front of him.

"Crap," thought Mike. "So much for keeping quiet."

But he knew the habits of the farm's owners and they would still be in bed. Mike went into the cornfield, dew causing the newly formed pollen to stick to his clothing until his shirt was almost yellow with the tiny specks. Sharp edges of the corn leaves sliced his hands until he finally reached back and pulled his gloves out. Sweat stung the tiny cuts as he yanked the tight fitting gloves onto his slippery, red tinted hands.

It took only a few seconds once he got to the 32nd row in. At that point Mike knew he could just hike down that row about 50 yards and he would hit pay dirt. The going was much easier.

Mike pulled out his shears and started clipping some of the buds of the plants. The plants were interspersed with corn stalks and had nearly the same rich dark green color. The leaves looked more like tomato plants than corn. Mike was careful to take no more than one bud from any one plant.

It took nearly half an hour to fill the bag, but when it was full Mike had enough to last him at least a week or two once it cured, unless his brother came round again.

"Heh!"

Mike turned and saw a sight that made his stomach turn and his mouth dry up.

"You son-a-bitch."

Mike heard the gun shot; it just didn't register in his rapidly disintegrating brain as the .22 slug bounced from side to side, ricocheting off bone, then smoothly gliding through the gray matter like a hot knife through butter.

Chapter Three

"The Lady of Troy"

Once the big rig had cleared the narrow opening of the gate, Ellie Carlson accelerated rapidly, not giving the young kid time to get out of the truck to shut the gate.

"I'm coming right back through," she said to his demand to stop and shut the gate.

He reluctantly gave her that, then lowered his head, already thinking what his dad would do if he found out, but everybody else was still asleep so he sat back to enjoy the view awarded him with the woman's shirt half opened. The truck and trailer would be long gone before anybody woke up and maybe just maybe he'd get a taste of that sweet thing next to him.

Ellie deftly swung the rig into the yard of the farm. The large white clapboard house looked much like the house her dad had moved to over by Yellow Pine. Green shutters bordered each of the windows and several of the lower level windows actually had red geraniums in window boxes.

"Pretty house," she commented.

"Yeah, Mom says, 'If we have to live in the damned country, at least we can have a decent house.'"

"The yard is beautiful. I bet you do the mowing and trimming."

"When I have to."

"Nice horse."

"We've got five of them. All Appaloosas."

"I've got two Quarter Horses."

"Is that what you haul in the trailer?"

"Nope."

As she started her turn to the left and swung by the wide-open barn door, she caught movement out of the corner of her eye. She knew part of her cargo was no longer in the trailer.

"Can I look at your horses?" Ellie queried as she slowed the truck down to a stop and began opening the door."

"Ah, no, you'd better get going. Besides, Dad doesn't like strangers by the stock. He thinks they might carry disease."

But Ellie would not take no for an answer.

As she hopped her 5 ft. 10 inch frame down from the heights of her Ram Truck, she heard the distant pop of a rifle. Instinctively she knew it wasn't a big gun that she had heard, but her instincts also told her to reach under the seat and grab her own Glock. The young man's shock was immediately transformed into panic as he grabbed for the door handle.

"Hold it right there! Sheriff's department! Don't move!"

"Goat" Carlson:

"I'm getting too old for this crap," "Goat" said to himself while outwardly not betraying any of the emotions running through his gray-haired head.

His legs were aching and so was his back and he'd only been in the trailer a few minutes before he'd had to kneel or stoop down with the other seven lawmen quietly waiting as Ellie tried to talk her way through the gate into what Drug Task Force intelligence had determined was a "Minnesota Gold" production center. He tried to hear bits and pieces of the conversation, but the exhaust of the truck kept rumbling out of the oversized tail pipes.

When Ellie and he had come up with the idea of using the trailer as a Trojan Horse, he had not thought through the natural consequence that it would be his newest and only woman deputy who would end up driving. All had agreed that it would be easier to buy into a woman rather than a man getting stuck at the front of the gate. It was the first time his daughter had been in this kind of action and while the pride was there, so was a touch of concern.

A jerk of the trailer nearly knocked him over and one of the deputies yelped as his feet slipped out from under him and his hand landed in a pile of manure left over from previous occupants. That deputy received a look from the other seven occupants that would have sent a lesser man home crying, but not Jim Barton. He was the jokester in the bunch and seldom took anything seriously.

"Goat" watched the rig's progress up the lane and warned two of the deputies to be prepared to disembark as they got to the barn they knew was close to the turn-a-round in the yard. "Goat" had done a Google search on the address and had gotten a satellite photo of such detail that he thought if anyone had been outside when the picture was taken they would have been able to i.d. them from it.

"Go!" motioned "Goat"

Two deputies deftly jumped from the open door at the back of the trailer, drawing weapons as they landed and skidded into the barn door, one on either side.

"Hold on," commanded "Goat"

The truck rolled to a stop.

"Leave it to Ellie to figure out a way to stop the truck in just the right place," thought the proud father.

He heard the cab door open up. He put his hand to his mouth, signaling the remaining deputies to keep quiet.

In the distance he heard what had to be a gunshot and immediately heard his daughter yell out.

"Go! Now! Go!" hollered the sheriff at his deputies and into the mike attached to his shoulder as he unwound his own stiff body and followed his deputies out of the now stopped trailer.

Within seconds two sheriff's cars and police cars from Harmony and Milton came flying in, kicking up dust. Officers jumped from their cars and hid behind them, guns at the ready.

"So, where'd the name come from?" asked Ox.

"It's a derivative of O'Banion and I got the name from the O'Banion who was a big shot in Chicago in the 20's. He was one of Al Capone's contemporaries."

"Yeah, Right."

"Honest."

"Since when would you pick a crook as a hero to name yourself after?"

"All right. Here's the real story. O'Banion was one of the people I read up on back in law school…I don't even remember why. When I was picking out a name I wanted to give myself a name in your honor, so Paul Banion and the Ox."

"Give me a break. If you don't want to tell me, don't."

Ox and I had been walking across the barnyard to the single story white dairy barn located about 100 yards from the house. It was a quiet morning, with heavy dew from the night before coating the grass, equipment, and the wires overhead. The shimmer reflecting from the droplets looked like diamonds coating everything. I couldn't help but think it was a grand morning.

"What do you suppose that's all about?" Ox asked me as a big blue Dodge pulling a 5th wheel trailer rolled by on the dirt road two stone throws away from the house.

Two Maplewood County deputy cars followed the nice looking rig and two police cars branded with names of towns that I recognized, from my previous research into the geography of my new home, as two little bergs within 20 miles of each other. All four cars had passengers.

"Don't know, but I'll bet we read about it in the paper tomorrow," I said with more than a bit of relief that the law enforcement vehicles had not turned into our drive.

"E.Z.", started Ox.

"It's Paul," I interrupted.

Ox gave me his famous stare then continued:

"Yeah, I know, but you'll always be E.Z. to me. The only paper we get comes once a week and it will include news about Millie Nelson having her grandchildren visit this week and who played cribbage with the nursing home residents."

My curiosity pulled me toward the green pickup sitting in the yard. I wanted to hop in and follow the parade that had just gone by.

"Don't even think about it. You've got chores to do."

Sometimes I hated Ox.

We walked into the barn through the milk house. The opening of the doors stirred the cattle and there was a cacophony of chains as 65 head of 1500 lb Holsteins struggled up from their prone positions. Almost immediately the bellows of those cows with the fullest udders greeted us. They were ready to be relieved of that burden of white.

"Shut the doors and windows," hollered Ox. "We've got to spray."

I complied by pulling shut the big barn doors at each end of the long white building. As I traveled between the doors I closed the windows on first one side, then the other. By the time I was done Ox had shut off the big ventilation fans and had pulled out a large aerosol can. A slightly blue-gray mist started at the ceiling and drifted down.

"You'd better get out of here."

The mist had already reached me. My eyes watered and the back of my throat gagged back its reflex to let loose. We waited outside for five minutes and returned into the barn. I accepted the urge to hold my breath as I quickly reversed the procedure of windows and doors. Up and down the alley way my boots crunched on the black pebbles that were dying and dead flies. They were everywhere.

"You can sweep up while I get the chains moving," ordered Ox as he handed me a two-foot wide broom. "Just sweep everything into the gutter."

By everything he meant the straw and manure that had found its way onto the walkway behind the cows. I proceeded posthaste up the aisle and happened to glance up to see Ox standing about 30 feet down the way. My experience with Ox is that whenever he stops work to look at me, I'm in for one of his practical jokes. My hesitation saved me as the cow just to my right reared up her back, just short of the t-shaped electrical device above her front shoulders and let fly with a forceful stream of piss that shot half way across the walk.

When she stopped, I looked up to Ox expecting to see him back at work. And, ostensibly he was, pushing feed in front of the cows. But I caught the movement of his eyes and knew my torture wasn't over. I just didn't expect it from the same source. Sure enough, I no more than stepped behind the fountainous cow only to hear her cough loudly.

It was a deep cough followed by two shorter ones. Each cough brought forth from her rear end, yesterday's alfalfa, corn silage, and grain mix well processed through all four of her stomachs and taking the unmistakable form of manure. Her aim was perfect as the first barrage hit my shoulder and splattered upward. The second hit waist high and the third covered my brand new Red Wing boots.

Ox howled.

I swore; and I never swear, but when it covers you from head to toe, it is not manure, it is shit.

Chapter Four

"Bad Guys Finish Last"

"Don't move…I mean it. Don't move or there will be consequences," said a motivated Ellie Carlson.

She pointed her gun at the young man who had just unwittingly escorted her onto the farm that investigation had shown was a production facility for half of the marijuana being sold in a four county area. Her dad, Sheriff Carlson, had been searching for weeks for a way to approach and move in on the bunch of criminals that had moved in at the end of March, shortly after the farm had been sold.

Neighbors had reported to "Goat" that the fencing was just a little bit more than what you would normally expect on a farm that was raising just a couple of beef cattle and a few horses. They had also reported that every effort to be neighborly had been more than rebuffed. People had actually been run off.

Shelley Robison, the closest neighbor and a classmate of Ellie's had called Ellie herself and told her that she was really suspicious of the people she saw coming and going. Ellie knew her friend wasn't about to exaggerate something like that so an investigation with the joint Drug Task Force had been started. It had been through that they had actually been able to get an informant planted with the gang.

The Task Force had submitted their report to "GOAT" just two weeks ago and Ellie had seen the look in her father's eyes and knew that he wasn't going to let this one lie. He had organized the raid, with her help, into one of the most imaginative plans she had ever seen in her short career.

Now Ellie was holding her pistol on the youngest of the seven people their intelligence work had told them would be in residence.

"Ellie?"

Ellie's look, nod, and thumb up told her dad that she was fine. She slapped her spare set of cuffs on the kid and moved him into the barn where she turned him over to Jim Barton, before moving on to her assigned position on the right flank of the house. She took time to slide into the bulletproof vest Jim had handed to her as she left the barn.

The deputies all moved forward in sequence, one team covering the next as they slid forward from the right, middle, and left. Ellie couldn't see the team approaching from the rear of the house, but knew that "Goat" had sent the two police officers from Harmony and Milton around to cover that location, expecting that if there were to be trouble it would hit them head on from the front of the house rather than the rear.

"Maplewood County Sheriff's Department! We have a warrant to search the premises," announced the deep voice of Sheriff "Goat" Carlson. He gave a count of five ticked off on the fingers of his left hand, then gave a nod to two deputies who had approached the front door. They used a sledgehammer to force the dead bolt lock out of its nest in the doorframe. They stepped back long enough for three other deputies to go running through the door with armored shields at the ready and guns drawn.

Ellie quickly checked her own weapon and moved forward. She could hear shouting from the officers inside and her acute hearing also picked up a female screech as well as the shattering of glass. The adrenaline burst caused her breathing to quicken and her heart to beat rapidly. Her bowels felt liquidy.

"Lord, don't make me fill my pants."

Out of the corner of her eye she caught movement and brought her gun up. It was a child…a little girl standing in the corner holding a teddy bear in one hand and a blanket in the other. Ellie was torn between moving forward with her team or breaking off and caring for the blonde haired little one.

"Shanna!" shrieked a blonde in bra and panties.

Ellie followed the blonde's movements with her gun and responded to the frightened mothers pleading eyes with her own decision to break off and stay with them. The mother's attire provided an excuse not to do a weapons search so Ellie told mother and daughter to stay put. She pulled out her primary cuffs and attached one end to the mother's wrist and the other to the lamp attached to the wall.

"Stay put and you'll be safe," Ellie commanded, and then moved forward.

Ellie peeked around the corner into the kitchen. It was a large kitchen with all white appliances except for an avocado green dishwasher. The floor was clean except for the gentleman lying there. He was half dressed and without socks. His hands had been placed behind his back and it was only with considerable effort that he was able to lift his head and turn it to face the Sheriff's daughter.

"Hi, Ellie."

"Goat" was p.o.'d and when "Goat" was p.o.'d he was not a good person to be around.

"I thought you said there were 7 adults in here. Nobody said a damn word about little kids or even teenagers. And, where the hell are the men. We got one damn guy here and he's an informant."

Carlson had called the head of the Drug Task Force shortly after the scene had been secured to express his anger and animosity with the Task Force in that the intelligence had been faulty or else they had missed out on at least two miscreants.

"I don't know Chief…"

"Don't call me Chief," interrupted "Goat"

"Sheriff, we found the stuff," hollered a deputy, obviously winded from hiking through the field he had just exited. "It's about 200 yards out in this corn field and there is a bunch."

Another deputy came from the back of the barn and announced:

"They've been drying and packing the stuff in the old hen house out back. And, the hog barn has about a hundred grow lights and tables all over. Looks like they were about to start growing stuff indoors too."

"So what am I going to do… put one damn teenager, two housewives, a baby and my own informant in jail?"

"There were fresh tracks going out to the field and we found a 4-wheeler by the barn. And, the horses and steers that were in the pen by the barn are gone. The two guys must have been out in the field when we hit them."

"Why would the horses and steers be gone?"

"To cover tracks… or to ride or both."

"Goat" looked with disdain at the deputy who'd made that suggestion. Then realized that he didn't have a better explanation.

"All right, you two wait here for transport with these desperate criminals. Ellie, you call social services for the kids. Jim, you organize our guys to search the perimeter to see where they may have come out. Bob and John, you guys can head back to your own towns and keep your eyes and ears open along the way. Get going… and nobody talks to the press but me! Understand?"

"Goat" directed the last to Jim Barton whom he had heard was talking about running against him for Sheriff this fall.

Then he pulled Ellie aside.

"Before you go, see what you can get out of these two ladies. Be sure you Mirandize them. And get that one some clothes. I don't want these deputies distracted."

Shelley decided to take her break early. Her boss had still not arrived and she knew that the door would need to be locked when she left. Small town attorneys did their own thing and Shelley had no doubt that Steve either had an early tee time or else had gotten engrossed in conversation over at the Milton Café. As Shelley opened the unlocked door of her car she caught of whiff of her husband. Well, it wasn't really her husband but what she was pretty sure he'd been smoking lately.

"Funny," she thought to herself. "It didn't smell that way this morning. It must be the car heating up from the sun shining in through the windows."

Shelley backed the car into the alley and headed over to the drug store. Normally, she would have walked, but she felt she needed to get there and back as quickly as possible. Her birth control pills would be ready to pick up along with Mike's butt cream. Now that was a combination. She realized that the thought of Mike was actually disgusting her lately and his latest problem with his rear end certainly wasn't helping. She figured she'd have yet another month when her pills really weren't necessary.

"Don't slow down," commanded a voice from the back seat.

Shelley's heart jumped.

"What…"

"Shut-up and keep your eyes on the road," directed the voice. "Head out of town and get to Highway 10."

"No."

Shelley's long blonde hair was suddenly jerked back, snapping her head against the headrest.

"I have a gun pointed straight at your back. Now do what I tell you."

Shelley picked up speed and went through the first stop sign she came to.

"Where is that damn cop when you need him," mumbled Shelley to herself. "He's always sitting at that intersection."

"When you get to Highway 10, pull over."

She drove the five blocks to the highway, praying that someone would see her and wonder what she was doing. On the one hand her terror stopped time from moving forward and on the other hand she arrived at the highway intersection much too quickly.

"Now what?"

"Turn the car off and hand the keys back here… Now, keep your hands on the steering wheel while I get out."

Shelley's relief at her guest's exit was short-lived as he opened the front door and sat on the passenger's seat.

"Go right and head to Cedar Grove."

Shelley drove the 15 miles in quiet terror. The man, who she recognized as her neighbor, was sweaty and full of what she knew, was corn pollen. His hands and face had tiny scratches and were oozing tiny trails of blood. She was certain this was not going to end well. As they traveled, the man pulled her purse up from the floor and went through it. He kept her cell phone and took the cash, about $50, from her wallet. When he saw Mike's family photo, he looked over to her and was about to say something, then thought better of it.

"All right, let me out here… I want you to drive over to Clipton without stopping... I will be coming right behind you so I'll know if you stopped and there will be nothing that will keep me from finding you... Understand?"

"Yes."

"Go."

Shelley was so tempted to swing down toward the Court House and the police station, but she knew who her passenger had been and if she knew him, then she knew he knew who she was and where she lived.

Oakdale was as far as she got when she realized she really had to go to the bathroom. She swung to the right at the first intersection and found a city park with an outhouse. She barely made it in the door before her body betrayed her first from one end, then the other.

Ten minutes later she came out of the cement block building with its two-seater toilet and walked to the fountain in the park. She thought about the geraniums and how nice they looked, then took a handkerchief from her purse and used it to wash her face. A piece of gum began to remove the taste of the bagel, which had not been nearly as good the second time through her mouth.

My back ached with the use of new muscles. It had been 15 years since I had milked cows on my grandfather's farm in Wisconsin and I had forgotten some of the tricks of the trade including how to use my legs instead of my back. I found myself experiencing pain in the lower back and in the upper quads of my leg muscles. But I would not give Ox the satisfaction of seeing me in pain.

"Watch that 58 cow. She likes to kick when you put the milker on."

"OW!"

"I told you."

My grandfather had told me that there was usually a reason that a cow kicked and that it was my job to figure it out. I went down on my haunches and took the rag to the teats of #58. She attempted to kick me again.

"You know I think this cow has a cut on the outside of her teat," I hollered at Ox. "What to you do for that?"

"You're right," Ox commented from the other side of the cow. "She must have stepped on it sometime in the last day or two. Let's strip her out by hand and see what she's got."

Ox gently massaged the quarter on which the teat was cut, then manipulated his hand around her teat and pulled. A yellow chunk came rolling out followed by off-white milk.

"Crap! She's got mastitis in that quarter. We'll have to treat the infection. E.Z., get me that tube up there on the shelf."

"It's Paul," I said as I handed him the tube.

He expertly stripped out more liquid, then inserted the business end of the tube up the teat and let the antibiotic go.

"We won't be able to milk her into the tank for a few days."

Ox had taken little convincing a little more than a year before when I told him about my plans. He'd been able to get a leave of absence from his job with Orange County and had used his experiences from his high school part-time job to map out a strategy for buying, stocking, and running a dairy farm in Minnesota.

I'd kept in touch through e-mail and a private chat room that we had set up. Together we'd searched for just the right place in the just the right community and had finally found the Mueller place just 8 miles from Harmony in West Central Minnesota. It had 160 acres, a nice house, a 65-stall barn and various other out buildings.

Ox had purchased the farm using a corporation that we had established when we first started our plan. The money had come from some of my enterprises with Tags. I know, some might think they were ill-gotten gains, but they were funds that would have disappeared into some Swiss bank account to be used by Tags and his minions if I hadn't gotten to them first. Besides, Tags never missed them, at least not until they were all gone. Altogether I had squirreled away a little over $2 Million using a special computer program that I had developed that rounded amounts down to the lowest dollar plus 1, 2, or 7 cents. For example, if a deposit was supposed to be $2,001.89 it automatically became $2,001.01 or $2,001.02 or $2001.07. I received at least 82 cents into my account. In the course of the three years that I used the program, I was able to generate nearly $1.3 million from thousands of checks deposited each day by the various companies owned and operated by Joey Titaglio. Shrewd investments on my part had generated an additional $700,000.

It took us another half hour to finish milking and get the feed pushed up in front of the cows. I did the pushing while Ox cleaned up things in the milk house. He disconnected the pipe line from the bulk tank, took out the filter to inspect it, then turned on the wash cycle that would scour the inside of the pipe line.

"Let's go feed calves."

I remembered feeding calves from grandpa's farm. It was a simple task of dumping milk or milk replacer that had been mixed up into pails in each of the calves' pens. The only challenge was with newborn calves that were still being bottle-fed.

"How many calves do we have?" I asked the Ox man.

"Three."

"Oh," came my disappointed reply.

"We have more cows coming fresh in the next two weeks."

Just then a real commotion could be heard on the other side of the barn as the cattle in the pens along the barn went running around the back of the barn and started bawling.

In his non-verbal way, Ox jerked his thumb toward the commotion. I knew he meant for me to check it out. I grabbed a pitchfork that was standing against the barn and headed back toward the commotion. Fifteen seconds later, the heifers in the pens came peeling back around the barn, followed by me; followed by 10 or twelve steers and 5 horses all hell bent on catching me and running me down. Ox laughed.

It probably was a funny sight, but I had all I could do to jump up onto the 2 x 6 railings that made up the fence line just as the whole bunch filled the space between the pens and the hay shed. The lead critters caught site of the hay and swung to the right. The second volley of cattle went running right on by, then tried to put on the brakes and were run over by the last three steers. The horses came trotting up behind, shaking their heads and blowing air and snot out of their nostrils.

After much milling around, checking out the cattle in the pen, then looking us over, the convoy of cattle and horses stopped in front of a stack of prime alfalfa hay and proceeded to destroy first one bale after another.

"What the hell…"

"Ox, are these ours?"

"Nope."

"What are we going to do with them?"

"Don't know."

"Well, someone is going to come looking for them."

"Might be the Sheriff."

That thought troubled me. I didn't think we were quite ready to be visited by law enforcement, but Ox was probably right. We had seen the parade of sheriff's vehicles following a cattle trailer just a couple of hours earlier. I'm not one to believe in coincidence.

"Goat" had been standing by his car for nearly two hours anticipating something to break. He had disbursed his troops to various assignments and none of them had checked in during the two hours. His impatience demanded that he contact them by radio, but his better judgment told him to stay off the air in case someone needed him or in case the sound of his voice coming across the radio would come at a bad time.

Ellie had stayed around until social services showed up to escort the two kids back to Hawks Hill. "Goat" had been tempted to keep the teenager in cuffs, but the social worker had insisted that she would not transport anyone dangerous enough to have cuffs on.

"Toss that cap to me before it gets torn."

"But Dad, I thought you were giving it to me," replied a mischievous daughter. "Warren Moon doesn't even play anymore."

"That cap is going to be worth something."

"Dad, should I head over to the Robison's place and let Shelley and Mike know what's going on?"

"I suppose you better. Don't tell 'em too much. I don't want word to get out until we know who's missing and where they are…Did you get anything out of the two women?"

"No, they were just too hysterical. And, the one with the little kid was beside herself. I'm not sure what they knew about what was going on. Do you want me to try again once we get them booked?"

They'd agreed that the Sheriff would handle any further questioning along with someone from the County Attorney's office. With that Ellie headed off.

Ellie deftly swung the pickup and trailer around and headed out the drive that just a few hours before had provided entrance for her and the team. She took a left out of the drive and headed to the intersection where she took another left.

"Mike's corn and beans sure look rough," she thought to herself.

She knew that Mike and Shelley had been having some personal problems, but now she saw that the problems seemed to extend to Mike's crops as well.

She remembered Mike was still working at the boat plant in Milton, so he might not even be home now unless he worked a night shift or would go in this afternoon.

Shelley was probably at work.

If nothing else Ellie would have a chance to walk around and make sure the missing desperadoes weren't hiding out at the Robison's.

Mad Max, the Robison's Rottweiler, greeted her. Max jumped up on the door of the Dodge to greet her. His stub tail was working its way back and forth at about 100 beats a minute. She knew Max wouldn't hurt a fly, but took her time getting out of the truck.

"Hi Maxie," she chirped. "I wuv you too."

Mad Max jumped up and put his paws on her chest.

"Hey! I don't let just any guy put their hands there," she joked as she tried to push him down.

That's when she noticed the red streak left on her hand.

"Are you hurt Max?"

Max started to howl like he was in pain, but Ellie could see no injury. It was then that Max grabbed her shirt and pulled her as though he wanted her to follow. They walked around the barn together, the dog dragging the woman.

"Oh, my God," Ellie exclaimed and suddenly knew that life in Maplewood County would never be the same.

"Goat"'s cell phone rang and, as he lifted it from its holster on the left side of his belt, he saw on the digital readout that it was Ellie who was calling him.

"Wonder why she's not using a radio," he thought to himself.

"Dad, you better get here right now," came a voice that "Goat" hardly recognized as his daughter.

"Ellie, are you OK? And, where is here," forgetting momentarily what he had known just minutes before.

"I'm at the Robison's."

"Do you need help?"

"Dad, just get here and call Doc Gilbert while you're at it!"

"Goat" knew that the reference to the Medical Examiner was meant as a message that there was at least one dead body that would have to be dealt with.

"Please God, don't let it be one of my guys."

"Goat" clicked the mike attached to his shoulder. He didn't want to break the radio silence, but the clicking sound might let his deputies know that they needed to check in.

The Sheriff walked over to his Ford Explorer. It had been driven over from Hawks Hill by one of the deputies who had transported the two women. With lights and sirens going, the grizzled veteran tore through the now open gate and headed to the Ingvaldson place where the Robisons had lived since her mother had moved to town and her new apartment.

It took him less than three minutes. He parked well back from the truck and trailer and walked around the barn where Ellie was busy tying up the Robison's dog. "Goat" had grabbed crime scene tape out of his SUV and set about marking off a perimeter from the body.

By the time he had completed that, Ellie had returned from the Explorer with two pair of disposable boots, two sets of disposable gloves, a digital camera, numerous evidence bags, and other paraphernalia. Since "Goat" had spent the best part of his career in crime scene investigation, he never went anywhere without at least the bare essentials for evidence collection and usually took care of those duties himself.

"Ell, you take notes," directed the Sheriff.

"Entrance wound appears above the right eye…Appears to be some sort of mucous or liquid around wound and blood is smeared."

"Dad, Max had blood on his muzzle. He was probably licking his face."

"Note that…It appears that the body did not fall here but was drug…but there are no obvious drag marks. Footprints…several of an animal, presumably the dog and some boots…"

"Those are mine," the young deputy confessed. "And, I saw that it looked like someone took something like a corn stalk or something and brushed the ground all around in every direction right up to the grass."

"Keep writing…Shirt is torn and a small piece seems to be missing right here on the back. Look…there is a tear in the pants on the back too. Looks like another on the front. Ell…do you see the little cuts on these hands? When I took off the gloves, there were obvious slice marks, almost like paper cuts."

"Dad, see those little whitish things on his shirt? I think that's from corn stalks…like the pollen or something. Could he have gotten cut from the leaves? Would they do that?"

"Sure, but what would he be…unless he was…how far is that farm? Sure, I'll bet he was out there in that corn field right where those marijuana plants were."

"Dad, are you thinking he's one that got away?"

"Well, he didn't exactly get away did he."

Just then Doc Gilbert showed up.

"Pastor," Pastor B. answered the parsonage phone for the 10th time that morning. He was getting a little frustrated that the Arndt wedding plans were happening this week, his only week this summer for a vacation. The wedding was still 6 weeks off, but that family had been putting off planning for months. Now they wanted everything done and they wanted it right now.

"Is this Pastor Brocks?"

"It's Brooks," came the short reply.

"I'm sorry. Pastor Brooks, this is Sheriff Carlson with Maplewood County. I understand the Robisons are members of your congregation. Is that right?"

"Aw...Can you tell me what this might be in reference to?"

"Well Pastor I guess I can if you can confirm that the Robisons are in your flock."

Pastor B. chuckled to himself when the voice on the phone used the term flock, especially when it came to the Robisons. They were hardly his sheep. Although he had married them six years ago and Shelley had been very faithful in her church attendance. Mike on the other hand, had not been.

"I guess I'm still wondering what this might be about."

"Look Brooks, I'm not one of your silly little ladies aid people trying to get a rumor started. This is official police business and I want an answer."

Pastor B. was taken aback and a little ashamed of himself. He never would have given the Sheriff such a difficult time if it weren't for those doggone Arndt women.

Just then his wife of 27 years came through the door in a hurry. She threw down the paper bags she'd been carrying and motioned to her husband that she needed to talk to him immediately.

"Would you hold on for a second, Sheriff?" queried the pastor and then didn't wait for an answer as he held the phone against his shirt.

"What!?"

"Something's happened at the Robisons," whispered the pastor's window on the community.

"Sorry, Sheriff. Yes, Shelley is a member and Mike comes occasionally. What can I do for you?"

"Do you know where Shelley might be?

"No." Silence.

"No idea at all."

"Well, I have an idea or two." Silence.

"Could you share at least one of those ideas with me?"

"She might be at work." Silence.

"Do you know where she works?"

"In Milton." Silence.

"Where in Milton?"

"She's Andy Ratcliff's secretary."

"Oh."

The Sheriff and Mr. Ratcliff knew each other from a number of cases Ratcliff had defended as a court appointed defense attorney.

"If I stopped by to pick you up, would you be willing to come with me to see Shelley?"

"Of course. If you think you know where she might be."

"You just told me she would be at her office."

"No, I told you where she works. I have no idea if she is there or not."

Well, would you be willing to come along with me to see if she is at work?"

"Sure, but can you tell me why?"

"When I get there," said the Sheriff, who figured two could play at this game.

"Sheriff, how did you know to call me?"

"I didn't. You were the *last* one on my list. I was hoping they were Catholic."

The Sheriff spat out a gob of sunflower seeds he'd been working over in his mouth while talking to the preacher. He knew the salt wasn't good for his blood pressure, but seeds were nothing on his pressure compared to ignoramuses like that fruitcake of a pastor. He couldn't imagine what his sermons were like.

"Probably taken from some book of sermons and he reads them," "Goat" sputtered to himself.

Just then the radio jumped to life.

"Sheriff?"

"Go Ahead Jim."

"We've covered the entire perimeter and have found a place where they must have come out not to far from the old Mueller place. We don't see any footprints except for cattle and a horse or two. Looks like the cattle kept on going down the road."

"OK. I guess its time to put out the word that we have a couple of desperados on our hands. Make sure we say they are armed and dangerous."

"You want me to notify the press."

"No, but you're going to have to. I've got a death notice to do."

"Who died?"

"Not on the radio… Jim, it may be connected to this morning."

"Oh. One of them?"

"Jim, run the release by Wally before you put it out. I want to make sure our County Attorney is aware of what's going on. He helped us get the warrants and I don't want him having any surprises. Tell him to call me on my cell phone if he has questions."

"OK. Over and Out."

"Goat" pulled up in front of the white house next door to Trinity Lutheran Church and gave a quick toot on his horn. He couldn't believe his eyes when the pastor came walking out with shorts and a Hawaiian shirt on.

"I'm on vacation," came the pastor's reply to the Sheriff's unspoken question.

"You sure are."

After calling her father on the cell phone, Ellie had waited for him before cordoning off the scene of the accident. She wanted to assume it was an accident, but knew it likely wasn't. A couple of pieces of twine string looped together had formed a leash of sorts and she had tied it around Mad Max. It had been a bit of a struggle to get him to leave his master alone. It wasn't that Mad Max loved Mike; it was that the dog in Maxie made him want to lick the small amount of blood that had trickled down from the small wound over Mike's left eye.

Ellie had no doubt about the life force having left poor Mike. His glazed over eyes, the smell of fecal matter and urine, and the flies already buzzing in and out of his mouth indicated no need for CPR or other life saving methods. A body didn't last long in the heat of July and if the Medical Examiner didn't arrive soon, there might just be an explosion of sorts.

What did puzzle Ellie a little was what kind of weapon could have done this to Mike. It was obviously a small caliber, probably a .22. She had no experience in weapons theory or practicality other than what she had seen on the numerous reruns of CSI that she had squirreled away on videotapes. They didn't teach you that kind of stuff at Alexandria Tech.

Her dad had arrived at the Robisons, checked out the scene, had her take some notes, and then given orders to Ellie to wait by the body. He wanted to track down the wife and let her know what had happened before the media or the local rumor mill got a hold of it. Ellie had suggested calling the local pastors to see if any of them knew the Robisons and where Mrs. Robison might be.

"Dad, Cool down before you leave," she'd told her father before he headed off to pick up the Lutheran pastor in Harmony.

"I've never been much of a churchgoing person, Ellie. You know that. But by golly this guy could make me convert to being a Methodist. He has to be the dumbest summanabitch in the county."

"Sounded like you gave about as good as you got."

"I know. I just hope this mess isn't tied into the mess around the corner. If it is, Jim Barton is going to make me look like an idiot."

"Dad, you know our informant is Shelley's brother. Just remember that it was Shelley who called me about what might be going on over there in the first place."

"I know. And, I know she's your friend. That's why I don't want you there."

Shelley drove her car back from Oakdale. As she did, she looked into every oncoming car and prayed that she wouldn't see her neighbor. Yes, she had recognized him as the person she'd seen that first week after the new neighbors had moved to the farm bordering her own. She'd stopped by to be neighborly and the blonde woman had been very nice, offering to invite her in for a cup of coffee.

Once in the house, the two women had hit it off right away. Even though the woman, Jodie something or other, had been in her early thirties and had a son who was thirteen and a daughter who was just about two, Shelley could relate to the woman. Both had been married early in life and both were living in places they would rather just visit.

They had just started their second cup of coffee, when the husband arrived. He was obviously not interested in company or even the blueberry pie Shelley had baked. After a few minutes Shelley had excused herself and driven out. As she did so, another car arrived with a man and woman in the front seat. The woman looked like a feminine version of the man she'd just met.

So as Shelley drove back to Milton she tried to think through what she should do. There were the threats made against her, but even more disconcerting was her knowledge that whatever had happened that morning was probably related to a conversation she'd had recently with her favorite deputy and classmate, Ellie Carlson.

Relief overtook Shelley as she used her key to unlock the still locked office door. Obviously Andy had still not arrived at work. She walked over to her desk and sat down to ponder her next steps. Just then the chime went off announcing the door had been opened. It startled Shelley and she knocked over the lukewarm coffee in her cup.

"Can I help you," she started while mopping up the coffee.

She glanced up from her chore to see a man in uniform whom she recognized was Ellie's father and her own pastor dressed in shorts and a flowered shirt. Both men took off their hats.

"Hi, Shelley. Is Andy around?"

"No, but I just got here so he may have come and gone," fibbed Shelley thinking that the two men didn't need to know that Andy probably hadn't even gotten dressed yet and that she had come and gone.

The Sheriff had a quizzical look on his face after her statement and it made Shelley wish that she'd told him the truth. She wondered why she hadn't.

"Shelley, I'm afraid we have some bad news. There's been a shooting. I'm afraid Mike is dead."

The words from her pastor chased all thoughts of the past hour out of her head for a moment, just like the void that comes just prior to a storm surge. Then the fear and anguish of her experience forced its way back into her consciousness.

"I should have gone to Clipton," she exclaimed to the two astonished men who could see no connection between what they had told her and what she had uttered.

"Sit down, Shelley."

"Pastor B. what happened? Where did it happen? When did it happen? I told him I'd do what he wanted!"

The Sheriff pulled out a pad and began to take notes. It never occurred to Shelley to keep her mouth shut, even though those words were always the first out of Andy's mouth whenever he spoke to one of his clients.

The cute girl climbed out of the truck and came walking over to Ox and me. I automatically pulled my cap down on my head, pushing my ears out ever so slightly. I've had enough experience with disguises to know that caps and hats were often the best thing to hide the true appearance of one's face.

"Are these your cattle?" I asked.

"Nope."

"Oh, I just figured with the cattle trailer and all…"

"Deputy Ellie Carlson," the woman clarified as she pulled her id out of her back pocket then hung it around her neck by the attached chain.

"I'm pretty sure they came from the farm down the road. I just swung in when I saw them lying by the hay pile. Figured they weren't yours."

"Yeah, they just showed up about an hour ago," I informed her. "We were just finishing up chores and were going to give the neighbors a call."

"I don't think anybody is there right now," she told me, making contact with her green eyes. "Can we just pen them up here until other arrangements are made? The County will pay you for any feed they eat."

I studied her instantaneously and knew she was nobody's fool. If I didn't handle this just right I'd have the entire department wondering who I was.

"Sure, no problem. As long as you are part of the deal."

She looked at me with a snide grin that made me hope she was a lesbian, because she sure wanted nothing to do with me. But the result was what I'd hope for. She left within minutes after doing a quick inventory of the alien animals. She asked for my name to put on the note pad containing the list and description of the animals. When I told her, I startled myself as I realized it was the first time I'd said the name out loud since it had become my moniker less than twelve hours previously.

I cursed my luck that something as stupid as some loose animals had brought the Sheriff's office to my door the very first day of my anonymity. Oh, well. It would soon be over with.

Ox poked me on the shoulder and startled me from my daydream that had envisioned the young detective in something slightly different than the jeans and plaid shirt she had on. My! My! How the last year and a half had taken its toll on me!

The Medical Examiner had finally shown up and with him had come a white Ford Expedition with deeply tinted windows. Swenson Funeral home had the county contract to haul away bodies from crime scenes, accidents, and other situations the Sheriff's department was called into. Swenson Funeral Home was not used by many families for their funeral services, so it always ended up being a battle between the funeral home a family chose and the one that hauled away the body from the scene. That alone made sad situations even more difficult, but Ellie remembered her Dad saying that old man Swenson knew how to grease the skids to make sure the transport service was always put out on bids and he always won the bid.

Ellie followed the Expedition out the drive and when it turned right, she turned left, back down the road that she had traveled earlier that morning, this time without the procession of police vehicles behind her. As she drove by the Mueller place, something out of place caught her eye. There were cattle out in the yard, mulling around with a few horses. She realized these might be the cattle and horses that had gone missing earlier. She swung her rig into the yard slowly so as not to startle the animals.

Two men were out in the yard talking and pointing at the animals, one just slightly bigger than the other, and both men ruggedly handsome under the obvious chore clothes that they wore. The smaller of the two pulled his hat down – a peculiar thing to do on a hot summer morning.

She had wanted to laugh out loud when they introduced themselves as Paul Banion and Ox. She had been tempted to call Ox "Babe", but after the morning she'd had didn't feel much like humor.

The smaller of the two, Paul, had tried to be funny and Ellie thought maybe had actually tried flirting with her. Ox said nothing.

It took Ellie a few minutes to talk through what they would do with the cattle and horses and in the end they had agreed to feed and water them for a couple of days until the County had time to decide what to do with them. Ellie had drafted up a list and description of the animals, written a note agreeing to cover costs, and, as an afterthought put her home number down under the County Sheriff's number. She would see if this Banion guy really was interested.

As Ellie drove out the drive and headed back to town, she called her Dad's cell phone and told him she'd found the critters that had disappeared. He confirmed that her actions were copasetic and told her to head back to change her clothes and get out to deliver the summonses that had been piling up on her desk.

For once Ellie decided that she could stand the monotony of delivering those official documents.

Chapter Five

"Till Death Do Us Part"

"Goat" Carlson:

It was obvious to the experienced Sheriff that the nice looking woman in front of them had something on her mind. She'd lied when she said she had just gotten to the office. That had been obvious from the spilled coffee and the fact that the pot was sitting there half empty. It was off, but "Goat" had walked over to it and felt the pot only to discover that it was more than lukewarm.

"Goat" was really puzzled by the response from Mrs. Robison when the funny preacher in the Bermuda shorts told her that her husband was dead. It was almost like she half expected to hear this tragic news. When she started talking what seemed like nonsense to him, "Goat" decided to start taking notes.

"Mrs. Robison, I'm so sorry for your loss," started "Goat" "Do you want Mr. Ratcliff or someone like him here before we talk some more?"

"I don't think so."

"Do you mind if I take some notes?"

"I guess not."

"Well, I doubt that we'll need them, but they might be helpful to us if something every goes to trial."

"Do you think that will happen?"

"It just depends on who did what."

"Goat" was pretty pleased with himself. Over the course of many years he had perfected the way he Mirandized unsuspecting suspects.

Shortly after starting the conversation, though, Mrs. Robison had a funny look take over her countenance, looked at a note on her desk and suddenly stopped talking. It seemed to be a pretty guilty response to "Goat" His original assumption that Mike Robison's death had been tied into the raid was probably false. That might just be best since he still wasn't sure how he would handle questions about the arrests of two women, a teenager, and a baby.

Pastor B offered to drive Shelley home from her office and to make some phone calls to her family and Mike's.

As he drove the newly widowed woman home he was puzzled by her repeated glances into the back seat and her constant checking of the mirror on her side of the car. It was as though she was looking for something or someone to be following them.

After several attempts to engage Shelley into some conversation, Pastor B gave up and thought back to how the Sheriff's attitude had changed in the course of a moment or two. As he thought back to some of the questions Sheriff Carlson had asked, Pastor B couldn't help but realize that the questions were intended to elicit something different than any other death notice he had ever attended.

As they drove into the farmyard of the home where Shelley's family had lived for nearly 100 years, Pastor B was surprised to see several deputies' cars. He recognized Jim Barton and drove up to where he was standing next to a four door Crown Victoria.

"Hi Jim"

"Pastor B.! Great to see you. What brings you out to our murder scene?"

It was only then that Barton saw that there was a passenger in the car.

"Sorry Ma'am."

"Jim, this is Mrs. Robison," Pastor B. said to his former parishioner. "She's here to make some phone calls."

"Ah, Pastor we're kinda going through the house right now and ahhhh… I ahhh… don't know that I can let her ahhh… go in there."

Just then a deputy walked out of the house caring a rifle in his glove-covered hands.

"What's he doing with Mike's rifle?" asked Shelley.

"Is that your husband's gun, Mrs. Robison?" asked Barton.

"Well, yes. Who else's would it be? What is that man doing with it? I don't understand. I thought someone shot Mike. He didn't do this himself did he?"

"I'm sorry Ma'am, I just don't think I can say anything right now."

"Jim, this woman has just lost her husband. She needs to make calls to family and friends before they hear about it some other way. You get on that radio and you get a hold of that pompous ass of a sheriff and you get him to at least let *me* get her address book so we can make some calls."

Pastor B. got out of the car and headed to the house as Jim Barton desperately tried to raise the Sheriff on his radio. The preacher had already returned with a white notebook and a small box and was getting into his car again when Barton came running up to the car.

"Sheriff says it's OK to get the address book."

"Thank You Jim," hollered Pastor B. as he turned the car around and stepped on the gas, throwing up a barrage of grass and gravel.

"I never could stand that man," Pastor B. muttered to himself.

"Oh my God! Oh my God! What have I done? What have I done," Shelley kept whispering to herself.

Pastor Brooks had been kind enough to offer to drive her back to the farm to collect a few things. She had actually hoped to be able to stay at the farm, but the deputies' presence had changed those plans so she decided she would have Pastor take her to her mother's new apartment and she would stay there. He could leave the car and walk home.

"I was kidnapped this morning," she suddenly blurted out. "My next door neighbor kidnapped me and took me to Cedar Grove."

Pastor B. nearly lost control of the car as he pulled to a stop. A car coming from the opposite direction slowed down as it approached then speeded up when they recognized the car and who was driving it.

"Oh great," thought Pastor B. "That's all I need, having the Dockerts seeing me in a car parked on the side of the road with Shelley Robison on the day her husband is found shot to death next to his barn."

He started the car again and pulled ahead to a field road where he swung in and followed the road to a spot just behind a grove of trees. The car was no longer visible from the road and the pastor turned to his passenger.

"Now, what in the world are you talking about?"

I really had a difficult time getting my mind off of the cute deputy that had left an hour or so earlier. Ox and I had finished penning the stray animals, then moved on to the rest of our chores. But I kept coming back to her red hair and freckles, those nice legs wrapped in denim and the shirt that had the top couple of buttons missing.

Ox had me feed the young stock then directed me to the calf hutches where three newborn calves were bawling for food. Dairy calves are always taken from their mothers almost immediately and are given milk from their mother that has been machine milked. A good producing cow might generate enough milk to feed three or four calves, often giving the equivalent of 8-10 gallons of milk every day. At $13 for every 100 lbs of milk, giving it to a calf didn't make economic sense for the typical farmer. The exception is the milk that comes from a cow during the first three days. It's called colostrum milk and is rich in nutrients and disease fighting antibodies that are important to newborn calves.

It was this colostrom that I was feeding the calves when Ox came running up with pistols for both of us.

"The alarm," said my little-speaking best friend.

While I was confident that my many arrangements to change my life from E.Z. Anderson to Paul Banion had been successful, I had directed Ox to set up a wireless infrared alarm system around the farm. It was costly and he had tuned it so the occasional deer would have to work to set it off. So it was, that when Ox announced that the alarm had sent a signal to his pager, he knew right away where the alarm had been triggered and that it had been set off by a vehicle of some type.

I followed Ox down a fence line, keeping a few paces back. We traveled quietly and with our pistols dangling along our sides. Both of us moved in a stooped fashion, pausing every 15 seconds to listen for any movement. A doe and two fawns jumped out of the hay field on our left side and startled both of us.

"Nice stand of hay," I thought to myself, realizing that the farmer in me was starting to take hold. "Wonder whose it is."

At the end of the corn field Ox paused, then stood up.

"Over by the woods. Looks like the neighbor's car."

"What do you want to do?" I whispered back.

"Gotta check it out."

We moved forward along another fence, this one in much better repair. As a matter of fact, it was woven wire topped at the 6 ft level with two strands of barbed wire. I was pleased that Ox had provided this extra protection and motioned to him my approval.

"Didn't do it. Other neighbors' fence."

"They got a reason to keep people out."

"Yep."

There could only be one reason to keep people out. Drugs. That's just what I needed next to my new home.

As we came to the end of the line, we paused again when both car doors opened and a woman in a dress got out of the passenger side and a relatively short man with Bermuda shorts and a wildly printed shirt stepped from the driver's side.

"You know em?"

"Yeah. Preacher and next door neighbor."

Neither of our guests had seen us and as they appeared to be doing nothing that was of our concern, we used our own sign language to make the decision to head back to the house. That's when that nice doe and her two fawns decided to jump out.

"Oh, man," thought Pastor B to himself. "What am I doing here?"

He decided it would be safer if he and Shelley continued their conversation outside of the vehicle. The last thing he needed was to have a distraught female make a move on him in her grief.

"Now, what do you mean, you were kidnapped?"

It was just then that something caught his eye. He watched as a big doe and a fawn, no two fawns came bounding out of the cornfield and raced across to the tree line. He followed their progress into the woods, then his heart sank.

There at the end of the field were two men. They had turned their backs and were headed down a trail by the fence.

"Did they see us?"

"What do you think?"

"Do you know who they are?"

"Don't you?… The big one is your neighbor… I don't recognize the one in the cap."

Ox and I hurried back to the yard without so much as a word between us, both of us lost in our own thoughts about what we had just seen. When we got to the house, Ox took my weapon and walked over to a vent in the wall, which popped open with just a slight pressure from his hand. In the opening suddenly appeared a Lazy Susan like contraption that held on it several boxes of shells, some gun cleaning equipment and two cases one of which Ox used for each of the guns.

"You're going to have to show me where you have your stashes," I told Ox.

He smiled back.

"You make lunch," he commanded me.

I went to the cupboard and the refrigerator to scout out our options. Ox had done a nice job of filling both with some of our childhood favorites, which surprised me since I doubted some of the California dishes we were used to were available here. Then it dawned on me that my mother was really a Wisconsin girl and that is where she learned to cook.

"How about some roast beef sandwiches and some of these cucumbers in a nice creamy Parmesan sauce," I hollered into Ox who had plopped himself down in front of the television set.

"Get in here," Ox hollered.

"We've dispatched an Eyewitness Team to West Central Minnesota where tragedy in the form of a murder took place early this morning. It's unknown at this time if the two stories are related, but we'll have more details on our 5:00 and 10:00 broadcasts."

"What is going on?" I asked after listening to the three-second teaser on Channel 7.

"Drug bust and murder… Next door?"

I figured Ox must be right. The parade of police vehicles going by this morning must have been the drug bust. I also began thinking about the consequences for us. The fact that the deputy had stopped by and indicated that the cattle and horses had come from down the road probably meant they were tied into it as well.

I assumed the murder was part of it too. That's just what we needed - a murder investigation going on right next door to my new habitat. What were the chances of that happening on the first day of my new life?

"I'll have lunch ready in just a couple of minutes."

"No time. Company," came Ox's cryptic reply as he looked at his pager. The signal showed a vehicle coming up the driveway.

"You stay here."

I didn't disagree with Ox, for coming up the drive was a white van with giant letters across its side indicating it belonged to the television station in Alexandria. I watched as he traipsed out the door.

Pastor B. and Shelley drove back to town in quiet, both lost in their own thoughts. Shelley starting to realize that life would never be the same with Mike gone and wondering how she would be able to break the news to his parents and siblings. Then realizing it might be even more difficult to tell the story to her own mother and brother.

"What have I gotten myself mixed up in," sighed Pastor B. to himself. "These are the things they don't tell you about in seminary."

His immediate concern was how he could help Shelley through this difficult time and at the same time keep himself out of any more difficulty with the elders of the church.

"Boy, their complaint about me not getting to the hospital to visit parishioners was nothing compared to what might happen if I don't handle this just right," contemplated the preacher as he swung into the apartment building's parking lot.

"Call me if you need anything. We'll talk after you've been to the funeral home and made those arrangements."

"Thanks Pastor B. You were wonderful."

The pastor hiked down the sidewalk as fast as he could. It was three blocks to the parsonage and he truly didn't want to stop and talk with anyone. He would have run if he could, but doubted that the Bermudas would stay up if he did.

Chapter Six

"Once Upon A Time..."

"Channel 7 is out in the parking lot," reported Jim Barton. "Do you want me to talk to them?"

"You mean you haven't already?"

"Goat" was not in a mood to put up with Barton. He'd been looking out the window of his corner office, watching for the news van to arrive. He'd seen Jim Barton talking to the "suit" who must be the on-camera reporter. The camera had been rolling. He was actually surprised that Channel 7 was the first one there. A local boy was a reporter up at one of the stations in Fargo and "Goat" couldn't imagine that the grapevine hadn't gotten to them first, especially since he knew that the local kid was related to his chief deputy.

"I tried to get him to say something, but he kept saying that you were the one responsible for everything. That so Sheriff?"

The 5'8'' reporter stepped out from behind Jim and moved forward to the Sheriff with his hand outstretched. The Sheriff immediately recognized his daughter's former boyfriend.

"Kevin," Carlson said with minimal enthusiasm.

"In the flesh."

"I thought you were with one of those Fargo outfits."

"I was, but 'CCO made me an offer I couldn't refuse. So I came home."

"Ellie know yet."

"Yes, I'm surprised she hasn't told you. I've actually got a date with her tomorrow night."

"She the one called you?"

"Nope. We got it off of the AP wire. I assumed it was the paper that put it out."

"Goat"'s blood pressure went from high to boiling.

"I've got to get myself out fishing," he thought to himself, knowing that his favorite past time was not going to be possible for some time to come.

"What can you tell me Sheriff?"

"Not much, Kevin. Jim's probably already told you that we had a successful drug bust on a farm just south of Milton. We confiscated over 300 marijuana plants, growing and harvesting equipment, and quite a bit of packaged product."

"What about the murder?"

"Well, we don't know yet if it was a murder. The medical examiner has to make a determination and we have a few more interviews to complete."

"Sheriff, we went out to the scene of both and I can't see how you can't connect the two. Is it possible that the victim, this Michael Robison, was shot by one of your people?"

"No!"

"Well, did he commit suicide?"

"We'll wait for the M.E. report before saying anything more."

"Sheriff, off the record?"

"OK," knowing it wouldn't be.

"We stopped at the Mueller place. Do you know the guy living there? He is one big, ugly dude."

"Barton, get in here," hollered "GOAT" ten seconds after the reporter left his office.

"How the hell did he know where to go? And what is this crap about the neighbor acting suspicious? And what the hell was he doing with information about the raid? And, where did he get the information that two of the people we were after got away and we have no idea where they are? And..."

""Goat", it weren't me. Maybe it was Ellie. You know she's dating him again."

"Goat" marched out to the dispatcher.

"Get Carlson on the radio," referring to his daughter formally.

After two attempts, "Goat" grabbed the mike from the dispatcher and put out the call himself while grabbing his cell phone and hitting her speed dial number. After two unanswered attempts, he threw the phone across the room into his office where it bounced off the back of his chair and landed on his desk.

"Oh, crap," sputtered Ellie as she rounded the corner and saw the courthouse parking lot. "That's all I need right now."

She was just in time to see Jim Barton's nephew and her one-time lover, Kevin Walters go into the main entrance of the courthouse. She was pretty certain that her dad had no idea Kevin was back in town working for Channel 7. Kicking herself for not thinking the whole media thing through, she parked the Dodge and trailer on the backside of the parking lot and hustled into the back entrance to the courthouse.

Ten minutes later the uniformed red headed deputy wended her way through squad cars until she found her own. She fired up the engine and headed back to Harmony. All thought of delivering subpoenas had disappeared with the discovery of Mike Robison's body.

"Car 54, please report."

"Car 54, please report your whereabouts."

"Car 54, where the hell are you."

That last had been her father's voice.

Her cell phone started to ring, but she was close enough to West Bend that she would be able to use the excuse that she didn't get a signal. Everyone knew that there was a 10-mile stretch where you couldn't get a signal.

She knew her dad was upset about a lot of things, including how the raid had gone. He was also upset about the murder, if that is what it was. There had only been two others during his tenure and both of those had been domestic. But mostly, she knew how he felt about drugs in his county. Growing up with him had been a real experience. His favorite quote had been:

You bring "Coke" into my house it better be brown, wet, served over

ice and plenty of it! You bring "Hooch" into my house it better have

4

legs, a tail and have a nose for quail, dove, duck, teal, or pheasant. You

bring "Mary Jane" to my house she better be cute, know how to shoot, drive

a truck and have long hair.

The trip took her only 23 minutes and she had broken one of her dad's primary rules. "Don't run lights and sirens unless you are pursuing or are going to an emergency situation." Well, getting away from "Goat's wrath just might qualify.

It only took a few minutes in her apartment to change clothes and put on her black slacks and white blouse. She walked down the hallway and knocked on the door of number 23.

"Shelley's down to Money's," reported the door plaques namesake, Ida Ingvaldson, referring to the local funeral home. "She needs you."

Ellie went down the steps and out the rear entrance of the building. She entered the code to her garage door. It was such a nice late afternoon that she looked wistfully at her bike, a Victory Vegas, but opted for the car.

The fire red Camaro roared to life and seemed to want to jump right into 4th gear, but Ellie never made it out of 3rd on her short trip to the funeral home.

Both of us had spent the afternoon talking through the information Ox had gleaned from the reporter and what we needed to do to deal with the certain-to-come interest in all things going on in our neighborhood. There were sure to be more reporters, but what was of more concern was the fact that law enforcement would be asking questions.

We tried to figure out the significance of the local Lutheran pastor's confab with our newly murdered neighbor's wife and could come up with no rational reason other than the obvious and Ox, who knew the preacher, thought the obvious was hysterical.

The news that two of the crew from the drug mill next door had gone missing was also a bit disconcerting. We decided to do a quick scan of each of our outbuildings, just to make sure the two crooks weren't there and to be certain we hadn't left something we didn't want a cop to find.

Ox had declined an on-camera interview and that decision had been readily accepted when the reporter spied Ox's smile, which Ox had degenerated with some black tooth makeup. Ox also kept his eyes crossed during his visit with the reporter. The latter was a trick we both had mastered in 4th grade, when I was E.Z. and Ox was Jackie Forester.

In the end Ox had gotten more information from the reporter than the newsman had gotten from him. That's my Ox.

Pastor B. wasn't sure what to say to his wife when he got home. Events had transpired so quickly all day that he had barely had time to catch his own breath let alone call his wife to let her know what he was doing.

"You didn't wear that!"

"Yes, dear."

"Here it comes," thought the good-natured preacher.

His wife had been the love of his life and the bane of his existence for 27 years. He often joked that they'd been happily married for 25 years. Then he would add, "That's not bad, 25 out of 27."

Funny, the only time Mary had laughed was the first time he told the joke.

"Mary dear, tell me what I need to know."

Mary looked at him over her shoulder, then continued ironing his surplice.

"Well, you already know that Mike Robison is dead...What you may not know is that it happened during a drug raid on that farm right next to their house. There was a shootout and Mike was killed out by his barn by a stray bullet that probably came from the Sheriff's own gun."

"And, Shelley must have gone right from her office and rendezvoused with a strange man, because the Dockerts saw her making out with him right in broad daylight. Can you imagine! Her husband not even cold and she's with another man."

Pastor B.'s body temperature went up with that last, as did the color in his face. But his wife never noticed. She continued with her verbal missive.

"The Sheriff suspects the big man that is farming the Mueller place may have had something to do with it too. You know the one. He's been in church quite a bit lately."

"Anything else, Honey?"

"Just that Shelley's brother was arrested in the raid and tried to use a little baby as a shield to keep the cops, I mean police officers, from shooting at him. Not only that, the Sheriff brought a stock trailer to the raid and left with those poor people's cattle and horses and took them all to his place."

"I sure hope Jim Barton runs against that evil man," she concluded.

Pastor B. smiled to himself as he realized that the Harmony grapevine had once again provided much more excitement than the truth ever could have.

"I'm going to go change and then run over to the office for a few minutes. I've got to call some folks about the funeral on Thursday."

"What funeral…you're not thinking of burying that woman's husband out of our church? Bartholomew Brooks, I'll never get the ladies to serve a meal after the funeral."

"Oh, I think there will be no shortage of people willing to be at that funeral."

"I don't know what to say," said a teary-eyed new widow. "He would really like that hunting scene in his casket, but that seems like an awful lot of money when his eyes are going to be closed."

Just then the ding-dong of the front door opening caused both Shelley and John Money to turn their attention to the door just in time to see Ellie Carlson walk through the solid glass entrance. Shelley stood up and walked to meet her. The two women hugged each other. Ellie pulled a handkerchief out of the pocket in her blouse and wiped Shelley's eyes then kissed her cheek.

Money watched discreetly from his office then moved forward.

"Hi, Ellie."

"John."

"What brings you here, Ellie?"

"What do you think?"

"We were just discussing caskets…"

"John thinks that I should have this one with the pheasants flying up…"

"Shelley, lets talk."

Five minutes later, the two women came back. Ellie took charge, laid out what Shelley could afford and challenged John Money to meet her budget. She had him throw in several extra bouquets and had made sure that the bill would be sent to her first. John had agreed to add a tent for the family and also to have three extra ushers at no additional costs.

"Ellie, do you have any idea what happened?" queried Shelley of her long time friend as they stopped by their respective cars in the funeral home parking lot.

"Oh, Shelley you know I can't say anything. Dad is being really closed mouth about it with me because he knows we are friends. Did he talk with you today?"

"Yes, but he was really strange and I was so out of it after Pastor B. told me that Mike was dead that I honestly don't know what I said."

They had agreed to talk some more when they got back to the apartment building, but instead they were greeted with reporters from the local paper and from three television stations. It seems that Jim Barton knew where Shelley's mother lived. Ellie quickly parked her car and ran around to the front of the apartment building to escort Shelley to Mrs. Ingvaldson's apartment.

"You're sure about this ballistics report you sent me?" questioned the Sheriff of the Minnesota Bureau of Criminal Apprehension. "No question about it being the gun?...I don't want to put words in your mouth... Well, I know you said the bullet was too fragmented, but you did say it was a .22 and you did say that the rifle I gave you had just been fired, and you did say the prints on the stock and the partial on the shells could be identified...."

"All right, I think I can get you some comparison prints within the next couple of days. Not a word to anyone about this."

The Sheriff returned to the notes that his daughter had typed up from their late morning at the crime scene. The ME's preliminary autopsy report was also sitting on his desk. The gunshot had definitely been the cause of death. The ME had found no other marks except for several small puncture wounds on the back and the thigh and the strange slices on the hands and face of the victim. Upon Doc Gilbert's suggestion, he had rushed some hair, blood and tissue samples down to Hennepin County's crime lab for spectrometry analysis.

A review of all the evidence told the experienced criminologist that 1.) Mike Robison was a drug user, 2.) Mike Robison's body had likely been moved, but a relatively short distance just moments after death, 3.) That Mike Robison had been in a cornfield shortly before death, and 4.) Mike had received at least one puncture wound prior to death and two after death.

"Ox, my damned back is really aching. How do you do it every day?"

We had just finished evening chores and Ox had insisted that I do all of the milking. He had helped me put the filter in the pipeline and made sure that the pipe went into the bulk tank. He'd shown me where the switch was to agitate the milk to keep it stirred up. He'd listed the cows that were being treated for this or that ailment and whose milk couldn't go into the bulk tank. Then he'd disappeared to "check on the heifers".

It took me nearly three hours to complete the milking compared to the two hours it had taken in the morning. I was a little slower then Ox and probably a bit more careful about cleaning the teats then he had been. I was also cautious going in and out between the cows, not wanting to repeat any of the misadventures of the morning.

"Wanna grill?"

"Sure Ox, you go right on ahead. I'm going to shower and shave."

When I came down from the bathroom I discovered Ox wasn't alone out on the patio. Sitting with him was the man whom we'd seen out by the woods. He'd changed out of his shorts, but the flowered shirt with peacocks was one I'd never forget. He turned to me as I came out the patio door.

"You must be Paul," he stated. "I'm Bart Brooks."

I walked over to the gentleman and shook his hand, looking at Ox quizzically.

"Preacher," he mouthed

"Jack has told me so much about you," began the preacher.

I jerked my head in Ox's direction. He shirked his shoulders and smiled, then shook his head.

"I know that both of you were trained as police officers and worked in law enforcement before coming here to Minnesota. Frankly, I need someone who is objective and has at least some law enforcement experience."

"Well, Pastor I'm not sure what you're looking for, but our experience was limited to being security guards on a college campus."

"Oh."

We invited the preacher to stay for supper, which was a mistake since he packed away more food than both of us combined. He especially liked my cucumber salad that had been left over from lunch.

Ox had grilled half-pound burgers to perfection. The meat was lean and really tasty. When I asked Ox where he'd gotten it, he replied, "Number 61."

The preacher had hinted around several times that he wanted to talk about something. I figured he was trying to find out if we had seen him out by the woods. Neither of us let on that we had.

By 8 o'clock he had finished half of our food and gotten nothing else from us, when he decided to leave.

"What do you suppose that was all about?" I asked Ox.

"Dunno."

"I'll do the dishes."

"Yep."

Early the next morning Sheriff Carlson was greeted by his favorite deputy, Jim Barton.

"Sheriff, did you see this bulletin from Cedar Grove County? A car was stolen from someone's driveway yesterday morning. I called over there. Keys were in it while the owner was delivering an Avon order. She came out and the car was gone."

"You thinking it's our guys, Jim."

"Could be, but how did they get to Cedar Grove?" queried the chief deputy. "Steal a car out by the farm or have a vehicle stashed away?"

"No, unless you guys missed something. You know it's almost 6 miles to get from that farm into Milton, but what if they headed across country instead of the roads? Pull out that township map."

"Geese, I never even thought of that. We followed the cattle trail to the west and south, but they could have gone straight north and it's not much more than a mile and a half. They'd have come in by the grain elevator and nobody would have given them a second thought. There's always guys who've brought grain in and leave their tractors at the elevator and walk down to the café."

"But how did they get from Milton to Cedar Grove?"

"An accomplice?"

"Jim, do you know who works in Milton?"

"Yeah I do. Are you thinking what I'm thinking?…No honor among thieves."

"It would sure explain a lot if Robison was involved in this thing."

"The Mrs. too?"

"Sure, why she just might have been carrying on with one of the two that's missing."

"What if there aren't two missing, but just one and the other is laying dead down in the morgue?"

"That sure would fit in with what she said at the office when that squirt preacher told her that her husband was dead," agreed the Sheriff.

"Wasn't it her brother we arrested with the women and children?"

"Yes it was," said the Sheriff, as he remembered what Jim wouldn't know – who told them about the drug operation in the first place.

"What do you mean you don't have Mike yet? He was supposed to come right to the funeral home," said a bewildered Shelley.

"I'm sorry Mrs. Robison, but Swenson hauled…I mean transported the body down to Minneapolis. The Sheriff insisted on an autopsy and wanted it done by the Hennepin County Medical Examiner. I just assumed you were told."

Shelley was disturbed by the news not only because it was something totally unexpected but also because the Sheriff hadn't said anything. Come to think of it, she realized, neither had her friend Ellie.

"Mom, I'm going to try to catch Ellie before she goes to work," she called out as she went through her mother's apartment door.

Ellie hadn't left yet but was in uniform and obviously ready to walk out the door when she answered Shelley's knock.

"Hi Shell…What's wrong?"

Shelley shared the information she had just gotten from the funeral home director. Ellie didn't seem surprised by the new information and Shelley began to feel a sense of panic tighten its grip around chest.

"Shelley, its pretty standard to ask for an autopsy in a death that isn't from natural causes. You know that. Dad's probably just being overly cautious. Let me call him to find out what's going on.

Five minutes later she came back into the living room from her bedroom where she had gone to make the call.

"Money's wrong, they just sent some blood and tissue samples down to Hennepin County. They were just going to call the funeral home to let them know they were ready to have Mike picked up. Now quit your worrying."

"Thanks Ellie."

"OK John, so we can plan on having the wake and a family prayer service tomorrow evening from 5 to 9. And the service itself will be at 11:00 on Thursday morning with committal in our cemetery…. Yes, I have the ladies taking care of a meal… No, I don't think we'll need extra chairs. We can get some from Good Shepherd across the street if we need them. You really think there will be that many?...Wow!...OK, I'll get there by 4:30…Thanks John."

It really irritated Pastor B.'s wife when she couldn't hear both sides of a conversation especially one that involved the juiciest news to hit Harmony in the 8 years they had lived there. Pastor B. knew that so when he got off the phone, he walked over to his wife and said, "I'm going over to the office to work on my sermon."

"That's what you said last night."

"Yes?"

"I called you there and you didn't answer."

"You know I don't answer the phone if I'm with someone."

Mary Brooks didn't tell her husband that she had actually walked over to the church to check on the candles, or at least that was the excuse she had planned on using. When she arrived at the church, not only was her husband not there, but his car was gone as well.

Mary trusted her husband completely, but she was very worried about him. He was such an innocent when it came to how people in the real world could take advantage of you. Bart had more than once reached out to his parishioners only to get in trouble. He had a different set of rules when it came to friendship, caring, and compassion. And, Mary Brooks was afraid that one day her husband's rules or lack of them would get him in trouble.

Ox woke me up the next morning and informed me that he had already gotten the chores done. I looked at the clock and realized that it was 7:30 in the morning. I was really going to have a hard time getting used to all the fresh air, the hard work and the huge amounts of food we were consuming.

"Sorry Ox," I begged.

"Cut hay today," was his reply.

Ox had spent the better part of a year establishing our farm, purchasing equipment, and developing an elaborate ruse informing people about who we were and what our plans were. In his scenario, we were cousins from California who had decided to come back to our Minnesota roots and start a dairy farm. He had planned to tell everyone who asked that he had quit his job in security and that I was trying to do the same.

There is a story about an old dairy farmer asking the question, "You know how to end up with a million dollars after a year of farming? Start the year out with two million."

And, to a certain extent it was true, so Ox and I had come up with a story about our grandfather leaving us enough money to get a start in farming and that it had been both of our lifelong dreams to do just that. For all the elaborate planning, fabricating, and downright lies we were willing to come up with, the plain truth was that nobody asked. That's Minnesota Nice.

"Called the neighbor lady. Offered to do up her hay. Said yes."

Interpretation: Ox had called the neighbor woman who had lost her husband the day before and suggested that the hay was at its prime and ready to be cut and baled. He had offered our services and she had agreed.

I knew what I would be doing the rest of the day and I could hardly wait. Driving tractor and implements was exactly why I loved

farming. You could have that cow stuff. Give me a nice John Deere
4020 with a haybine and I would be in seventh heaven.

After a quick breakfast of toast and an apple, I headed to the
shed where Ox was already hooking up the tractor to the haybine.
We each grabbed a grease gun and within a few minutes had greased
up both the rig I would use as well as the John Deere 6040 and Gehl
round baler that Ox was going to use on hay that he had cut on our
farm just three days earlier.

Ox took the vintage 1951 green pickup that he had fixed up
over the winter and led the way out of our driveway and around the
block to our neighbors. He had thrown an ancient bicycle into the
truck bed and informed me I could use it if I ran into any problems
with the tractor.

As we rolled into the driveway, I got sight of a sign declaring
Mike and Shelley Robison owned the farm. Ox had told me that it
had been in the family, Shelley's family, for nearly a hundred years
and was actually known as the Ingvaldson Farm.

The farmyard consisted of a nice two-story house with a
porch that surrounded nearly three-fourths of the house. There was a
separate garage and what appeared to be a tool shed. There were two
doors on the east side. One appeared to go into the house, the other
down into a cellar or basement. There was a large white barn with a
pen on one side. It didn't appear to have any livestock. A large red
machinery shed stood next to several grain bins and there was what
appeared to be an old hen house standing just to the north of them. It
was a nice yard, almost a duplicate of our own.

Ox got out of the pickup and climbed up on the tractor with me. He motioned me down a path that I negotiated carefully, continuously comparing the progress my tractor was making with that of the implement I pulled. At a gate, Ox jumped down and pulled back 5 strands of wire attached to four sticks of wood. He motioned me through the gate into the alfalfa field.

I took a refresher course in how to proceed with tractor and equipment and a reminder that I needed to take it easy until I had made the first round.

Ox stood off to the side and waved me on. I moved the throttle forward, engaged the power take off and let out the clutch. I was cutting hay. Ox watched me until I reached the side of the field. I knew he was concerned that I make the turn properly. When I had made the maneuver, I looked proudly back to him, but he was gone.

I had nearly made it all the way around when a movement got my eye. It was the same doe we had seen the day before but this time she bounded over the fence by herself. The wire twanged as she hit it. A split second later I glanced down to my right and saw light tan where there should have been only green. My reflexes were quick, but not quick enough as a fawn flowed up the conveyor and disappeared into the machine. A second fawn lay just three feet ahead of the same fate, oblivious to the fate of his brother and to how close his own demise had come.

I shut the machinery down.

I climbed down from the tractor and walked to the rear of the haybine, expecting a mess, but there lay the lifeless fawn without a scratch. It was dead, no doubt of that. I picked it up every so gently, aware that its mother was watching from the woods. I walked it over to the fence and laid it down on stubble freshly mowed with the thought that I would retrieve and bury it at a later time.

It was then that I spied, just feet away, a strip of plaid cloth hung up on a barb of the wire. It was ragged and less than two inches long and strangely there was what appeared to be denim on another barb no more than three feet further down. Upon closer inspection I noted that both pieces of fabric had been torn at a right angle to its respective mother garment. The denim's white under-thread was slightly discolored either from the rust of the barb or the tear of the owner's flesh.

I couldn't help but reflect that the owner of this field I was cutting could very well have been the owner of the pieces of material now waiting a decision from nature as to whether it would become a part of some rat's nest or coat the home of one of the Orioles dog fighting in and out of the woods.

A sharp bleating from the other fawn brought me back to the reality of the tasks at hand.

Chapter Seven

"When Harry Met Sally. No, When Paul Met Shelley"

Shelley left her mother's apartment a little after noon. She hadn't been able to eat anything except a saltine cracker with some egg salad on it. Her mother had made the egg salad several days earlier and it had tasted like it. Shelley would have loved to stop by the Milton Café for one of their "Heartstopper" burgers, but knew that it wouldn't look good for a newly widowed woman to be eating alone in the Cafe.

"I don't understand what I'm feeling right now," Shelley thought. "It's like I don't even miss Mike."

She headed out of town on Highway 210, hoping no one would see her. "A widow in grief should be with family and friends," she thought.

The trip out to the farm had taken less than 12 minutes. She pulled up to the mailbox to grab yesterday's mail and the Hawks Hill Daily Journal. She threw the accumulation onto the passenger seat, glancing at the paper as she did. Her heart skipped a beat when she realized that Mike was staring back at her from the front page of the paper.

The headlines read, "Local man killed in drug raid". Shelley pulled the car quickly into the farmyard and grabbed the paper to read the front-page article. She was shocked to see that there was speculation that Mike had been a part of the drug ring. The article even hinted that he was one of two people who had originally been thought to have gotten away during the raid.

Suddenly the previous day's trip from Milton to Cedar Grove with her unwanted passenger came flying back into the widow's mind.

"How could I not tell anyone about what happened?"

It was then that she heard the distant sound of a tractor.

"It's Mike...no, it can't be Mike," sobbed the woman with a new realization that her life with Mike had ended on day two thousand one hundred ninety-three.

"Oh how I hate you, Mike!"

The tractor rounded the barn and came toward the car, slowing down as it got to within a few feet.

Shelley quickly wiped her eyes and stepped out of the car, expecting to see her friendly if not quiet neighbor. Then she realized what she saw was a smaller version of the man she knew as Jack. This version had a keen sense of awareness betrayed by his blue eyes. It was as though he took everything in at once.

"You must be Jack's cousin. He told me you'd be showing up one of these days. It's so nice of you to take care of the hay. Fill your tractor up from the gas tank over there," Shelley said, indicated a large red tank on stilts.

"Hi. No need for that. Just trying to be neighborly. Ox and I are both very sorry for your loss."

"Ox?"

"It's what I call Jack."

"What do I call you?"

"Paul, Paul Banion."

At first Shelley thought he must be joking or that she had misheard what he said.

Shelley moved closer to the tractor to converse with this humorous stranger. As she got nearer the tractor, she was startled to see what appeared to be an animal laid across driver's lap.

"Is… that…dead?"

"Oh, I'm sorry," said Paul, realizing what the Bambi must look like. "It jumped right into the machine. There was nothing I could do."

"So what are you doing with it now?"

"Um…I…a…guess I'm going to…a…bury it." He mumbled.

"Well, you can't lug it around on your lap like that. I'll go get a spade and we can bury it in the woods over there," she pointed. "We have a little pet cemetery there."

Paul carried the animal over to where there were a number of wooden crosses, most with writing scratched on them. He lay the carcass down and took the shovel from Shelley. It only took a few minutes to move sufficient dirt to bury the tiny fawn.

"Now what?" asked Paul awkwardly.

"What do you mean," replied an equally awkward observer.

"Do you pray over it or something?"

"It's a dead deer," stammered the distraught widow.

Then she burst into tears again.

Boy did I feel stupid. Here I was hauling around a dead baby deer when I came across this poor woman whose husband has just been murdered. She had obviously been crying and how could I blame her. She seemed nice enough. She'd come right up to the tractor with a smile on her face. That is she had a smile on her face until she saw the dead deer. I thought she was going to crown me when she saw the poor thing.

I tried as best as I could to explain what had happened and she must have finally understood because the next thing I know we're talking about all of her family pets that have died over the years and we're walking down to the "cemetery". It took a couple of spades of dirt to make a hole big enough for the fawn.

I thought I was being the nice sensitive guy my mother taught me to be when I asked her if I was supposed to say a little prayer or something. Sensitive, yeah. I no more than get the words out of my mouth when she starts bawling. Then what do I do. Nothing. They don't cover that kind of thing in any FBI manual or dairy farmer manual, as far as that goes.

Without saying another word she turned and walked away from me, back up toward the house. I followed discreetly behind her until I got to the tractor. I was about to climb up onto the seat when I spied a pile of letters and a newspaper that she had put on the hood of the car when she went to get the shovel. If I left them, they'd blow away. So I picked them up and followed her up to the house.

As we got closer to the house, she turned her head over her shoulder and saw that I was following her. For whatever reason, she sped up and got to the door well before I did. Strangely, she held the door open and beckoned me in. I had just witnessed the strangest performance I'd ever seen. This woman had gone from grief to fear to seduction, I realized as I looked into her hazel eyes. Who am I to understand the female species?

"I…ah…came out to get some different clothes for tomorrow and Thursday," she informed me.

I knew not of what she spoke, but guessed it had to do with funeral arrangements. She seemed to assume I would know what she was talking about.

"Could you or would you have a cup of coffee or something with me?"

"O.K."

"I mean I just don't want to be in the house alone and I didn't realize it until I came up to the door."

"O.K"

"Here, just sit down right here while I make us something."

This was one strange woman, but I liked her. Perhaps it was her vulnerability that drew me to her. At the same time, she also dismayed me. After all, yesterday morning her husband had been murdered. Yet later in the afternoon Ox and I had witnessed the preacher and her having a little tryst out by our woods. Now she was flirting with me.

As she moved from the refrigerator, from which she pulled a canister of coffee, to the sink to get water, I glanced at the paper I'd brought in. I skimmed the article on the front page and had just about finished when I looked up to see that she was looking at me.

"It's not true."

I sure hoped it wasn't, because this was just too fine a lady to have to spend the next 3 years in jail on a drug charge.

Just then I heard a growling. I turned to face the reincarnation of "Tags" Titaglio's Rottweiler. Had they found me?

"Max, take it easy!" soothed the deputy.

"Ellie, hi. What are you doing here?" queried an embarrassed Shelley.

"I told you I'd bring Max back from the kennel. I was just going to drop him off here and put him in the barn, then I saw your car. Hello Mr. Banion. Is that your tractor out there?"

Paul looked at the young deputy and remembered his manners long enough to get up and move to the other chair so Ellie could sit next to her friend. He grunted an affirmative answer to her query about the tractor.

"I don't get it," he thought to himself. "I'm like a school kid with a crush on his teacher the minute this deputy walks into the room."

Ellie was more than a little curious as to what Paul Banion was doing with her friend. This was not a time, she figured, for Shelley to be opening herself up to strangers; especially after what she had heard at the Sheriff's office and read in today's Journal.

"I see you've got the paper."

"Yes. Can you believe what they are saying about Mike?"

"Shelley, have you given any thought to…" then she chastised herself. This was not a conversation she wanted to have right now in front of Banion.

"…to what you're going to do with Max now," as she changed the subject.

Shelley caught on and turned the conversation to options for Mike's dog, Mad Max.

The ignored Paul finished his coffee and took his excuses with him out the door. He knew when it was time for "woman talk." He was no dummy.

"Shelley, what do you know about that guy," started Ellie. "You've got to be careful right now. People are starting to wonder about all the things that have been happening."

"Ellie, he seemed like such a nice man. He and Jack offered to do the hay for me and I was just being neighborly and saying thanks."

"OK. But you need to be thinking about the future."

"Ellie, this farm has been in my family for a hundred years. I'm not going to sell it, no matter how much I want to get away."

"I'm not talking about the farm or that future. I'm talking about tomorrow and the next day and the day after."

"The funeral?"

"Yes, the funeral. But Shelley, Hon, I think you really need to talk with Andy about what's in the paper. What if they begin to put two and two together and get five? You could be linked to the drug ring or worse."

"Ellie, what are you talking about?"

"I can't say anymore," remembering her duties as a deputy and daughter. "But you need to talk to Andy right away."

It was hot. Probably the hottest day of the summer as Goat got into his Ford Explorer. While it wasn't a police package Crown Vic, the Ford had been equipped with lights and sirens and had the biggest engine he could order. It was white with the Sheriff's logo detailed nicely on both sides. It had leather interior, GPS mapping, stereo sound, heated seats, and wonderful air conditioning that took less than 3 minutes to cool down the whole vehicle.

Yesterday had been a disaster, but by the end of the evening last night Goat had realized that his strategy was going to work. He'd made sure that Barton had heard enough of his conversations with the Cedar Grove County Sheriff and the medical examiner from Hennepin County that even Barton could figure out what must have happened.

The result of his strategy of using Barton's contacts with the press had shown up in today's Daily Journal. Robison's death was being tied in to the drug ring, which it probably was anyway. And, suspicion was being directed away from any bungling that may have occurred during the raid. Even the Cedar Grove County Sheriff had agreed that the auto theft was likely just some kids joy riding.

The quickly arranged blood and tissue tests had shown a definite presence of THC, Tetrahydrocannabinol, and it had not only been in the blood, indicating recent use, but also in the hair, indicating prolonged use. His deputies had found nothing in the house, but that was to be expected. They hadn't spent much time there before the woman showed up with the preacher. They had found a gun though.

Goat had spoken with Wally Setten, the county attorney and knew that he should technically have had a search warrant, but he figured the entire farmyard and buildings were all part of the crime scene.

"Why," reasoned the Sheriff, "the decedent could have been shot in the house and made it out to the barn. Setten had looked at him skeptically when he said that. That guy knew more about what was going on than Goat liked. He had heard rumors that Wally was going to support Barton this fall.

The Sheriff smiled to himself as he contemplated some of the actions that he had planned that would take place over the next few days. He would get so much positive press that Barton might even think twice about running against him in November.

I quickly finished my coffee and the oatmeal raisin cookie that the widow had placed on a small plate for me. Neither of the women seemed disappointed to see me go. I hiked out to the tractor, fired it up and reversed the path I'd used to get to the Ingvaldson farm. It had been a good day.

As I arrived back to our farmyard, Ox was just parking the round baler in the shed. He had been able to get the whole field done and wanted to use the 4020 to move the bales off of the field over to the fence line where they would wait until needed this fall and winter.

"Done?" he asked.

"Yeah, but I hit a damn fawn."

"Venison burgers tonight?"

"No, it didn't do anything to the haybine, but the lady showed up just as I was bringing it home to bury. She got all teary eyed and upset so we buried it there."

"You comfort her," implying more than what was said.

"Ox, don't even go there. But I will tell you that I think that lady has got more problems then a dead husband. I could see finger print dust on several surfaces and she was saying that the Sheriff's men were in her house when she got there yesterday. She said they took a gun. And, something else. Have you seen the papers? I think someone is out to put her at the scene of the murder and maybe involved in the drug thing."

"That's what preacher was hinting at last night."

"I know. I thought he was wantin' to know if we had seen the two of them. I think he's worried about her. He may know more about what's going on then he let on last night."

"Funeral?"

"You know small towns, Ox. If we don't show up, there may be questions asked."

Chapter Eight

"That Was the Night"

Freshly showered after a long day, Ellie looked over her naked body as it appeared, gradually unconcealed, from her legs up as the fog retreated from the mirror in her bathroom. Her excitement at spending some time with Kevin was obvious as her body betrayed the fact that she'd not been with anyone since he'd left a year ago.

It wasn't as though there weren't opportunities, just not the right guy at the right time. Even now she wasn't sure if Kevin were the right guy or if the night after the death of her best friend's husband was the best time. And, there was this new guy in town whom she was intrigued with. Whoa! The thought of him triggered an even greater response.

"Maybe I should get back in the shower," she joked with herself. It was the first time she had smiled in three days.

She and Kevin had agreed to take things slow. Well, actually she had insisted and Kevin had finally agreed. To emphasize her resolve, Ellie had been sure to drive her own car to the restaurant overlooking the activity of a summer night on Otter Tail Lake. She told herself that if he moved too fast or if it seemed like Kevin was only interested in getting a story, she would up and leave on him.

Kevin had arrived first and was pacing up and down when Ellie walked in the door. He had forgotten just how great this redhead looked. Seeing her brought back some real memories, enough so that he had to turn away for a minute to get his thoughts and body under control. When he went to give her a hug, she rebutted the effort with an outstretched hand. He chuckled to himself, "so that's how it is going to be."

He ordered Champagne, then Caesar salads for them both. There was fresh Walleye for her and a nice steak for him.

The two former lovers were uncomfortable at first, but the contentment of two old friends soon took over.

"I hear your Dad is scrambling to clean up yesterday's mess. What was he thinking of with that trailer stunt?"

"It was my idea too."

"Oh."

"Kevin, can we just not talk about work?"

"Sure."

But his "sure" had only led to more questions as he came at things from first one angle and then another. Finally, Ellie had had enough and implemented her backdoor strategy

"Can you excuse me for a second? I need to use the ladies room."

One minute later she was in her Camaro and heading down County Road 7 to her home. She fumed the whole way home. "I should have known! Once a creep, always a creep."

The phone had been ringing when she walked into her apartment. Caller ID showed Kevin's cell phone number. She didn't answer. Luckily she'd not given him her cell number, keeping that part of her identity well guarded.

Fifteen minutes later, the buzzer for the secure apartment lobby entrance set off her phone again. She turned her television to channel 3 and saw that it was Kevin waiting expectantly. The phone rang again and then again three minutes later. Ellie watched, stewing over the loss of her Walleye and the loss of an evening.

The lobby door opened and Ellie observed her friend Shelley and Mrs. Ingvaldson enter. They appeared to chat with Kevin for a couple of minutes, and then Shelley took the key from her mother and opened the door. Kevin marched in with them.

To her surprise, her own door did not receive the anticipated knock. Instead, she heard muffled voices and footsteps go past her apartment and down the hall.

"Shelley, what are you doing," exclaimed the deputy to herself. "There are only so many ways I can keep you from hurting yourself."

Chapter Nine

"Mr. Green Jeans"

I was really starting to get the hang of chores by now. It was the third morning that I had milked. Well, all right, I admit that I slept in yesterday, but Ox had gotten me up on time this morning and I had to confess that the summer air was really doing me well. Once again, Ox encouraged me to handle the milking duties by myself and at the rate I was going I could easily have knocked off a good fifteen minutes from my previous attempt at manipulating the milk from these bovine beauties.

I was just approaching the half way mark, when Ox came running in to tell me to take the milkers off of the three cows I was draining of their white nectar.

Once they were off, he stepped back into the milk house and suddenly there was silence where just seconds before had been the steady hum of vacuum pumps sucking their quarry dry.

"Come here," Ox motioned as he stuck his head through the solid wooden door that led into the 16 X 24 foot room that housed the bulk tank and milk pumps.

I walked over to him wondering what in the world would cause him to halt my progress in achieving what would have been a new record for milk solicitation from the 65 four-legged assets ensconced in our barn.

I could have nearly cried when I spied the reason for Ox's insistence on my interruption of milking endeavors. There, still spewing its white contents, was the pipeline, not directed into the bulk tank, as it should have been, but instead focusing its now thin white juice into the sink. I had neglected to install the business end of the pipe into the receptacle where it would have dumped its gallons of produce into a cooling environment designed to keep this wonderful beverage cool and refreshing.

"Few hundred dollars down the drain," came Ox's dismissal of the lapse in judgment on my part.

"Literally," came my humiliated reply.

"Forgot the filter too."

It was not one of Paul Banion's best days. Ox was a little blue also. I won't say the obvious lest those indulging in the reading of this narrative would immediately dog-ear a page and put us away. Oh, I can't resist it.

"You might say we were Paul Banion and his blue Ox, uh Babe."

Pastor B. nearly lost the toaster strudel that he had been savoring just moments before. His practice of late had been to rise early, take a brisk, if not short walk around the block and return just in time for the coffee to have completed brewing so that he could pop a toaster strudel into the toaster without fear that the coffee brewer and toaster on the same circuit would overload the limited capacity and cause the breaker to disengage.

This morning he had forgone the walk in lieu of watching the morning news. Since Kevin Walker had returned, Pastor B. enjoyed watching the cut-in from the Alexandria station at 6:25 and 7:25 because Kevin was often the reporter. Kevin had been in Trinity's Little Lambs youth group when the Brooks had moved to Harmony. It was kind of exciting to see someone on television who you knew.

"In an exclusive interview with this reporter, Shelley Robison, wife of slain drug kingpin in Maplewood County, admitted that she had transported another of the gang members from Milton to Cedar Grove two days ago shortly after the raid carried out by Sheriff "Goat" Carlson and his daughter Deputy Ellie Carlson came to its unsuccessful conclusion. We'll have more on this story tonight at 6 and 10. Reporting live from Harmony, Minnesota this is Kevin Walters."

Pastor B. tried to pick up the pieces of his strudel and succeeded only in spreading the icing over his pant legs. He knew the story that ran on the news this evening would have a devastating impact on the community and on his nice little world. He also wondered what else poor Shelley might have told Kevin.

Sheriff Carlson had stopped at the Crystal Lake Café on his way to work. He tried to do that two or three times each week. He ordered his usual, peanut butter toast and black coffee and was just starting to get the peanut butter off of the roof of his mouth when he noticed that a couple of the patrons were getting louder and louder. They were actually laughing and it seemed to Goat that he might even be what they were laughing at.

He looked at them with a steely glare that had been known to put the fear of God in lesser men. It did little to these two jokers other than to make them laugh even louder, albeit with an attempt to hide their mirth.

"What's with you two?"

"We hear you was arrest'n a baby and her mommy while the real crooks were getting' a taxi ride from their next door neighbor."

"What are you talking about?"

"Didn't you hear…that lady what lost her husband on Monday in the big drug raid…while you was arresting those folks, she was hauling the bossman out of the county. Told that reporter what grew up over there in Harmony all about it. Was on the news this morning. He says they's gonna be a lot more on the news tonight."

Goat threw a five dollar bill next to the cash register and was out of the parking lot less than 30 seconds later. His radio was burning in his hand as he rounded the corner onto highway 210 with out bothering to stop for the stop sign.

She looked on in disbelief as the morning news cut in showed Kevin Walters standing outside of her mother's apartment building. Shelley couldn't believe it. She had been talking to her best friend's boyfriend, not a reporter.

"How could you do that to a friend?" she questioned the television.

Her equally puzzled mother sat on the couch across from her daughter. The two of them had been surprised to see Kevin standing in the lobby entrance when they had returned from the funeral home.

"I've been waiting for you," he had said as they came in the door. "Shelley, I just wanted to offer my condolences for Mike. Mrs. Ingvaldson, so nice to see you again."

And just like that it had seemed the most natural of circumstances to invite this Harmony alum, who was now a celebrity of sorts, into their apartment for a cup of coffee. They had visited for nearly an hour, Kevin drawing Shelley out from the depression she'd felt for several days. They had talked about life on the farm, what Mike was doing, what Shelley was doing, the kids whom Mrs. I. (all the high school kids had called Shelley's mom "Mrs. I.") was teaching in her second grade class. It had been so relaxing. Perhaps too much so, for Shelley had passed on to Kevin in confidence what had happened in the half hour or so just before the Sheriff had walked into Andy's office.

"Kevin, at the time I was so scared. I knew right away who it was in my car and he insisted that I give him a ride from the office over to Cedar Grove. But I had no idea about the raid or that Mike would end up dead."

"Shelley, why didn't you tell the Sheriff?"

"You know, I was OK by the time I got back to the office and I think I probably would have called someone, but just then Mr. Carlson and Pastor walked in and it was like my whole world came to a crashing end. My first thought was that my neighbor, whatever his name is, had killed Mike and would come after me. Then the Sheriff started asking me questions and, like a dummy, I answered them."

"What kind of questions?"

"Oh, you know like where was I this morning and how did I get along with Mike and if I knew how to handle a gun."

"A gun?"

"Yeah, that's the question that made me stop and think 'what's going on here?'" Then I saw Andy's note."

"What note?"

"Andy gave me a note when I first went to work for him. It's a reminder for whenever somebody calls and they've been arrested. I'm supposed to say: 'Don't say a word until Mr. Ratcliff is there with you.' So I decided I should take his advice."

"Do you think the Sheriff was going to arrest you?"

"Oh, Kevin. I don't know. I was so confused and just not myself by then that I don't know what he was doing."

"Does anyone else know about your trip to Cedar Grove?"

"Just mom and Pastor B."

"Pastor B.?"

"Just in general terms," had said Shelley realizing that this last information might be best kept private.

"And Ellie doesn't know?"

"Kevin, weren't you supposed to be with Ellie tonight?"

"Yeah, but our signals got crossed and it didn't work out," half-truthed the reporter.

By morning, the reporter had developed Shelley's tale into a full-blown narrative of love triangles, trysts, intrigue, and law enforcement ineptitude with a promise of more information yet to come. Shelley was devastated, but not nearly as much as Ellie.

It appeared to Ellie that it might be another year before she would get "lucky". Since she and Kevin had gone their separate ways, Ellie had focused first on completing her criminal justice degree, then on finding a job and keeping it.

That job just might be in jeopardy if her father had seen the teaser that Kevin had on the morning news. The innuendo that her father had done less than stellar work had been eclipsed only by the fact Kevin had mentioned her own name.

"This might be the day to deliver those subpoenas," thought Ellie, not looking forward to being in the office with her father around. It was just as she approached Crystal Lake that she saw her dad's car come flying through the stop sign at the intersection onto Highway 210. His lights and siren were not on, but he was making time. She slowed her own vehicle down and signaled a right turn. "No sense in getting to work to soon," she contemplated.

A few minutes later she pulled into the Crystal Lake Café parking lot. Three men were standing between a couple of pickups, slapping each other on the back and having a good time. "Probably sharing fishing stories," expected the deputy. She parked her car and started for the restaurant, feeling safe in the knowledge that her dad had long since departed his favorite spot for breakfast.

"Hey, deputy! You just missed your boss. Yeah, he was here investigating. Looking for bad guys! Seems he's misplaced one or two."

They roared with laughter at what had to be an inside joke.

"Hi Ellie," came the greeting from the waitress behind the till. "You want to give your dad his change? He left in a hurry."

"Just keep it. I'm sure he meant to leave it as a tip."

They both smiled at the redhead's little joke. Sheriff "Goat" Carlson never left a tip anywhere.

"Kevin's back in town."

"Oh, I know it," replied the deputy.

"The guys were talking about a story he's working on. Saw it on the news this morning. Anything to that lady killing her husband and running off with one of the druggies?"

Ellie's frown reminded the waitress of previous discussions and questions that she had attempted with the Sheriff's daughter. All to no avail.

"All right, you can't blame me for trying. It really does make for good conversation around here."

"Yep, I can imagine it would. There are all sorts of stories that would make for good conversation."

The prompt was all the middle aged woman needed to remind herself that three months earlier her own son could very easily have been the source of such a conversation, but a young deputy, new on the job had quietly handled a tricky situation involving a certain young woman with a promise from mother and son that "it will never, ever, ever happen again".

"This one's on me," quipped the server as she delivered a coffee and Danish.

"Let's put it on dad's tab," replied the smiling face.

Chapter Ten

"That's A Bunch of Bull"

Ox and I hauled our weary butts out of the barn about 10:30. Once the pipeline had been put into the bulk tank and Ox had made sure the filter was all set, he had insisted that I go ahead and finish the milking. I had decided to wait until I was done milking before I ran the barn cleaner. Ox evidently ran it at the same time that he was getting ready to milk, but I calculated that at this point in my new career I could only handle one thing at a time. Earlier events had demonstrated my incapability to do even the one thing well.

I was able to complete the tasks at hand – milking, then feeding, then barn cleaning, with no more negative consequences. Once again, my ego began to assuage itself from its lowliness experienced when my compatriot exuded a real and significant lack of confidence in my milkmaid (or would that be milkmaster) abilities.

The Ox-man peaked around the corner from the addition on the barn that held three pens for cattle that needed to be isolated because of disease, treatment, or because they were ready to calve.

"One coming," he hollered.

My excitement at this news flash was palpable. It had been over 15 years since the last time I'd been anywhere near a live birth. That had been on my grandfather's farm. Now the first birth was about to happen on my farm.

"I'll be right there," I intonated right back at my birth mentor, for Ox had gone through this many times in the months since he'd taken on operation of the farm.

Ox turned to me as I came through the four-foot wide entrance. He held his hand to his mouth to indicate I should be quiet. I looked across the tubular steel gate and saw number 81 lying on her side, straining. Two cream colored feet were at the ends of two black and white legs stretching out from 81's rear end. Mucus coated the legs and hung down the six inches or so to the straw covered floor.

Despite my attempts at quietude, 81 sensed my presence and struggled to her feet. The calf legs disappeared back into the swollen vulva from whence they had been protruding. Number 81 blew air and snot from her nostrils and rushed at me. I stepped back just in time to avoid having the arm I'd swung over the top rail smashed against it.

"Better step back," came the command from my tutor.

I did.

It took five minutes or so for 81 to settle down. During that time she voided her bladder and I watched Ox toss in some more straw. She bellowed her pain a few times then sank down, first on her front legs, then her back. The calf's feet once again peaked out from their hiding place. Ox looked at his watch.

Number 81 was a cow that was having her third calf and as such was less apt to need assistance from us midwives. Suddenly she lay on her side and began to push. Within seconds the legs once more were out nearly as far as they had been before. She made several more pushes in the intervening minutes and as she did each push I would look to my coach in anticipation. By the third push, I began to see anxiety on Ox's face.

He gradually opened the gate and walked into the pen. 81 was used to his presence and seemed to sense that he was there to help. Even so, just as Ox got close to her, she raised her head and made as though to get up. Like a Lynx pouncing on its prey, Ox leaped for the cow's head and held it down using the chain that encircled it. He then straddled her neck, thus obviating her rise from the straw padding upon which she laid.

"Grab those chains and handles hanging on the wall," Ox directed me.

I did.

Ox then directed me into the stall, which I accomplished hesitantly, assuming that Ox's 200 lbs could keep 81's 1600 lbs under control.

"You sit here," directed my consultant, pointing to the place that he currently occupied.

I did.

Reluctantly.

I could feel the warmth of 81 radiate up through my pants and immediately my groin area started to sweat, along with the rest of me.

Ox quickly grabbed a bucket of soapy water and doused his hands and arms with its contents. He then got down on his knees behind the cow and gently followed the line of the legs up into the cavern from which they protruded.

"Head twisted," he reported.

He pushed the legs back in a ways, and then reached in again. A dribble of fecal material oozed out of the cow's rectum as she strained against the intruder. He appeared to stretch the opening and slightly repositioned the legs. The efforts he was expending were taking their toll on Ox and on 81. She jerked as though to get up, put her attempts were futile.

Ox then grabbed the chains and handles from the soapy water and took one end of the chain and made a loop, put it around the calf's leg, then did the same with the other end.

"Gotta put it up high enough," he informed me. "Otherwise could just pull foot right off."

I watched then as he placed the handles strategically on the chains. He then began ever so slightly to exert pressure on the chains.

"Gotta pull down, not out. Come here."

I did.

He directed me to take the handles and continue pulling. I looked up to 81's head. She was straining, but you could see that she was exhausted from the effort. She wasn't going anywhere now.

Ox now reached back into the dog-tired (or is that cow-tired) animal. He shook his head. It did not seem to be going well.

"Dry," he reported.

When labor goes too long, the mucus, which acts as a lubricant for the calf's travel up and out of the birth canal, can be used up. Such evidently was the case.

"Pull harder."

I did.

"Again, but don't jerk.

I did and I didn't.

I was reaching the edge of my own endurance and strength. Then suddenly, as though the plug had been pulled, everything let loose and I went stumbling back, dragging a huge calf along with me.

"Bull," lamented Ox, for in the dairy business, female calves, or heifers are the desired result.

Ox scooped up some straw and rubbed the calf dry. It wobbled its head and attempted to voice its opinion on our abilities, but nothing came out. Ox used his hand to scoop some gunk out of the calf's mouth and was rewarding with a bleating. The cow let out a soft groan in reply.

"Let's leave 'em."

"Nice calf."

The words startled us both. We looked through the tubes of the fence to see a man standing there in uniform and a straw hat of western design. I recognized him, but barely, from the unflattering photo that had been on the newscast last night.

"I've never seen two characters look as guilty as these two," reflected the Sheriff to himself. "I wonder what they've been up to."

The two men in the pen scrambled to right themselves from the straw covered floor. Both brushed the straw off of themselves, but in the process spread birth matter, blood, and manure over their already dirty clothes.

"Carlson's my name," the Sheriff said as he reached out his hand, then thought better of it when he saw the condition of the two men's hands. "I'm Sheriff."

"Jack Forester,"…"Paul Banion," replied the two men almost simultaneously.

"What's the story with you two?" probed the Sheriff, not one to mince words.

"Sheriff, how about a cup of coffee?" said the smaller of the two men.

"Too hot. I'll have some water though."

The three men walked through the barn and across the yard in silence. When they got to the house, Paul and Ox took off their boots in the entryway. They then invited the Sheriff into the kitchen. Paul pulled out a glass from the second cupboard he looked into, took a pitcher from the refrigerator and filled the glass for the Sheriff.

"Sheriff, we're going to go wash up quick and change clothes. Just take us a minute or two."

"Sure. You just take your time. I'll look around."

"Ah, OK. Here's yesterday's paper. Nice picture."

The Sheriff was a keen observer of the criminal mind and of their behaviors associated with it, or at least he fancied himself that way. He certainly had caught on that the one named Paul didn't know where the drinking glasses were. He also noted that there were only a couple of glasses in the cupboard.

The Sheriff ignored the paper put in front of him, obviously a ploy to keep him from having a "look around". He stood up and walked over to the cupboards. They seemed pretty bare for two strapping big guys to be eating off of. He opened the refrigerator and saw about the same thing. There were some cucumbers that looked a few days old. He dipped is finger in the sauce. It tasted like a creamy Parmesan, just like his wife used to make.

The freezer revealed a little more food, mostly frozen meat. The wrapping paper indicated that it had been processed by Harmony's Meat Market. The quantity certainly indicated that it had come from at least a half, maybe even a whole animal. "Maybe old Harold will know something about these two," the man contemplated.

"New coffee maker, new towels, new refrigerator, new dishwasher, new washer and dryer, new freezer, lots of new things you have here in the kitchen. What are you two up to?" he once again asked of himself. Most farm homes the sheriff visited had old appliances and glassware and dinnerware that had survived generations.

A glance into the living room and dining room showed little in the way of photos, collectables, plants, or even that lived in look that comes in every farm home because the occupants are always too tired to do much in the way of housekeeping. But this place was immaculate, especially considering that two guys were living there. The Sheriff wished he could take a look in the roll top desk that set against the wall in the dining room. He figured there would be a treasure trove in there.

"Ahem, can I help you find something, Sheriff."

"No, just getting fidgety. When you get to be my age you can't stand to sit too long. All right guys, tell me about yourselves."

Minnesota nice evidently no longer survived. Paul laid out the story, with few details, that the two Californians had agreed would be the chronicle of their journey to the Minnesota farm. The Sheriff gradually warmed to them, especially when both indicated that they had been in law enforcement, albeit as security people at a local college. By the end of an hour Paul's natural affability had started to win the grizzled old detective over.

The Sheriff still had his doubts about some of the aspects of their stories, but they truly seemed to be friends if not cousins and they had given him information that he could check out, if he had a mind to. Soon the talk drifted back to what had brought the shamus to the Mueller place in the first place.

"I see you still have cattle and horses penned up. They are looking good. Any interest in keeping them?"

"I take it the owners are not going to be in a position to want them back," asked Banion.

"No. Well, so far all we have in custody is the two women and they're not talking. We're going to have to keep feeding and taking care of the animals, no matter what happens. I guess if you have the feed and don't mind, we'll just keep them here. Then when the courts make their decision, the animals will likely be forfeited. By then you'll probably have nearly their value used up in feed, so we'd just settle by turning over title to you."

"Sheriff, let's just say that we will continue to do the neighborly thing and watch out for the animals. We'll keep track of the feed and when you've got a plan, we'll settle up."

"Sounds fair enough. You boys going to the funeral?"

"Probably."

"Good, I'll see you there. Might be a surprise or two you might want to watch out for."

With that, Sheriff Carlson drove off slowly in his white Explorer. He had much to ponder and he knew that he had left just enough information behind him that those two California boys would be doing some pondering of their own.

"Funny thing," thought the Sheriff, as he turned right onto the tar road, barely taking note of the gray car going past him in the opposite direction. "I could have sworn Kevin said that one of these guys was ugly as sin, with rotten teeth and crossed eyes. These two were both fine looking young men."

"Probably not the only thing Kevin's gotten wrong," he said out loud with pleasure.

Chapter Eleven

"Oh, What a Tangled Web"

Shelley drove by the Mueller place and couldn't help but think of the good looking young man with the funny sense of humor whom she had met the day before. She was half-tempted to stop in to see him and try to explain what had happened to her on the day Mike had died. Strangely, she was attracted to Paul, not in a sexual way, but he seemed to be such a good listener. She had been just about ready to talk to him about what had happened when Ellie had arrived with Mad Max and warned her off.

"Jeez, that's the Sheriff," she exclaimed to herself. "Wonder what he is doing there."

All thoughts of stopping to see her new friend were immediately dashed. Shelley figured she had better just go on to her own home and feed Max, pick up the mail, check on the chickens, and make sure her horse still had some hay. Her brother, freshly released from jail, had offered to do it for her, but she had declined wanting to get out and get some fresh air.

She rolled the car up to the mailbox, even though the car was on the wrong side of the road. The window squealed its way down. Another thing Mike said he would fix but hadn't. There were a couple of bills, a few envelopes that looked like they were sympathy cards, Mike's farm magazine and her own Readers' Digest.

Yesterday, it was just after getting the mail and breaking into tears that Paul had come gallantly in from the field to comfort her.

Shelley remembered the emotions she felt as the two of them shared the intimacy of laying to rest the beautiful little deer. She had wanted so much to reach out to him for a hug.

That memory caused her to look over to the row of crosses just by the woods. There were 6 or 7 family pets buried there and now too was this shared event to be a reminder of loves lost and found.

"Paul, my friend, what would I do without you."

Just then an older green pickup drove in the drive. At first Shelley's breath came a little faster as she thought it was Paul behind the wheel, then she realized it was the bigger version, Jack.

"Mrs. Robison."

"Please, call me Shelley."

"Just stopped by to check on your place. Wasn't sure if you were back yet."

Jack had just uttered more words to her than she'd heard him say at one time in the nearly one year that they had been neighbors.

"Where's Paul today?"

"Got him baling hay."

"Be sure to say 'hi' from me and tell him I want him for supper one night next week."

Ox stood dumbfounded as the widow traipsed on in to the house, stopping to pick a flower on the way to the porch.

"Pauly, what have you done?" wondered Ox of his friend who was just then baling his 33rd square bale of the afternoon.

Ox told me shortly after the Sheriff left that there was another field of downed hay that needed to be baled. It was high quality hay evidently because he suggested that it should be square baled. I remembered that my grandfather always took the very best hay and square baled it for the cows. The big round bales would be used primarily to feed the animals outside.

Ox had me use the same tractor that I had handled well the day before to cut hay at the Robison place. This time the 4020 was hooked up to a brand new John Deere 348 square baler with a bale ejector. I had told Ox to buy used equipment whenever possible so he had traveled the state trying to find used tractors, wagons, drills, and other equipment. But he had found that there were certain things we'd be better off buying new and hay balers had been among those items.

This baler was a thing of beauty. It slurped up the entire width of the windrow of hay, compressed it into 80 lb bales and then flung them 30 feet into the air to land in the hay rack being pulled behind. I could adjust just about everything the baler did, but Ox told me not to.

By the time I had made the first round of the field I was feeling pretty comfortable with the baler and my ability to judge where to position the tractor relative to the rows of hay. My thoughts began to drift back to our conversation with the Sheriff. It had been obvious that he had stopped by to gather information. I was sure that he had gotten very little from us, but he had also dropped some hints about the investigation and his terminology sounded ominous.

Just then I noticed that the sound of the knotter had changed over the last few minutes. I turned just in time for the wind to catch tufts of alfalfa from a broken bale that was struggling through the air and not making it to the wagon behind. Oh, how I hated hay chaff down my neck. I also hated mechanical problems.

I shut off the PTO, turned off the tractor and stepped down, my boots crunching the three-day old stubble of the field. I walked back to the baler, threw open the covers. "Yes, obviously something is wrong," I muttered under my breath. "Ox, where are you!" I screamed in my head.

It was beyond me. Of course most things mechanical were beyond me. Ox and I would have to talk about having a radio on the tractor or carrying cell phones. That would have to be a conversation of the future, but for right now I was stuck in a hay field nearly a mile from the home place and with a $25,000 piece of equipment I knew nothing about.

I took a sip of water from the bottle I had squirreled in the compartment under the seat and looked out over the expanse of field to see how best to travel. I started out going diagonally across the rows toward the field road, but soon changed my mind as every three steps I would either have to jump over the windrow or step on it. I decided to walk parallel to the rows and even jogged a time or two. It took me less than 7 minutes to get to the dirt road that would eventually lead me back to the farm.

"Want a lift?" came the shout from the gray Grand Prix that had just moments before gone flying by kicking up dust. It had evidently turned around.

It was my neighbor Mrs. Robison. "Now what to do" I thought quickly to myself.

Saying "No" when it was 92 degrees was stupid. But getting into the car with this lady might be more stupid. I opted for more stupid.

"Where to?" the woman asked me as she put the car in gear.

"Oh, just to our place," was my reply.

"Trouble?" indicating the tractor and baler way out in the field.

"Yeah, something with the knotter."

"Mike always used to get Nelson equipment out of Cedar Grove, but there is a new repair shop in Harmony now too."

"I'm sure Ox'll be able to fix it."

"What's the story with you two guys?" It was the second time in just a few hours that the same question had been asked.

"Not much. We're cousins and best friends. Wanted to start a farm and did. Thanks for the ride."

But before I could get out of the door she reached across and grabbed my arm.

"How about that supper?" reminding me of her earlier request.

"Let me check with Ox. Thanks again."

I hightailed it to the house without even looking around. That is until she honked her horn.

"Sunday works for me," she hollered through the now open window.

I waved and turned back to my destination – a cool drink of water, and a cool house. Hopefully Ox would show up soon too.

Chapter Twelve

"The Enemy of My Family Is My Friend"

Pastor B arrived at the funeral home shortly after 4:00 PM. He was surprised that he was the first one there. As a matter of fact he wondered if Shelley would even be there by 5:00.

At 4:30 a woman whom Pastor B recognized as Mike's mother arrived and with her came a younger woman with two young children trailing in behind her.

"Hi Pastor. I'm Sarah Robison, Mike's mom. I didn't know if you would remember me from the wedding or not. This is my daughter Margo and her children Sympathy and Hope. Bob will be coming in a few minutes."

Pastor B. did not remember either woman, but then it had been almost exactly six years since the wedding. He had looked in the church records and seen that Mike and Shelley had just celebrated their sixth anniversary on Sunday.

"Nice to see you again," he fibbed. "Can I help you with anything?"

"We're wanting to set up a little panel board with some photos and such of Mike's life. Don't suppose Shelley would have done that."

Pastor B. detected just a little bit of resentment, but these poor folks were going through some tough times so Pastor B. chalked it up to that.

"I'm sure Shelley will be here any moment. Her mother called to tell me she had to run out to the farm quick to check on things and get the mail."

"Humph! No one else could have done that?" muttered Mike's sister. "You two get over there and sit down. NO RUNNING AROUND."

"Oh this will be fun," contemplated the preacher.

Just then a young man entered wearing a t-shirt and shorts, no socks, and some rather beat up Adidas.

"Robert John Robison, that is nothing to wear to your brother's wake. You are more like your father every day."

"Your right, Old Lady. I can't stand you either."

Mrs. Robison tried to slap her errant son but missed. He laughed.

"I've got other clothes in the car."

Just then John Money walked in and introduced himself to Mike's siblings and parental unit. He offered to take them in to see Mike before others arrived, but Pastor B. suggested that they wait a few minutes for Shelley.

At 4:47 Shelley and her mother arrived. Shelley had in her hand a few cards that had obviously been mailed. She was about to put them in the basket set aside for cards when her mother-in-law stopped her.

"Don't you think you should open them? There might be money in them. You can't just leave them setting there like that.

Shelley looked with barely hidden disgust at her mother-in-law and said, "This is Harmony, not Minneapolis," referencing the city Mike's parents and brother and sister had moved to since the wedding.

"Well, I'm going to put them in my purse just in case," said the older woman with contempt.

Seeing the potential for conflict, Pastor B. stepped forward and offered the services of the funeral home.

"John has a fire-proof safe here and I encourage all the families to have him keep the cards in it until after the funeral. His people will take care of the cards and memorials here and at the church. It's all a part of what you're paying for."

Shelley "harrumphed" her victory. Mrs. Robison shot daggers through the pastor and Margo Robison went chasing after Sympathy and Hope, getting close to neither.

Shelley realized after she dropped Paul off that she was going to have to really get going if she was to make it to the funeral home by the 4:30, which is when she had told Pastor and John Money she would be there. A quick drive back to town helped. She jumped in the shower and was nearly finished when her mother started knocking on the door.

"That Kevin Walters fellow is on the phone for you," her mother reported.

"Tell him I'm not here."

"I already told him you were."

"Tell him I'm in the shower."

"I already told him you were out of the shower."

"Tell him to kiss off."

"I will with pleasure."

Shelley and her mother left for the funeral home ten minutes after they were scheduled to have arrived. When they arrived at the home, she immediately spied her mother-in-law's car. It was inappropriately parked in a handicap parking space. The widow pulled out her cell-phone and dialed the local police department just up the block.

"Jenny, that you. Yeah it's Shelley. Yeah it's tomorrow. Say we are just at the funeral home getting ready for the wake and there's a car here parked in the handicap space without a handicap license or one of those things on the mirror. Well, maybe John should come up here and at least ticket the car. Let them know they shouldn't park there. Thanks Jenny."

Shelley's mother had already made the journey to the door when Shelley came running across the parking lot to catch up with her. They went in together, but Mrs. Ingvaldson excused herself to "freshen up."

It didn't take long for the long-term animosity between Mike's family and Shelley to rear its ugly head. Pastor had diffused most of it, but it still lay there like the proverbial pink elephant in the center of the room.

John Money opened the doors to the main parlor and invited the family forward to view Mike. Shelley went first. She brushed

Mike's suit as though there were lint on it. She knew she should feel something more than relief and tried awfully hard to pull up some emotion, but the last year had taken its toll. Without kissing him or touching him, Shelley turned and went and sat in the front row, ready to receive well wishers.

Mike's mother was a real study in contrast. She went forward with Margo and Rob supporting her on either arm. She was sobbing.

"Oh brother," thought Shelley.

Mrs. Robison laid herself prostrate across Mike and kissed the cool forehead and attempted to clasp the hands of the corpse. Then she did the most peculiar thing. She stepped back and snapped a picture, first with her digital camera then another with her cell phone.

"I sent it to your dad," remarked the now calm mother.

Rob stayed up longer then his sister and mother. Shelley had gotten along with Rob most of the time. He seemed to be taking it particularly hard so Shelley calculated that perhaps it would mend some fences if she went up there a stood with Rob for a few minutes. She got there in time to hear him say his goodbyes and offer a little gift.

"Enjoy, brother. You gave to me in life. I give to you in death. Consider us even."

And with that Shelley watched as Rob snuck a rolled cigarette, obviously marijuana, just inside the casket where no one would see it.

"What are you doing?" she whispered forcefully.

Then she put her arm around him as though to comfort him but surreptitiously and pinched his ear.

"Get over there and sit with your mother."

"Oh, baby. You know how I like this."

After the give and take, Shelley cautiously reached both hands forward, with one she touched the cold wax of Mike and with the other scooped up the cigarette. She then walked over to the small family room where they had left their coats and purses and quickly hid the butt in the side pocket of her handbag.

The rest of the evening was a steady stream of friends and well wishers. Classmates came and went as did other members of the church. Several teachers showed up, fondly remembering antics that Mike had pulled in high school. Several of his co-workers from the boat plant in Milton came, as did the plant manager. The owner of the company had sent flowers.

As people came and went they would often, but not always stop briefly to visit with Shelley or Mrs. Robison, the senior. No one talked with Shelley about the circumstances of Mike's death, but she could hear the undertones of conversation and knew that they were talking about what had happened.

At about 7:00 Pastor B. called the family and friends who were there together and had a prayer, then encouraged folks to reminisce about happier times. By 7:30 they had finished that part of the wake.

At 8:30, the older Mrs. Robison came over to Shelley and made their excuses.

"Margo just has to get the kids to bed."

"OK, I'll finish up here and stop by to see you."

"No need, we'll be in bed."

And with that Mike's mother walked out with her daughter and granddaughters.

Rob came up and asked Shelley if she wanted to do anything, but Shelley just gave him a look and he too left.

Shelley was just about to leave herself when her friend and classmate Ellie Carlson walked in. She came forward and gave Shelley a big hug. They then walked up to the casket together.

"He looks pretty good compared to the last time I saw him," commented the deputy.

"Was it pretty bad?"

"No, it looked like it happened pretty quickly."

"I've been so wrapped up in my own stuff the last couple of days. I guess I never even thought about what you must have gone through finding him there like that. Where was he?"

"Behind the barn."

"Ellie, can we get out of here?"

"Sure, Hon. Let's just leave your car here and we'll take mine."

Ellie had been tied up most of the day delivering the subpoenas that her father had given her. When she finally got home, she realized she'd never make it for the prayer service at the funeral home, so she took the time to grab a bite to eat and a quick shower. She left home at 8:30.

"Ellie," came a shout from across the parking lot at the funeral home. Ellie responded by looking over to the people standing by their car and giving a half-hearted wave. They looked vaguely familiar.

"Ellie Carlson, you get over here right now."

Now Ellie remembered that gruff, gravely voice. It was Mike's mom. It had been a couple of years since she'd seen her.

"Probably saw her out at the farm," realized the deputy. "What can I do for you Ms. Robison?"

"You can damn well tear this ticket up."

"What ticket is that?"

"Says here it is for parking in a handicap space."

"Can't do that Ms. Robison."

"Well, Robbie says you're a deputy."

"I am. But this is a City of Harmony ticket."

Ellie was puzzled that Robbie knew she was a deputy. It had only been six months and she knew she hadn't seen him in that time. They had a brief fling when she had been a senior and Robbie a sophomore. It had lasted two dates and had ended abruptly when Robbie produced a bottle of hard liquor and offered her a drink on the way home from the Hawks Hill Cineplex.

"Sorry Ms. Robison. You say hi to Robbie now."

Ellie had then gone into the funeral home to pay her respects to Mike and to check on Shelley. She could just about imagine what kind of shape her friend would be in if her mother-in-law had been anything like what Ellie had just experienced.

The red head had not been far from wrong. Her friend stood there looking bewildered. Ellie walked up and gave Shelley a hug. Then they went hand in hand up to the casket. It was a shock for Ellie. The last time she'd seen Mike, he'd been lying in the dust with flies crawling in and out of his mouth and with an obvious bullet hole just above his right eye.

John Money had done a good job of fixing the hole and providing Mike with a calm look on his face that probably belied the last few minutes of his life. As she looked at him, Ellie couldn't help but think about the autopsy results that her dad had let her read late that afternoon when she'd completed her rounds.

"What do you think?" he'd asked as he tossed the report on her desk, then pulled up a chair.

As she read the report, it reinforced her own supposition that Mike had been shot elsewhere and his body carried or hauled somehow to the spot where she'd found it. The three puncture wounds were strange. The ME reported that one was peri-mortem and the other two postmortem.

"Dad, why didn't you call in the Crime Bureau to investigate the body and the scene?"

"You're talking to the best damn investigator in the state. That's a copy you can take home tonight. I'm meeting someone for dinner."

Now she was standing next to her good friend in front of the body of her friend's husband laying in a casket with a suit and tie.

Shelley started to ask questions about what Ellie had seen, which made the deputy very uncomfortable. She suggested they go somewhere and talk. A few minutes later they were headed out of the parking lot and down the main street of town that then turned into a state highway that led out of town.

"Do you want to stop at Four Corners for pie?"

"No. Do you mind if we just drive out toward the farm."

"OK"

As she drove, Ellie recounted the story of Ms. Robison in the parking lot with the ticket. Shelley laughed so hard she cried, then confessed that she had been the one to call the Harmony police. That made Ellie reciprocate with her own laughter.

"What's that?" asked Ellie as they came to the intersection of the two dirt roads near Shelley's house. "I see some light out in that corn field."

Ellie drove on to the field road, and then turned her lights off, thinking that if someone were in the field, they would assume the car had driven on. She took the time to pop the cover off of the dome light of her car and loosened the tiny bulb. She reached in the back seat and pulled up a pair of jeans, a t-shirt, and some boots. Within minutes she had wriggled out of her slacks and blouse and into the jeans and boots.

"You sit tight," she ordered Shelley. "If I'm not back in 20 minutes, dial 911 and tell them who you are and say that an officer needs assistance. Then tell them where we are."

With that Ellie opened the glove compartment and pulled out her ID, a small Maglite and a .22 pistol she kept for special occasions. She opened the door and scurried out and down the field row to the gate. She took the time to close the gate behind her, then walked as quietly as she could down the fence line to the approximate spot where she'd seen the lights.

Stealthily, the jean-clad deputy moved through the corn as quietly as possible. After 8 minutes had passed on her watch, she was nearly to the point she had guessed was where her quarry had been. She could see nothing. She stood still, held her breath and tried to tune her ears to the slightest sound.

"There," she thought. "I could swear I just heard something."

It was then that she felt the tap on her shoulder that startled the crap out of her. She jerked her head around and was greeted with a bright light that blinded her momentarily. The fist meeting her jaw brought even brighter lights, although they twirled around. She felt a sharp knife slice through her cheek, and then met the ground face first. Before she dropped her weapon and her consciousness, she got one shot off.

Chapter Thirteen

"It Only Hurts When I Laugh"

Ox told me that he thought number 83 was going to calve sometime during the next few hours so we used that as our excuse for not going into town for the wake of our neighbor, whom I'd never met. Ox had met him and actually had gotten along pretty well with him, or so he said in his anemic use of language. It was the new widow that I was hoping to avoid, for in the last two days she had seemed to be present at every turn and that kind of involvement wasn't what I needed right then.

"Alarm," Ox warned just after we got in about 9:30 from checking the cow. He quickly checked the reading and reported that it might have been a deer since whatever had set of the alarm had crossed a fence onto our property and then almost immediately crossed another to get off.

We had both just settled back into our chairs out on the deck, thankful for the mosquito repellant that both of us had put on in anticipation that our bug zapper would not get them all. Off in the distance we heard a car backfire. It had been almost identical to the sound we'd heard just three days earlier and from almost the same direction. We looked at each other and shook our heads. The early morning sound had been forgotten by both of us until its twin was heard seconds before.

We looked at each other and realized the sound was not a car backfire and neither had the sound on Monday been a car.

"What?"

"I don't know."

Indecision was not something that either of us was used to and it ate at both of us. Our first response from our training and past six years of experience urged us to get to the heating grate in the wall where Ox had stored our weapons and pull them out, then go look at a way "to protect and serve." That part of our lives had to be put on hold and I knew my best friend well enough to know that it was killing him too.

Five minutes of looking at each other, looking past each other, and trying to come up with conversation that would take us away from the temptation was suddenly punctuated with the sound of an engine and gears not in harmony with each other. We looked out across the yard onto the dirt road that ran along our property and saw the headlights of a car. Those lights told the story of someone attempting to destroy a perfectly good transmission as it jumped forward, then rolled, then jumped forward again.

"Camaro," commented Ox. He knew his autos.

A minute later the sounds of engine and transmission out of sync came closer as twin beams bounced unhealthily into our yard then swung around before coming to an abrupt halt.

"Help!"

Both of us jumped from our chairs and raced to the car. As I got closer I recognized the face and momentarily wanted to turn around and run. Ox must have sensed it because just then he gave me a little push.

"What? What?"

"Call the police! Call the police!"

Ox looked at me at the same time I looked at him. We had no intention of inviting the local constabulary to our humble abode.

"Shelley!… Shelley! Stop screaming!… Now tell me what's wrong," that as Ox helped the distraught woman from the red Camaro.

She took a deep breath, and then started to sob.

"It's Ellie. I think she's hurt. Come with me. Please."

"Where? Where is she?" I shook her as I asked the question.

"In the field."

I watched Ox steal away up toward the house. I was sure that he was going to get the necessary equipment to take on this assignment that the widow woman was giving us. I attempted to get more information from her, but was unsuccessful. Just then Ox pulled the old green truck up to us and said, "Get in."

Without words, for she no longer could speak, Shelley directed us out to a spot on the dirt road right near a field entrance. We told her to sit tight, and although she protested that Ellie had made her do the same thing, we insisted.

In the distance we could see flashes of light and I thought at first it must be some nearby airport. However, Ox straightened me out with the single word, "lightning" and we both attained a new sense of urgency. Within seconds a low rumbling interrupted the still of the hot night.

"About four miles away," predicted Ox the weatherman.

"How do you know that?"

"Know lots of things."

The banter between the two of us relaxed us momentarily. There was a sudden burst of energy and noise just off to our left. Ox swung his flash light abruptly and caught a doe and fawn in its beam. The two animals froze as if a magician had cast a spell on them. Ox dropped the light and we could hear their progress off to the west of us.

"There…a light," reported Ox.

And sure enough, it was now dark enough that even the least bit of luminosity would catch our attention. We moved forward slowly, for the beam was stationary and low. Both of us pulled our weapons from under shirts that had been previously tucked in. Ox motioned me forward, indicating he would cover me.

I inched forward, clunks of dirt turning to dust under my boots. Another flash of light, this time closer, illuminated a mound of something that was starting to uncoil itself, moaning as it did. Two more giant steps, "Captain may I?" and I was next to the pile. I reached forward and was startled when my hand was grabbed by a vice and I was looking down the business end of a .22 pistol.

"You son of a bitch," growled the heap. "Freeze!"

I froze. But it wasn't necessary, because in the next instant the redhead who had "captured" me was out cold, having fainted from the exertion of my "capture."

"Ox, it's OK."

"One mile," came Ox's report after a significantly brighter flash. We had only a few minutes before weather would hit us.

Both of us have enough experience to know that someone who has been knocked out should not be moved except by trained medical personnel. We were going to have to make an exception.

Ox turned the woman onto her back. The light I now held showed me that the woman was the lovely deputy who had stopped by. Ox stooped down and, I was proud to see, used proper lifting techniques to pick up his burden. I led the way out of the field, listening for Ox's breath to become labored so that I would have an excuse to take over the load, but Ox was in superb condition. It took us only a few minutes to rapidly trace back our steps.

Shelley met us at the field entrance and came to life as she saw her friend. The frightened little woman barked orders to both of us as to where to put her friend. She had me sit on the truck bed, my back against the truck and hold her friends head while she ministered to her and checked her thoroughly.

"Jack," avoiding my nickname for my friend. "You get up there and drive. Go slow, but hurry."

"Back to your house," came her reply to Ox's unspoken question.

"Hi Hon, what's up," started the Sheriff as he answered his cell phone. The phone number readout had indicated his daughter's cell phone so he was startled to hear a man's voice.

"Sheriff, this is Paul Banion. We met this morning."

"Mr. Banion, you had better have one hell of a good reason to be using my daughter's cell phone."

"Yes, sir. I do sir. Your daughter has had a mishap. She's seems to be all right, but we thought we should call you and her phone had your number in memory."

"Who's 'we'?"

"Well, sir, Ox and me. And then there is Mrs. Robison here also. She's the one that came and got us."

"Shelley?"

"Yes, sir."

"Where is Ellie?"

"She's at our place, sir. And, again she seems all right; other wise we would have called an ambulance."

"I'll be there in 10 minutes."

"Yes, sir."

Nine minutes later, a white Ford Explorer whipped into the Mueller place with lights flashing. It splashed through a couple of puddles that had accumulated from a thunderstorm that had just passed quickly by. The Sheriff immediately saw his daughter's car with the two men who owned the farm standing on either side of it. The shorter of the two was just shutting the passenger door as the Sheriff arrived.

"They are inside, sir. Right this way," indicated the one named Banion.

All three men walked to the house.

"In the living room with Shelley. Can I get you something Sheriff? Coke, Iced Tea, water?"

"Not right now."

"Ellie, are you all right?"

The Sheriff's daughter looked up from the pillow upon which her head lay. She removed the ice pack from her face and the father immediately saw that the left side of her face was rapidly becoming swollen and discolored.

"Who did this to you?" came the anguished inquiry. "Was it one of these two? Was it Kevin?"

"Dad, cool it. I don't know who did it."

She then recounted her activities of the previous hour. Shelley filled in the rescue blanks that Ellie was unaware of. After the questioning and the retelling of the story, Goat had settled down enough that he realized right now he needed to be a father more than a police officer.

"Let me get you some more ice. I'll get you something to drink too."

He walked into the kitchen, but neither of the farmers was there. He heard some humming and conversation just down the hall and decided to find its source rather than to go digging through the freezer himself. Not that he hadn't done it before.

He got to a door on the right from which the sounds were coming and knocked then entered. Laid out before him was a very nice office with computer, fax machine, scanner, copier, file cabinets, and more. The copier was where the humming was coming from.

The two farmers were standing at the copier, engrossed in whatever was being spewed from the machine.

"Ahem, can I get some more ice for Ellie and maybe a glass of water?"

Like two kids caught in the cookie jar, both men turned around and as they did, hid behind their backs the documents they were looking at.

"Oh sure Sheriff. I'll get it for you."

The Sheriff noticed Banion surreptitiously take the sheets from behind his back and hand them to his partner, giving the bigger man a look that meant something to him but was lost on the lawman. Banion then walked ahead of the Sheriff out the door and down the hall to the kitchen.

"I'm going to go out to check on that cow again," reported Ox.

The Sheriff noted that the big guy seemed to be carrying something under his unnecessary jacket slung over his arm. He watched through the window as the man progressed across the yard. He stopped briefly by his daughter's car and the Sheriff watched closely to see if the dome light came on, but it didn't. A few minutes later Carlson could see lights go on in the barn where there had been none previously.

He turned his attention back to the ice pack Banion was handing him and the water glass that was also put forward. Banion smiled at him, then led the way into the living room. The Sheriff couldn't help but think someone had just put one over on him.

Ox took the drive as slowly as he could, but the crackling of lightning and the banging of thunder spurred him on as he drove the green pickup with his precious cargo in the rear. Now it's been a while since I've had the head of a beautiful woman in my lap so I was naturally a little bit concerned that my body was going to double cross me and reveal the strong attraction I'd sensed when first I'd met the delectable woman now laying against me.

Shelley attended to the deputy by holding her hand and repeatedly patting my leg. My senses were being attacked by two lovely women. I really needed a cold shower, especially after the vixen in my lap moaned what was hardly a whimper of pain. The slight movement I felt was difficult to handle at best. It was then that God answered my prayer. It started to rain. No, it started to pour, then hail, then pour.

Ox swung up as close to the house as he could, then jumped out. By then we had our victim ready to be transported to the house. We all raced to shelter, just as the heavens opened up. We slipped and slid through the door, laughing at what the cascade of summer nectar had done to our clothes and hair.

"Ox, put her on the couch," I ordered as I went to the bathroom to grab towels. "Shelley, there is an ice pack in the freezer."

"Do you think we should call an ambulance?" questioned Shelley as she returned with the ice.

"No, I'm OK," replied Ellie despite the fact the question had not been addressed to her.

"Well, is there anyone else we should call," I asked.

"My dad."

I asked the casualty what his number was, but when I tried it there was no answer. "Try his cell phone...I can't remember the number...It's on my speed dial."

It was obvious that she did not have her phone on her person and I did not see a purse. Before raising the alarm that it might have been left out in the field, I decided to check her car. I trotted out to the car and opened the driver's side. Surprisingly, there was no light that came on. I looked at the dome light and saw in the dim light cast off from the yard light that Ellie had used an old trick that I had used a time or two. I pushed the bulb back into its socket and immediately spotted Ellie's purse in the back seat.

As I reached for the purse, a brown file folder flipped down and a couple of pages popped out. I saw immediately that they were autopsy drawings. I pulled the purse up to the driver's seat and sorted through the various pockets. The outside pocket provided quite a little surprise. Inside it was a rolled cigarette of some sort that was still fresh enough that it had not disintegrated. I'd seen neither woman smoke, so the coffin nail caught me off guard. I also knew enough to realize that it was likely not your standard Marlboro brand.

It was then that I spied another, smaller purse with a cell phone sticking out of the pocket.

"Much more appropriate for a lady," I said to myself.

Sure enough, the cell phone reported in bright print, "Ellie" when I flipped it open. I scrolled through the outgoing calls, assuming Ellie had recently called her father and sure enough there it was, "DADDY". I had a hard time thinking of the man I'd met earlier in the day as being "DADDY".

The phone call was brief if not difficult. I sensed Ellie's father was not happy to hear my voice on the end of his phone.

While I was out by the car, my inquisitive nature drove me to look at the file. I had almost made it through five pages when Ox came out to see what was keeping me. I popped the bulb back out of the dome light. Just then the white Explorer came rolling in. I handed the papers to Ox who hid them down the back of his pants and under his shirt.

"Copy and put back in the car," I instructed Ox and the Sheriff jumped from his car and came at us.

It took us nearly an hour to get our guests taken care of and on their way. I watched through the window as Ox returned the file. The Sheriff watched too, but he didn't realize the door could be opened and shut without the telltale sign of the dome light.

As they left both Ox and I got lovely little kisses on our cheeks from the maid and the maiden. The ones I received were much more enthusiastic then the ones Ox got or at least that's what I told the Ox-meister.

We both looked forward to retiring for the night and dreaming nice warm thoughts about a delectable redheaded deputy and a newly widowed blonde.

The walk from the house to the car was interminable. She knew her father well enough to know that his relief and concern was about to be replaced by a lecture and interrogation. Now she wished that they had taken Shelley's car, for it was obvious that Shelley would not be able to lurch Ellie's four-speed Camaro back to town.

The Sheriff had reluctantly agreed to Shelley driving his Sheriff's car with a stern warning of, "Don't touch anything."

Ellie had gone to her car while dear old dad showed Shelley how to handle the complexities of his Explorer. When she got there, the first thing she noticed was the file folder, now sitting on the right side of the back seat instead of behind the driver's seat. She supposed that Paul had moved it when he got her cell phone. She quickly hid the folder on the floor, hoping her father had not seen it.

Her father returned from the Explorer and explained that Shelley would follow them to the apartment building, then the Sheriff would head home from there.

"You're sure you don't need to see someone. That's really turning into a shiner."

"Let's just get it over with, Dad."

"What do you mean?"

"I mean the lecture and the grilling."

"What are you talking about?"

"Never mind."

They traveled another mile in silence. Then the Sheriff could contain himself no longer.

"Can you tell me what, exactly you were doing out in that field without backup?"

"It wasn't any big deal, we saw a light."

"NO BIG DEAL!" interrupted the Sheriff. Anytime you take your weapon out of its holster to fire it, it is a BIG DEAL!"

"Who said…"

"Don't even go there, young lady. That big guy gave me your gun. Said he found it in your hand. I smelled the barrel. It had been fired. I'm going to let it slide 'cuz it wasn't your regular piece. My point is that you were concerned enough to take a gun, to tell Shelley she might have to call for help, and to take you ID with you and you DIDN'T REPORT IN OR CALL FOR BACKUP!" he shouted.

Silence.

"And another thing, what was the purpose of smooching with that Banion guy?"

Ellie knew better than to answer that question. Her father had been hard on many a young man as she grew up. She was not about to explain what had transpired on the ride in from the field. She'd been startled by the reaction Mr. Banion had as she lay in the bed of the truck with her head on his lap. Had she been more with it, she'd have made some comment like, "is that a banana or are you happy to see me," using her Mae West imitation. As it was, the sensation had disappeared when the sudden downburst had hit them.

That man sure wasn't like any farmer she'd ever met. Of course neither was the big guy.

Ellie was saved further conversation when her father looked in the review mirror and saw Shelley roll the Explorer up to the cement guard on the parking lot. Everything would have been all right, but for some reason Shelley goosed the 4-wheel drive up and over the eight inch barricade, landing the SUV with its step bumper, squarely on the cement.

Chapter Fourteen
"Mourning Ablutions"

Pastor B. and his wife had just finished their morning devotion and prayer time. Like most mornings when the good pastor faced a particularly challenging occurrence with a large audience, the pastor was conflicted that morning with two very strong urges. The first such inclination was to coerce his wife of twenty-seven years into the bedroom to relieve some built up tension. It had been a practice that they had indulged in for nearly twenty years with equal passion on both of their parts. In the last seven years, the other compulsion was much more apt to win out.

"Hon, do we have any…" Before he could finish she had turned from the cupboard with a bottle of Imodium.

"You know me way too well," answered the pastor as he grabbed up the bottle and headed to the bathroom where he proceeded to provide a concert of sound and smell that would be repeated at least once more before he headed for the church at 9:30.

At 9:15 the good pastor had received a phone call from his favorite Sheriff. After listening to the lawman for three minutes without interrupting, the pastor implored to Sheriff to abandon the plan that he had just laid out.

"Sheriff, I will not put up with that kind of activity at my church or at anything remotely connected with my church. I don't care if you think someone might get away. That is your problem, not mine!" …"Well, can you at least tell me who it is that you are going to arrest?" ..."Sheriff, only under those circumstances. And I will warn you Sheriff that I am not one to be trifled with. If you don't follow what you've just laid out, I will be making calls to 'CCO, to Fargo stations and to the newspaper"... "No, it's not a threat. It's A PROMISE," and with that he slammed the phone down, looked at his wife, and then headed rapidly to the bathroom.

"Jim Barton, you had better run for Sheriff," he mumbled as he flipped on the fan in the bathroom.

Ellie Carlson woke up with a start. She had been dreaming, she remembered that. She tried desperately to recall the last part of the dream. The deputy in her knew that it was important.

"Let me think," she said out loud as she stared at the ceiling, trying to concentrate.

The effort was rewarded with some rather erotic thoughts about the previous night. Of course she knew that it was all a dream, even though it was pleasant to recount. In her dream, she and Paul, for certainly she must call him by his first name now, had been in the back seat of her Camaro.

"That had to be a dream," she chuckled to herself.

In her dream, Ellie was trying desperately to get comfortable, but no matter what she did, something kept rubbing her back. Finally, she shoved Paul out of the way and saw what it was...but she couldn't bring into focus what it was that she saw.

The redhead crawled out of bed, hurting throughout her entire body, which puzzled her because she'd only been hit in the face. She walked into the kitchen and filled her coffee maker with water and coffee. The sight and sound of the water going into the container suddenly generated a tremendous urge to go to the bathroom. While she sat there, the dream came back into focus. She leaned forward and looked through the open door. Sitting on the kitchen table was the file folder she'd brought from the office.

That was it. The folder. When she tried to look at it last night, she'd been too tired, but her mind must have registered something because now she saw it so plainly, what the Ellie in her dream was trying to deal with. The papers in the folder were out of order. Someone had been looking at the file.

"It had to have been Shelley," surmised the rookie, "while I was out in the field."

We pushed through chores as quickly as possible. We now had two fresh cows that had to be milked separately. Number 83 had been standing proudly by a newborn calf when we got to the barn in the morning. Ox kept the cow's attention focused on him while I had spirited the young calf out. She had been standing and sucking on 83's engorged teats, so we weren't worried about the calf.

I moved the calf outside to one of 15 calf hutches that Ox had built himself during the winter. They were made from three and a half sheets of plywood on a 2 X 2 frame. The front of the hutch was open but surrounded by a sixteen-foot long wire panel that was 48 inches high. Both ends of the panel were attached to either side of the hutch.

Ox had given me a bottle of blue liquid and had told me to douse the calf's umbilical cord all the way to the gut. He had taken a mean looking pair of pliers and inserted a couple of metal tags into her ear, one on each ear. He had made note of the numbers. This was evidently a special calf.

"Warrior calf," reported Ox.

I had been away from the farm too long. Warrior was evidently the name of the sire that had been used when this particular cow had been inseminated. But that was all I knew about him, the bull.

We were close to being done with chores when Ox told me to head to the house and shower up. I didn't argue, as I knew it would be tight for both of us to get showered and changed in time for the funeral.

As I walked to the house, my thoughts went back to the autopsy report and other notes that I had gone over very early that morning. Lots of information, but not much in the way of facts that would lead one to conclude anything in particular.

The shower felt good, but it dawned on me half way through it that I didn't have any clothes appropriate for a funeral. The only halfway decent slacks I had were the ones I'd worn for two days while I jumped from one plane to another and from one city to another. "I might just have to beg off of the funeral," I thought.

But Ox had thrown a pair of slacks and a dress shirt on my bed. He also had a nice pair of loafers lying there. Once again I realized how blessed I was to have Ox as a friend.

I walked in to the kitchen just as Ox was hanging up the phone.

"Preacher," he reported. I remembered the man who had visited us a couple of days earlier and wondered what he might want.

"Says, the Sheriff is going to be arresting someone after the funeral."

"Why would he be calling you? And how in the world does he know that."

"Don't know and don't know."

"I wish that preacher would say what's on his mind," I volunteered.

Ox headed for the shower while I finished combing my hair and brushing my teeth at the kitchen sink. Mom would have been so proud.

"Mom, please. I really have to go pee!"

Shelley had been waiting for a long time for her near sixty-year old mother to complete her morning routine in the bathroom. She glanced at the kitchen clock and realized they needed to get a move on if they were to get to the church on time. On time meaning before Mike's mother arrived.

"Finally, Can I take my shower now too?"

"Yes, dear. We have plenty of time. I'll make us some toast and coffee."

"I already ate."

"What did you eat?"

"I made myself a sandwich."

"For breakfast?"

By then Shelley had shut the door and turned on the shower so she felt no need to continue the give and take.

Shelley's thoughts turned from the shampoo she was working into her long blonde hair to the file folder she found in Ellie's car the previous night. It had been too dark in the car to read much of it, but she had realized it was Ellie's file on Mike's murder. What had startled her was the list of suspects she'd found typed up on the second page.

Shelley had wanted to drive Ellie home so she could talk with her about it, but her father had insisted that she not operate the Camaro. Then he'd gotten mad because she'd run his car up and over the cement barrier in the parking lot.

The sting of the shampoo rolling into Shelley's eye brought her back to the task at hand. Her mother didn't believe in modern bath gels, exfoliates and conditioners so she was going to have to make do with mom's bar soap. The shower felt good to Shelley. She knew she was going to need to feel clean on this day. There would be so much to deal with.

After his fourth trip to the bathroom, the Imodium kicked in and Pastor B. felt like he was in control once again. He would have just enough time to take a quick shower and get dressed. It was going to be a hot day and he knew that wearing the cassock alb would only make him warmer. He thought again what a great invention an air-conditioned gown would be for preachers.

While he showered, he ran through his sermon one more time. It was unlike any funeral sermon he had preached before, but this was his first murder. His bowels growled as he remembered John Money's prediction of four or five hundred people attending the funeral. That was nearly twice what his church had ever handled. When he had told his wife, she had insisted on driving to Alexandria to buy a new dress. She had been thoughtful enough to bring back a new pair of shoes for him.

"Bart, you have a phone call," hollered his wife through the half open door. "It's Mrs. Arndt about the wedding."

"Tell the woman it will have to wait until tomorrow."

"She wants to know about a song her daughter wants sung at the wedding."

"It will have to wait until tomorrow."

"It's a song by that band out of St. Cloud called Nate Diggy Dog and the Dog Diggers."

Just then the hot water ran out and Pastor B was inundated by a cold blast of effluent that shriveled up everything including his patience. He stepped naked out of the shower, grabbed the phone from his wife, and said forcefully into it, "Tomorrow," then pushed the "End" button.

"That wasn't Mrs. Arndt. There was a call waiting. Whoever it was said he wanted to talk to you about giving himself up."

"Oh boy," thought the preacher.

The Sheriff of Maplewood County was a picture of sartorial splendor. He had opted not to wear his dress uniform. He reserved that for fallen law enforcement officers, government officials, and others whom he had respected in life. Mike Robison did not qualify. Besides there would be lots of uniforms showing up anyway.

He pulled his best white straw Stetson out of its box and mounted it onto his gray head. He proceeded to check various angles in the mirror and decided that his left side was his best and most photogenic. He would need to plan on that side being to the cameras at the press conference early this afternoon.

He hadn't even bothered to contact the press since he was certain most of the local and even some stations from Fargo and the Twin Cities would have crews there. It was a slow time of the year for news and experience told him that the hints he'd put out over the last few days would bear fruit – abundant fruit.

He walked to the bathroom and ran the electric razor over his face a second time then splashed on some Old Spice.

"Beth, you would be proud," referring to his departed wife of thirty-five years. "Mount up," he said to himself with a grin and shrug of the shoulders that positioned his western cut blazer into place. He tightened his bolo tie as he walked out the door. His gun holster was snug on his left side and barely visible. He never minded if it showed a little.

Chapter Fifteen

"If You Don't Spit Green, Get Off My Lawn"

Pastor B decided to walk the short distance to the church. He would be riding with the Funeral Director out to the cemetery so a car was superfluous. As he rounded the corner he was shocked to see that there were already cars backed up two blocks from the church and on both sides of the street. He waved to a few people he knew, but many of the faces were unfamiliar to him.

"You were right John," affirmed the pastor to the young funeral director. "There are cars parked around the block already."

"Nervous, Pastor?" questioned the black suit clad undertaker.

"Only that we have enough food for the lunch after the funeral."

The quiet summer morning was punctuated by the sound of a diesel engine in low gear. Both men looked toward the parking lot alongside the church as a large truck with a huge disk on top moved slowly along the building, just making it under the power lines that came into the corner of the structure. The truck had almost made the journey when the left front dropped about eight inches, pulling the vehicle off to the side abruptly.

The driver attempted to move forward, but to no avail; then backward with minimal progress. The beautiful green yard, so carefully manicured by the trustees all summer long, was turning to green and black stew.

Another truck with similar equipment but much more compact came rolling out of the parking lot and scooted up the same yard with little difficulty.

"Hey!" yelled the pastor, "you can't go there and you certainly can't park there."

"Hey, Father, we've got a generator, but is it OK to plug into the church."

"I am not a Father. And no, it is not OK. Get that rig off of the yard."

"Problems Pastor?" came a voice the pastor recognized but did not welcome.

"Yes, Sheriff. Would you please get these people out of here?"

"Let me talk to them."

By then there were four trucks from different stations.

Ten minutes later the Sheriff tracked down the pastor who by then was trying to prepare himself for the family prayer.

"Pastor, " began the Sheriff.

"Did you get them off?"

"Ah, no, but I got something even better."

"And what is that?"

"They are willing to make a nice donation from each station to help cover the cost of repairs."

Somehow the pastor doubted that his church would ever see a dime, but he needed to move on with preparations. He turned from the Sheriff without reply.

"Hi Jim," the pastor said across the room as he saw his former parishioner and potential candidate for Sheriff.

The warm greeting to his Chief Deputy was not lost on the current Sheriff.

The Sheriff wasn't exactly excited about the large number of people attending the funeral. First of all, he'd had to park nearly four blocks away, right in front of the pastor's house. Second, his plans for the afternoon did not include having to deal with a few hundred people watching him make an arrest. The media would be fine, but you never knew how people might react when they saw someone they knew being arrested. And finally, these were all potential voters and his experience was that when you gathered together voters you had better know what was going to be said and who was going to say it.

The little episode with the television satellite trucks had also perturbed him. Sure they had agreed to pay for damages, but it had put the Sheriff at a disadvantage. Luckily none of the reporters had been involved.

"Sheriff, anything in particular we should be doing?" asked his chief deputy.

"No, I'll tell you when and where to be," replied the Sheriff. "Nothing will happen until after the funeral."

"Are we supposed to direct traffic?"

"I'm not having my deputies being traffic cops."

"Then I'm not exactly sure why you have four of us here. With Ellie off today, we're kinda short staffed."

"Check in with me after the funeral. I'll have something for you to do."

"I'd like my mother sitting with me in the front row. And, we'd like to be alone in that row."

"Shelley, it is so tight in there already. We really should fill each row."

"You're right John, I want Ellie to sit with me."

"Ah, Shelley, it really should be family. Your mother-in-law?"

"No!"

John Money walked away from the widow muttering under his breath something about not being paid enough.

Shelley had made one last visit to the casket, then she and her mother were escorted down to the basement where the family would gather for a prayer prior to going up to the church. She asked the usher from the funeral home to find her friend Ellie and ask her to come be with the family. She had appeared five minutes later.

Ellie had just decided that she wasn't going to be able to find a seat in the main part of the church when an usher came up and asked her to step out. She had assumed there was some kind of emergency although officially she was not on duty, having taken the day off to spend with her good friend.

"Mrs. Robison has asked that you come down and be with the family."

"Oh, OK."

Ellie was more than a little puzzled by this request, but realized that Shelley's only other family was her mother and her brother, who no one had seen since he'd been released from jail.

The deputy was dressed as anything but a law enforcement officer. She had worn a black skirt and jacket with a white blouse underneath. She wore heels and sheer nylons which she knew set off her legs. To accentuate her green eyes and red hair she'd worn a favorite kerchief around her neck.

Fifteen minutes later Ellie walked arm in arm alongside the young widow. Mrs. Ingvaldson came directly behind them. The three women sat alone on three chairs that had been set directly in front of the first pew. Mike's mother, his sister and two little ones, and Mike's brother Robbie, who despite his attempts to hide it, was limping, followed them.

Ellie had noted not only the limp, but also saw that Rob seemed to avoid shaking hands with people. She had tried to get a good look at his right hand but Rob had avoided any contact with her. Ellie had her suspicions about how Rob might have hurt his hand.

Ox and I made it to town in, what we figured, was plenty of time, but had to park nearly two blocks away. We hightailed it from our truck, through the alley and into the church parking lot where we watched several trucks attempt to find space to park. Then one of the trucks, mounted with satellite equipment, made for the lawn next to the church.

"Too wet, gonna get stuck," observed Ox. And he was right.

The first truck suddenly skidded and slid toward the church. Each of the next trucks seem to have less trouble as the further they got from the church building the firmer the grass was. As we walked past the second truck we saw the preacher, who nodded in our direction, come running forward with another well-dressed man I'd not met. It was obvious that the preacher was not happy.

As we rounded the corner and started to mount the steps into the church, our old friend Sheriff Carlson met us as he was coming down the steps.

"No room in there boys," he said nicely to us as though we were long lost friends, "Better head across the street, they've got televisions over there with a link to cameras."

We decided to take our chances and got into the church just as a beautiful redhead was being escorted out by an usher. Ox grabbed a folding chair from behind a door. How he knew it was there, I don't know. He pushed me forward and directed me to sit where the woman had just vacated her seat, then he set his folding chair down and ignored the stares of people on the edge of pews on either side of him.

We sat that way for ten minutes or so when, by some unknown signal, everyone stood up. The family walked in. It was then that I realized the woman dressed in black whose seat I had taken was now walking arm-in-arm with Shelley. It was the deputy. I couldn't believe how, as a law enforcement officer trained to observe things, I had missed identifying her as she came out of the church.

It was a strange parade that walked to the front of the church. Shelley, Ellie, and an older woman took the chairs. Two more women and two children followed them. Then came a scruffy looking kid in his early twenties. I glanced at his hands, which he continuously was rubbing. They had tiny cuts on them, and seemed to be bothering him.

I looked at my own hands and realized that the sweat that had started to blossom on the tops of my hands was really irritating. It was then that I realized that my own hands resembled those of the punk who was now sitting directly behind Shelley. And, I knew when and where my hands had received their ill treatment.

Goat watched as his suspect walked into the church. He knew that the criminal was unaware of what awaited them. The Sheriff had positioned himself in the balcony overlooking the sanctuary, wanting to keep an eye open for trouble, not that any was anticipated.

The lawman watched as the pastor walked down the aisle, turned and raised his hands ever so slightly. Immediately the congregation stood up, many turning their heads to the back of the church. The widow came out from under the balcony and the Sheriff was shocked to see a familiar redhead walking alongside her. A woman the Sheriff knew was Mike's mother accompanied them. The

Sheriff chuckled to himself as he saw that, looking down from on top, the older woman had obviously thinning hair.

Then came what must have been the sister dragging two little knee biters along with either hand. The woman walking in with her didn't seem to notice what was going on. Another person came right behind and at first the Sheriff couldn't tell if it was a man or a woman, but was convinced by the time "it" had reached the third pew in, that he was a man, of sorts.

Goat saw that someone was standing in front of a chair in the aisle, and then realized it was Forester; and Banion was sitting next to him. Someone two rows ahead of the farmers lifted what had to be a digital cell phone and must have snapped a picture just as the widow passed.

"Wouldn't you know it," he remarked to himself, "it's Kevin Walters. I suppose that photo will end up on the news tonight."

The Sheriff couldn't see the television cameras, but knew that several must be positioned in the back of the church. There was a small video camera being operated in the balcony by someone the lawman recognized. He surmised that he was transmitting the signal to the church across the way.

It took just a few minutes for the family to be seated. The Sheriff was surprised at how few there actually were. In the end there was an entire pew that sat empty behind the family.

The preacher lowered his hand and the congregation sat. He announced a hymn that the organist played through once. It wasn't one the Sheriff was familiar with so he just hummed along.

According to the program he'd received there would be another hymn sung at the end of the service and a solo would be sung by a Mary Brooks.

"Must be the preacher's wife," surmised the constable. "Not bad if it's the woman sitting up by the organist. Wonder how preacher man scored that lady?"

Carlson looked down at the cleric who had sat down in the front of the church and wondered what he might have on underneath the gown.

"Probably his Bermuda shorts and that god-awful shirt with flowers."

Chapter Sixteen

"It's My Funeral and I'll Cry If I Want To."

Pastor B. got up from his chair and walked over to the pulpit. He paused briefly at the altar and said a little prayer between himself and the God whom he had been serving for 25 years. This was the first time he had preached at a service for a murder victim. With all of the rumors related to the drug ring going on next door to the victim, his compassion and concern for Shelley, and his desire to come across just right for the TV cameras in the back of the church, he was truly conflicted.

He started by reading the obituary then paused and looked up to the audience, which filled the church to overflowing. He knew that there were more people watching the service from the basement, where television monitors had been set up and also from across the street at Good Shepherd Lutheran where, thanks to technology provided by the local high school, another 200 or more people had been seated.

"Dear friends in Christ. While the words I've just read detail the short life of our son, our brother, our husband, our friend whom we knew as Michael Norris Robison, they could just as well have been the obituary of the city of Harmony. For you see, in the last few days, life in this town as we have come to know and love it has ceased to exist."

"Some of you are here today because you are neighbors or co-workers and you are expected to be here. Some are here because you knew and loved Mike. Some are here because you are curious about who is here and what might happen. Some are here representing the public, because, while most deaths are private, this was not. But there is one who is here who is celebrating what has happened in our community."

"If no one hears the gunshots, do they not happen? Were it only so! Murder and drugs and crime are such ugly words when they appear outside of a mystery novel. They are on our lips now as we ponder what could have gone so wrong in our little town that we must now speak those words about a person we knew. He was our friend, our co-worker, our classmate, and our neighbor. Today a family none of us knew well has been destroyed by drugs and another has ceased to exist because of murder. We don't know how they were connected or even if they were. But we cannot as a community look upon one event without seeing the other and in them see a reflection of who we have become. We have more questions than answers, more anger than fear."

"Oh Evil One, what has caused you to visit this horrible tragedy upon our peaceful community? Did you see something in us that we were not aware of? Did you see a weakness that you could take advantage of? Or did you see in our apathetic strength a challenge, an opportunity to cause us to question our own faith?"

"Evil One, did you think that because we were in a lull and church attendance was going lower with the activity of summer that this was a time to strike? Not so Evil One, for it is to our churches that we will turn and be lifted up by Word and Sacrament and the fellowship of those who worship your enemy."

"Evil One, did you think that our community does not love its children, that we have no time for them; that they are a burden to us? What causes you to think that? Is it how we treat them in our schools and in our neighborhoods? Do you see us so involved in work and play that we forget how precious they are to us? Did you think that the evil weed and meth and crank and other addicting things could replace our love for them? Not so, Evil One, for what you have done has caused us all to grab our little ones and hold them close; to caress them with love and to show patience and understanding."

"Did you think, Evil One, that because there is anger between spouses; that more of us are not living up to our marriage vows; that some of us are living in sin; that there is sexual abuse and violence, that you could cause us to turn from those we have committed our lives too? You are so wrong! Today I see husbands and wives hugging and silently committing to themselves that no matter how bad things get your way will not be the answer."

"Did you pick a Christian community for some evil purpose, Evil One? Did you think we would question our values and beliefs? Did you think that those who are momentarily weak in their faith would turn to you? Did you expect us to turn from our churches, our Sunday Schools, our parochial schools, our pastors and teachers and our Christian friends? IT WILL NOT HAPPEN!"

"Yes, Evil One, we are wise to your tricks. You use tragedies like this to cause doubt in those who are questioning, to cause anger when there should be pity, to hate when there should be understanding, to fear when there should be respect, and to blaspheme when there should be prayer. You cause us to blame He who is blameless and to cry tears of woe when we should be celebrating mercy."

"But we will not let you win, Evil One. Our clergy are already helping us to understand; those closest to the tragedy will be provided comfort and compassion; neighbor will reach out to neighbor knowing that we must be more sensitive to each other; we will turn to our churches, our schools, our clubs, our youth organizations; and we will, as a community, resurrect ourselves as a stronger, more vibrant, more caring town. We are coming to a clearer understanding of how you work and what evil you can bring to us in our lack of vigilance. We know you walk about as a roaring lion, seeking whom you can devour. But not here, Evil One. MOVE ON!"

"In our community, our strength is in the Lord and in each other."

And with that there was silence.

The Sheriff had not been paying a lot of attention to the proceedings in front of him. The preacher's sermon had just been so much background noise as far as he was concerned. He wanted to look over the audience and also to keep an eye on his suspect. He noticed suddenly that there was no sound and felt like he had really missed something. Actually, he felt a little like someone had said something about him and he had missed what it was.

The woman next to him was quietly sobbing and Goat noticed that the man behind the video camera had wiped his big bulbous nose across the sleeve of his shirt.

"Obviously, I missed something," thought the Sheriff. "It doesn't look like there's a dry eye in the place."

The Sheriff was genuinely baffled by what was transpiring. He didn't think that Mike Robison was that well known let alone liked. His own daughter, a class mate of Mike's, had little good to say about him despite the fact she and Mike's widow were close friends.

The preacher's wife got up and started her solo, but had to stop and start over again, she was crying so much. Goat watched as the preacher got out of his seat and went over by the organ, whispered something to his wife, gave her a little hug then proceeded to sing a duet instead of a solo. Even the Sheriff had to admit they did a really nice job of it.

The pastor gave the benediction, according to the program, then told the congregation that a lunch would be served downstairs and that those who did not wish to travel to the cemetery could start the lunch. He led everyone in a prayer that started with "Come Lord Jesus.." which the Sheriff mumbled along with, half remembering the prayer from his youth.

The final hymn started and about half way through, John Money came up with one of his ushers and they wheeled the casket out. The pallbearers followed the casket. Then John came back and ushered the family out. His wife was there too, helping to direct traffic.

When he saw the family start to leave, Goat headed for the stairs and unceremoniously stepped over and around other people in the balcony. He hustled outside and caught sight of Jim Barton.

"Jim, you and the boys stick around here now. I'm heading out to the cemetery. I want you ready to make an arrest when I get back."

"What? What are you talking about Goat?"

"You heard me."

"Yeah, I heard you, but I don't believe you. Who are we arresting?"

But the question went unanswered as the Sheriff scooted across the parking lot and quick-walked to his car some four blocks away.

The young widow had been a nervous wreck by the time the pastor had finished his prayers with the family down in the basement. She had thought that having Ellie with her would help matters, but there was only so much the former classmate could do, especially with Mike's mother still fuming over the ticket she'd gotten the night before.

Shelley realized she was being difficult with John Money, but was also adamant about not having that woman sit with her in the front row. Mike's mother had practically abandoned them after her move to Minneapolis and she wasn't about to share these special moments with the old bitty.

The trip up the stairs had been difficult because the whole way was laden with people, most of whom she didn't recognize in her grief. Ellie had finally taken her arm when she had stumbled over a television cable lying in the back of the church. They had walked arm-in-arm down the aisle. When they'd gotten to about half way down the pathway, Jack Forester was standing there and next to him was Paul.

Shelley tried to smile at the two neighbors, but wasn't able to get more than a grimace out.

As they approached the front of the church, Ellie had pinched her arm just in time for her to see Kevin Walters. Kevin had his cell phone out and held it up in front of them. She couldn't believe he would actually be snapping a picture. By now it was probably on the way to the station.

The casket lay in the front of the church. It was a simple gray casket, for in the end Ellie had helped her realize that she was going to need her money to survive on. A pall with a cross on it covered the casket. And, covering the pall was a large bouquet that John had "thrown in". It had a ribbon on the right side that said "husband" and another that said "son".

Half way through the first hymn, Shelley had started to sob quietly. It was only the second time she had cried since the Sheriff and Pastor B. had made their trip to her office.

"Why is it that I cry now?" she asked herself.

Ellie patted her arm.

The rest of the service was a blur. Shelley heard the sermon, but it just didn't seem to be about Mike or her. It had been awfully quiet following the discourse and Shelley finally understood that something momentous had occurred to bring the full church to absolute silence.

That surmise was confirmed when Mary Brooks, who had never been at a loss for words, wasn't able to sing her solo.

When the service was over, Shelley reversed her route, this time following Mike's casket out. She was escorted, along with her mother and Ellie to her car that was waiting in front of the church behind the hearse and another car from the funeral home. Ellie got behind the wheel, but couldn't start the car without keys.

Shelley sorted through her purse. She gave out a little exclamation when she realized that the cigarette she'd confiscated from Rob was still in her purse. She calculated that as soon as they returned from the cemetery she'd have to flush it down the toilet.

"Shelley," said Ellie, "you're doing just fine. We're almost done."

"Yeah, Hon. I'm really proud of you," reiterated her mother.

"Thanks. I can't believe all the people who were there."

Chapter Seventeen
"Alone At Last"

Ellie was concerned about her friend. She hadn't cried in three days and then during the service she totally broke down.

Ellie was also concerned about her father, the Sheriff. She glanced up to the balcony as they walked out of the church and had seen him forcing his way out, stepping over, around, and through people who got in his way. Something was up. Her father was usually so much more in control.

As she drove the two miles to the cemetery, she realized that the deputies she had seen at the church, including Jim Barton, were not there to direct traffic. That seemed strange to the deputy, since she had taken the day off and her dad seldom concentrated his officers at one site without pretty good reason.

As they swung into the cemetery she could see that about half a mile back was an old green pickup truck. Paul and Jack most have decided to make the trip to the graveside. Ellie thought that was really kind of them.

I really dislike funerals. Yet, I also know how important a funeral is in the overall grief process. But I still hate funerals. I think it is because each time I attend a funeral, I'm reminded of my grandfather's memorial service.

It wasn't too hard to make the decision, following the church service, to hustle over to our vintage Chevrolet and join the throng heading out to the cemetery. Ox drove and I sat reflecting on the message and on the day.

For us the day had started with the birth of a new heifer calf that would someday be the foundation of a bigger and better herd. To now be focused on the dead seemed like a not so rare dichotomy that those of us in farming (yes, I know, I've only been doing this four days) see on a daily basis.

We barely made it up to the graveside in time to hear the pastor complete the committal service. Then people started heading to their cars and taking the journey back to the church basement where hot dish, Jell-o salads, and little ham sandwiches no doubt awaited them.

I've always been intrigued by the history contained in a cemetery, so Ox and I took a few minutes to walk around and look at the names and dates on the headstones.

"Norwegian side is over there. This is the German side," reported a deep voice.

We turned to see the Sheriff standing with his hands on his hips and his legs spread apart as though he was ready for a shootout.

I don't know about Ox, but I had all I could do to keep from laughing. I must have smiled wickedly though.

"Well, boys I want to thank you again for helping my daughter out. But I'm warning you right now, I don't want her involved with a farmer."

And with that he turned around and strutted off, back to his white Explorer. The man had been born one hundred and fifty years too late.

I looked at Ox and Ox looked at me. This time we could not restrain our laughter. Old Wilhelm Schoephoester was probably rolling in his grave, because two grown men had all they could do to keep from rolling on it.

Her sister-in-law had once told Shelley that she should start a family with Mike. All Shelley needed to do was bring her sister-in-law and her two kids to mind anytime she started thinking about a family and she had the best birth control device money can't buy.

In that same conversation Margo had said, "It is unbelievable pain followed by complete and total joy."

Shelley felt like she had just given birth to a new life – her own.

She almost wanted to sing out as they drove back to town. She actually thought about telling Ellie that she would drive back, but decided it might be unseemly. The widow wanted to dance for joy, not because she hated Mike, and she probably did, but because she felt free for the first time in six years.

Free to watch the television shows she wanted to watch. Free to cook the supper she wanted to eat. Free to call the friends she wanted to talk to. Free to ride her horse without Mike making some comment about a "hay burner". Free to sleep as late as she wanted. Free to go to bed without fear of being pawed all over. Free to buy a dress without first asking for permission. Free to own more than one purse. Free to leave her facial cream on the bathroom counter top without finding it in the garbage can or worse. Free to have Ellie over for dinner. Free to have her mother over to dinner.

Free to have Paul over to dinner Sunday night, she remembered.

"Oh, yes," she thought to herself, "there are going to be some freedoms I will enjoy more than others."

"Timing is everything," thought the Sheriff as he followed the car back to town. "I've got to make sure we don't have a situation that could get out of control, but I also want to make sure that there is maximum coverage."

As he rolled across Highway 210, he noticed that one of the trucks from a Twin Cities station was coming down Main Street. He hoped that the others had not left. His hopes were dashed when he arrived at the church to find the only truck remaining was the one that had gotten stuck.

Old Albert Arndt was there with his son's tractor trying to pull the rig out of the church lawn.

The Sheriff climbed out of his Explorer and hustled over to the truck.

"You boys might want to stick around. There just might be some news here today."

"Who are you? Oh, yeah, the Sheriff. Say Sheriff we'll get a check sent here to the church. You think a couple of hundred will do?"

"No, I'm saying there is going to be something newsworthy happen in the next few minutes."

"Well, the reporter has already headed back to Fargo. I doubt we can get him back. Sorry. You just let us know if you schedule a press conference."

The Sheriff turned away just in time to see his quarry enter the church.

"Gotcha."

The Sheriff accelerated to get to the door just ahead of the woman he had surmised was the mother of Mike Robison.

"You're the Sheriff aren't you?"

"Yes, ma'am and you are…"

"I'm Laverne Robison. Mike was my son. Say, have you figured out who did it?"

"We're getting very close."

"Well, I think you should look at Shelley."

That caused the Sheriff to stop in his tracks.

"Why is that, Mrs. Robison?"

"Vernie, I go by Vernie."

"All right, Vernie. What do you know that I should know?"

"I know that she didn't love my son. I know that she seems to be more interested in the money that folks have given than she has a right to be. I know that she didn't seem all that broken up over

Mike's death. I know that she and that preacher sure seem to be cozy."

"Anything else?"

"Isn't that enough."

"Well, it certainly gives me something to think about."

"Say, while I have you, is there any chance you could get this taken care of," she said as you pulled from her purse the ticket she'd gotten the night before.

"You just leave it with me. I'll take care of it."

Trying to catch someone's attention or even having a conversation in private was virtually impossible for Pastor B. all day long. There were several people the good pastor desperately needed to visit with and the sooner the better.

There was the Sheriff whom Pastor B. knew was going to do something before day's end that they would all regret. He'd seen the Sheriff sitting up in the balcony and from a distance had spied him talking to Jack and his friend out at the cemetery.

There was Shelley Robison. Not only did he want to console her as a part of his duties as pastor, but he was also very concerned about some things that he'd heard and also the intimation the Sheriff made that there would be an arrest.

There was Jack Forester and his friend Paul, both of whom needed to receive an explanation of what they'd seen a couple of days earlier when the pastor had been visiting with Shelley out near their woods. But Pastor B. also knew instinctively that the two men had more going for them that what met the eye.

And there was his wife. He'd never seen her breakdown like she had in the funeral service. Something must really be troubling her.

Chapter Eighteen

"The Game is Afoot...Long"

Ox and I almost decided not to go back to the church for lunch. We still had a few chores to take care of and Ox thought that since the wind had been blowing all morning, the hay at the Robison place would be ready to bale by the time we got back to the farm. As we drove by the church on our way out of town, I spied the Sheriff talking with some of his men. Just then the men dispersed in several directions. I've seen enough police action in my day to know that the countenance that was on each of those men's faces was serious and that something was about to happen.

"Pull over. Let's go back to the church," I said to Ox.

He looked quizzically at me.

"Something's going to happen back there," I replied to his unspoken question.

He did a U-turn and swung into the parking lot. We both jumped down from the pickup and headed for the back door that, Ox explained, led to a set of stairs that went directly down to the kitchen. We walked through the kitchen, to the surprise of a number of ladies who were busy with dishes and serving.

As we walked through the kitchen door, we saw that most of the people had eaten but were sitting around visiting. A few were congregated by the woman we now knew was Mike Robison's mother. A few more were with Shelley. Ellie was just coming from the beverage table with two Styrofoam cups filled with coffee. She smiled at us and mouthed a silent hello. She nodded her head toward the table where she and Shelley were sitting.

Ox and I each grabbed a chair and sat down, waiting for events to unfold.

Just then the Sheriff walked up to the table and parted the visitors like Moses parted the waters.

"Mrs. Robison," he said to Shelley, "I want to express my sincere sympathy at your loss."

"Thank you Sheriff. I don't know what I would have done without Ellie."

"Now Shelley Robison, I hereby place you under arrest for the murder of your husband, Michael Norris Robison. You have the right to remain silent…"

Ox and I watched as the Sheriff motioned for one of his deputies to come forward and handcuff the now bewildered woman.

Absolute quiet was the order of the day as the entire room began to notice that something was happening. Ox and I both stood up.

"You boys stay right where you are," commanded the Sheriff. "Take them into custody for obstruction if they move an eyelid," he directed his deputies.

"Father, may I speak with you in private."

"No," came the gruff reply from the Sheriff to his daughter.

"Mrs. Robison, may we search your purse for a weapon?"

Shelley nodded her reply in shocked silence.

"What's this?" questioned the Sheriff as he picked up the lone cigarette in Shelley's purse. He then deposited the cigarette in a small baggie that he pulled from his jacket pocket.

I was surprised by his actions, but decided that now was not the time to say anything.

Ox and my eyes followed Ellie as she stood up and looked around the room. She was obviously looking for someone. When she didn't see anyone she walked quickly to the door that led to the stairs up from the basement of the church.

Our attention came back to the deputy who had handcuffed our neighbor. He was saying something to Shelley and she was nodding her head, again in silence. The deputy started for the kitchen with his prisoner. The ladies from the kitchen had all come out and were standing by the serving window awestruck.

"Jim, what are you doing?" questioned the Sheriff.

"Taking her out the back way."

"You will do no such thing. She goes up the main staircase."

The deputy seemed to know that it didn't pay to argue.

I heard a "harrumph" from behind me and turned to see the pastor standing there. I had assumed that Ellie had gone to find him and if that were the case, she wouldn't find him unless she came back downstairs.

"I genuinely don't like that man," said the pastor, obviously referring to the Sheriff.

"I heard that preacher," came a reply from the Sheriff who was now crossing the room toward the main staircase.

Just as the group got to the stairway, Ellie reappeared with a well-dressed man in tow. I figured the guy had to be either a banker or an attorney.

"Damn that father of mine," cussed Ellie Carlson under her breath as she walked briskly across the fellowship hall and up the stairs to the main part of the church.

She had looked in vain in the hall for Andy Ratcliff, Shelley's boss and a well-known defense attorney in that part of the state. She'd finally found him out by his car visiting with Shelley's brother who had opted not to be a part of the family for the funeral. It was obvious that they were talking business but that hadn't stopped Ellie from running up to him.

"Andy, Andy," hollered an out of breath Ellie. The two men had turned to her.

"Andy, James, you've got to come right now. Dad is arresting Shelley for Mike's murder!"

Both men were incredulous and started to follow Ellie back into the church. However, by the time they had descended the stairs, James was no longer with them. Ellie puzzled about that, but only momentarily as the attorney and deputy ran headlong into Jim Barton, Shelley, and Sheriff "Goat" Carlson.

"Hold on Sheriff," commanded Andy. "What do you think you're doing?"

"Arresting a murderer."

By then the attorney was red faced with anger as he realized what the Sheriff was up to.

"Jim, did you know about this?" questioned the attorney.

Barton stood shamefaced and shook his head.

"I thought not. Sheriff, I'm going to ask you nicely to take the cuffs off of Shelley…No, you wait and listen. If you do that, I'll not call my friends at the paper and let them know what you tried to pull…No, you wait and listen. Tomorrow morning at 10:00 my client and I will present ourselves at Wally's office and we'll look at what you have…Oh, I can tell you haven't even bothered to let Wally know what you were going to do, have you?"

Ellie was certain that her dad had not bothered to contact the county attorney. The two men hadn't seen eye to eye for a while and Ellie knew that he had given her father some grief over the "enlarged crime scene" search that the deputies had done of Shelley's house.

The young deputy also knew from reading the file her father had given her two days before that this wasn't just a frivolous action Goat was taking. The reading of the file had been exactly why Ellie had encouraged her friend to talk things over with Andy. She realized now that the widow had probably had too many other things going on and had put it off.

"Well," she thought, "Andy's involved now."

Pastor B. was beside himself when one of the ladies from the kitchen found him in his study. He had hidden out there, hoping that the Sheriff would not find him, assuming that the lawman would not do anything ill-advised with out first talking it over with the pastor.

His phone call earlier in the day from someone who wanted "to give myself up" had led him to assume that the culprit the Sheriff was about to apprehend was a man. He had even ticked off the possible candidates, some of whom he doubted were guilty of anything other then coming into the Sheriff's sights.

Pastor B. got to the basement in time to watch the exchange between the attorney and the Sheriff.

"Boy, if I'm ever in trouble that's the lawyer I want on my side," thought the preacher.

"Shelley, come on up to my office. Please you too," the pastor offered the attorney and his new client.

A few minutes later they were all ensconced in the Pastor's small but adequate office.

"Shelley, you need to tell your attorney here what you told me last Monday," said the minister.

Shelley then spent the next ten minutes going through what had happened to her the morning her husband was found murdered. The attorney sat through it all without asking any questions.

"Shelley, your pastor here and I are both covered by privilege. Can you think of anything that would lead the Sheriff to suspect you? Anything at all, no matter how small?"

"I honestly can't. I know they were in the house when pastor and I came out to get some phone numbers."

"In your house? I thought the body was found out in the yard?"

"I guess Ellie found it back behind the barn."

"Did you give them permission to go into your house?"

"No, they were already in it when we got there."

"I can vouch for that," chimed in the pastor. "As a matter of fact, Jim Barton had to check with the Sheriff to see if I could even go in to get the phone numbers."

"And did the Sheriff give you permission?" queried Ratcliff.

"No," chuckled the pastor. "I'd already gone in and gotten what Shelley needed by the time Jim got hold of the Sheriff."

"Was there anyone in the house with you…anyone from the Sheriff's office?"

"No."

"Give me a dollar, you too Shelley…All right, now I'm officially both of your attorney's"

"Why do I need an attorney?" asked the preacher.

"I hope you don't."

Chapter Nineteen

"The Definition Of Fair: I Win, But Not By Much"

"Well, I almost made it," thought Goat to himself as he directed Barton to take the cuffs off of his prisoner. "If we had just made it up the stairs and out to one of the deputies' cars I would have saved so much time and energy. Now I'm going to have to play games with this damned attorney again."

Goat had had a run in with Andy Ratcliff earlier in the week. The defense attorney, who bragged that he had been number 1 in the number 1 class to graduate from the new University of St. Thomas School of Law, had gotten the two women who had been captured in the raid on Monday released without bail. The Sheriff and his men had not even had time to question them.

The Sheriff remembered that the attorney had been masterful in putting forth just the least little doubt about the Sheriff's voracity: "Your honor, these women have young children to care for, they were not aware that someone, whom the Sheriff can't even identify, was growing marijuana in their field. And your honor, these two ladies have family in the area and are simply not a flight risk."

The Sheriff also remembered that the young pipsqueak Setten had sent over from his office to handle the arraignment hadn't even put up an argument.

So, now the Maplewood County Sheriff's office would once again suffer an embarrassment at the hands of Andy Ratcliff. Goat was steaming by the time he left the church. And, as he left the church he saw his would be quarry enter the pastor's office along with her attorney.

"Wonder what that's all about," thought the Sheriff. Then he recalled the phone call he'd received from Jim Barton on the day of the murder. Jim had reported that the preacher and the victim's wife had arrived at the farm and wanted to go in the house to retrieve something. By the time Jim had called him and gotten the clearance, the preacher had already gone into the house and come out with something.

The Sheriff went back in the church and found his chief deputy.

"Jim, remember that call that you made to me from the Robison's, when preacher and Shelley showed up. You told me the preacher brought something out with him. What did he take out of the house?"

"He took an address book."

"Are you sure?"

"Well, that's what he said he was getting."

"But you didn't see what he took."

"No, I was talking to you on the phone."

"And no one went in with him," the Sheriff said incredulously.

"No."

"And, why was that, may I ask."

"Well, he's a pastor… I know him…He was my pastor."

"Um, well he's not mine."

The attorney in me applauded the man who had come to Shelley's rescue and embarrassed the Sheriff into releasing her. The lawman in me felt for the Sheriff. I'd been there more than once in my career when a lot of hard work had been undermined by a too smart trial lawyer.

I was probably one of two or three people standing in the room who knew the contents of the case the Sheriff had against the widow. I would probably be looking at her as a prime suspect myself, especially after finding the marijuana in her purse.

But I also would have used some common sense. In the Paul Banion book of common law etiquette, you don't arrest someone at a funeral, and if you are running for election in the fall you don't make widows and children cry.

Ox and I decided that we'd called enough attention to ourselves and headed for home. We checked the maternity pen and saw that both new moms were doing well. A third was getting close to calving and would bear watching throughout the day.

It was too early to do chores, I'd had a good lunch, it had been an emotionally draining day, I thought it would be a good time to take a little nap in the hammock Ox had out on the patio.

"Gotta bale hay," was Ox's reply to my suggestion.

I took the repaired square baler out of the shed by first hooking it up, under Ox's watchful eye, to the John Deere 4020. After first pinning the draw bar to the baler, we put together the power take off. We then greased every ball bearing and grease zerk we could find. Finally, after Ox checked to make sure I had enough twine string, I headed off to the Robison's to bale the hay I'd cut three days earlier. Despite the rain of Tuesday night the hay had dried well on Wednesday and Ox assured me everything would be fine by the time I got out in the field that afternoon.

I pulled out of our drive pulling a baler and three hayracks behind me. It was a long procession extending nearly a hundred feet behind me.

"Wow!" I exclaimed to Ox, "I stretch out forever."

"No problem," said Ox. "Just don't back up."

Upon which advice I immediately began thinking about all the places along the way to the Robisons where I might have to back up if I didn't know exactly the way to get there. Now, those who have experienced pulling anything at all can only imagine the fear and trepidation upon which I entered the journey.

The ten-minute journey took me nearly a half an hour in first gear. I bumped it up to second gear on a straightaway, but then put it back into first after turning the corner. Despite my caution, I barely made the turn into the farmyard of the late Michael Norris Robison.

"I wonder where the 'Norris' came from," I thought remembering that I'd asked myself the same question during the reading of the obituary only a few short hours earlier.

I cautiously drove through the yard and out the field road next to the barn. As I rounded the corner, I saw a gray car come in the same drive that I had just traversed. I assumed it might be Shelley and further conjectured that she probably didn't want or need company other than her attorney and or her friend Ellie. Besides, Ox said that he would be coming over to pick up the first rack of hay within the hour, which meant I had better keep moving.

It was just about then that the laws of physics and Murphy collided with each other and the third wagon banged hard into the fence post upon which the gate to the hay field was hung. Luckily I was not going very fast or both the wagon and the fence post would have been traumatized. As it was, the rack tipped forward onto the right front wheel and moaned unappreciatively at its juxtaposition to the post.

I was able to back up just enough to relieve sufficient pressure that the rack dropped back to all fours, but I saw immediately that the third rack would not make it through the opening without some significant repositioning.

I had to crawl under the rack to take out the hitch pin. It was really tough to do and I had to pull forward on the wagon's tongue with one arm as I undid the pin with the other. As I struggled, sweat formed on my brow and I wiped it away. It was then that I felt it.

As I lay there, trying to catch my breath, I suddenly felt a presence. I glanced to my left and came face to face with the brown and black face of a dog. Not just any dog, but a really big dog. I was sure it was the same one I'd seen a few days early. He crawled forward on his haunches and joined me, plopping his head on my abdomen.

"Nice doggy," I said. "Shoo, Shoo."

"Having problems?" came a question from someone other than the dog.

I cocked my head enough to see a pair of legs encased in jeans that extended upward out of my line of vision and downward to a pair of athletic shoes. I assumed it was Shelley.

"Ah, not until just now," I replied. "Could you call off your dog?"

"He's just saying 'hi'."

"I'm sure. It's just a little difficult for me to move."

"Here Max, come on Maxxy. That a boy. Good Maxxy."

I struggled a bit more. Finally the pin came out and I dropped the tongue and crawled out from under the wagon.

It was only after I had crawled out from under the wagon that I heard the grating sound of something being pulled ever so slowly across bare ground. I turned around to see the wagon I had just unhitched drawing away from me at a snail's pace. It was then and only then that I realized that there was a slight incline going into the field. Not enough slope to notice, but obviously enough to encourage my wagon to become wayward.

"Is it supposed to do that?" asked the lady in jeans.

"Yes!"

I ran for the wagon and got to it just as it started to pick up momentum. I didn't have time to reach down and grab the tongue, which would have given me some control. Instead I snatched the rack itself and tried to attain some purchase on the square tubing that made up the cage into which the bales were tossed. The beast carried me with it, cussing and swearing. I tried desperately to use my new boots as brakes, much as in the manner of Fred Flintstone, but to no avail. The road ahead of me, or would it have been behind me, had a curve in it and I anticipated that the twist in the path would have some impact on my miscreant. It did. The jolt threw the tongue of the wagon ninety degrees and flipped me clumsily off of my feet while still holding onto the rack.

It was then that Max decided to join in on the chase, followed by his master or would that be mistress. In any event, he started snipping at my feet. His mistress started yelling and chasing after all three of us, the wagon, the wagon master, and the dog snapping at us both.

The wagon stopped with a jolt and I regained my footing. The back of the wagon had kissed a three-foot wide oak tree about 20 feet off of the path. I looked around to see if any damage, other than to my ego, had been done to equipment or person. I found none.

I decided there was little I could do alone with the aberrant wagon and I certainly would not request assistance from the observer standing near the road. She had changed from her earlier attire and was now dressed in a white blouse and blue jeans. I brushed myself off of the dust and debris that had accumulated on my person over the previous minutes.

"Are you all right?"

"Just fine."

I walked up the slight incline with as much dignity as I could muster. Max seemed to enjoy standing by the wagon and barking as though reminding me of my blunder.

I fired up the diesel engine of the 4020, caught a fine whiff of diesel exhaust that reminded me of the buses traveling the finer streets of New York and moved into the field. I climbed down from the tractor after positioning it just so. I was about to detach the number two rack when Shelley came forward with a large block of wood.

"Mike always used this," said Shelley as she tossed the block behind a back tire on the wagon.

"Thanks," I said, "I'll remember that."

I repeated the process of unhooking a wagon, this time with much greater success. I mounted the tractor again, engaged the power take-off and heard the now familiar click, clack and clunk of the baler devouring its ribbon of hay and expelling the by-product of square bales into the large rack trailing behind. I tipped my hat to the lady and let out the clutch.

Off to my left, nearly on my horizon, I caught sight of a doe and fawn scurrying across the field and leaping over a fence. Glancing back to the road, I saw that Shelley had seen them too. She smiled and nodded to them, then gave a little wave. Right then and there I knew that between the two of us, there was only one murderer, and it was I. I hoped the doe would forgive me for bumping off her Bambi.

Chapter Twenty
"My Brother's Keeper"

It surely seemed odd to Shelley that for three days following her husband's sudden death she had only cried once, and that while sitting in the car at her own home. Then the day of the funeral came and she hadn't been able to quit crying. First it was during the service; then it was when the pastor had led the mourners in prayer at the graveside; then it had been when the Sheriff had arrested her; then it was sitting in the pastor's office while her attorney explained a few things.

"I have no more to give," thought Shelley as she drove down the dirt road and into her own drive way.

Not even the sight of her new friend driving through the yard and out into the field had an impact on Shelley.

"I wonder what he thought," contemplated the distraught woman as she reflected back on the incident in the church basement, knowing that Paul had been there to see the whole thing.

It only took the blonde fifteen minutes to go inside and change into jeans and one of her dad's old white dress shirts. She had some chores to do and then wanted to take a long horseback ride through the woods. Riding was the best way she knew to clear her head and do some "right thinking", as her dad used to call it.

Shelley went over to the barn and took Max off of his lead so he could run and get some exercise as well as take care of some other business. Like a shot from a cannon, Mad Max took off toward the field road. Shelley jogged after the dog. Normally she wouldn't worry about him, but she remembered the look of fear that Paul had the other day when Ellie brought Max into the house.

She found both Paul and Max under the wagon playing. Paul had asked her to call the dog, but Max had been so enamored of the young man, she'd had all to she could do to get him to come out.

Paul had parked the wagon down the hill with some difficulty. She'd then shown him how her dead husband used to block the wheels on a wagon so they didn't roll. He'd thanked her then started up the tractor and taken off. After just a little ways down the windrow, Paul had turned around and smiled at her. She nodded her head and smiled, then given him a little wave.

She watched him head down the field and go over the hill, the baler kicking out beautiful green hay bales about every thirty feet. Max had tried to follow Paul, much as he used to follow Mike up and down the fields. But Shelley had called Max back and this time he had obeyed, no doubt anticipating a treat.

As mistress and dog walked back to the farmyard, Shelley's thoughts went back to the meeting with the attorney immediately after the funeral.

"Shelley, obviously Carlson thinks he has probable cause to do what he did. Can you think of anything that would make him think you could have done this to Mike?"

"No, not a thing."

"Shelley, we need to tell Mr. Ratcliff here everything," the pastor had chimed in.

The look on Andy's face, a face she knew so well, was devastating to Shelley.

"Ah, pastor I hope you're not hinting at something here…"

"No, NO!" interrupted the pastor. "It's just that there was a lot more that went on that day than what anyone knows."

"Shelley?"

Shelley had then laid out the trip from Milton to Cedar Grove then on to Oakdale. Pastor B. had chimed in about him and the Sheriff visiting her office. Andy was especially concerned about the way Carlson had asked certain questions.

"Did you at anytime believe you were waiving your rights?"

"Well, I realized that I probably needed to keep my mouth shut."

"Good. Did you at anytime give permission to the Sheriff to search your house?"

"No"

"I can vouch for that," interjected the Pastor. He then proceeded to tell about his adventure going into the house.

"Did Deputy Barton see what you had taken out of the house?"

"No, he came back just as we were driving off."

"Did anyone else see you together?"

Silence.

"I take it someone else did see you. Well, let's leave that alone for now. Shelley, I want you to come in to the office by 7:30

tomorrow morning. And, ah, Pastor I need you to stay away from Shelley for the time being."

The latter had startled both the pastor and Shelley.

Shelley needed to relax. She brought Mocca, her Palomino gelding out from his stall and tied him to the hitching post. She loved the smell of horses and leather and the feel of a saddle under her. She brushed Mocca, then saddled him and took off down the drive.

Just short of the road was a narrow path that headed back into the woods that surrounded the house. She followed that path for 300 yards then came out along a fence that separated her place from the neighbors. She followed that fence down to where it intersected the road, then rode for nearly half a mile along that fence line. Then she turned back to reverse her path.

She loved this ride because she went up and down a few small hills. She would gallop Mocca up the hill, anticipating the view afforded. Often she spied wild animals like fox or wild turkeys, deer or coyotes. Once she actually saw a moose, although no one believed her. As she topped the final hill on her journey back, she was surprised to see her brother James at the bottom of the hill walking toward the fence.

She watched as he moved forward cautiously and wondered what might have prompted him to be out there that afternoon. She'd been disappointed when he had not bothered to come early enough to the funeral to sit with the family. And she especially wondered about his disappearance as she was being arrested.

Just as he was about to climb over the well-maintained fence dividing the two farms, Mocca decided to welcome him with a whinny. Startled, James looked up the hill and saw his sister. He waved, and then started to walk toward her.

There are times in a pastor's career when his faith is challenged. Most pastors look forward to those times as opportunities to grow spiritually and to strengthen their relationship with God. This was not such a time for Pastor Brooks.

After Shelley left his office, the attorney stayed behind to talk with him. By the time the meeting was over Pastor B. would have taken the first bus out of Harmony, had there been such a bus.

"Pastor, we don't know each other which is probably a good thing. I'll keep my manners about me."

Pastor B. had known something was about to come his way.

"Do you have any idea what your cute little stunt with the address book may have cost Shelley, let alone you? That sheriff is out to get re-elected and he may just be running against one of his own men. He needs to solve this case. He has become the laughingstock of the media and this little arrest antic that he pulled downstairs is just going to put salt on the wound."

"I thought that…" attempted the pastor.

"Your job is not to think. It is simply to pray and you had better be doing a lot of it. If I read the Sheriff correctly, he is right now conferring with the County Attorney about obstruction of justice charges against you. My guess is that you will be forced to testify against Shelley, or at least tell them what she told you."

"But I can't…"

"Pastor, you're not doing your job again. Pray. That's it. Keep your mouth shut. If anyone, and I mean anyone shows up from the Sheriff's office or County Attorney, you call me and keep your mouth shut until I get here. You don't even offer them coffee. Capeesh?"

"Yes, pray…keep mouth shut…call you."

"Very Good! Now I'm going back to my office."

Pastor B thought how simple life would be if what he promised his new attorney could actually happen, but Andy Ratcliff did not know Mary Brooks. The pastor knew something was tormenting Mary and he prayed it had nothing to do with Shelley Robison. "See," thought the pastor, "I'm praying. Now if I can just keep my mouth shut."

As Pastor B. walked the four blocks from the church to his home, he contemplated how he would explain to his wife the events of the last four days. It was not a conversation that he was looking forward to. Over the twenty-seven years of their marriage he had kept few secrets from his wife. He also had never talked with her about private concerns of his parishioners. Now those two things were colliding, as he knew his wife would have to be prepared for his possible arrest or questioning.

"Hi Mary," he said to the figure stooped over the garden in front of their house.

There was no reply. The minister went up to the steps leading into the house and sat down on the second from the top step, leaning his back against the top one.

"Are you all right?" he asked after sitting for what seemed like an interminable time.

When again there was no reply, the cleric reached down to his wife's shoulder and caressed it. She shifted away and started pulling weeds in earnest. The preacher moved to the edge of the stairway and reached for his wife's chin. When he lifted it, he saw that she had been crying.

"What is it, Luv?"

After twenty-seven years, Pastor B. knew his wife and that knowledge led him to do the unobvious. He stood up and made as though he were going in the house.

"I think I'll make myself a cucumber sandwich from those cukes the Arndt's dropped off."

"No, wait."

"All right. Come here and sit by me."

She lifted her body from the ground, brushed off some grass clippings, then removed her garden gloves. She walked over to the steps and sat down next to her mate. He put his arm around her.

"What will people driving by think?"

"They'll think I'm a pretty darn lucky guy to have such a beautiful woman sitting next to me."

"Tell me about her. Do you love her? When did it start?"

The Farmer Stands Alone
Bill E. Schultz

It was the first day that Ellie had taken off since she had started work in the Sheriff's department six months earlier. True, it had been for Mike's funeral and she probably could have gone back to work in the afternoon or gone and spent some time with Shelley, but it was such a delicious day that Ellie decided to spend it at the beach.

Now Maplewood County has over 1,000 lakes in a state that boasts of having 10,000 lakes, but the plain truth of the matter is that there really are only a few public beaches. She opted for the one on Portage Lake, located about half way between Harmony and the city of Maplewood. It is a small lake, with limited parking for beach goers, but afternoons are generally not busy.

When she arrived at the beach, she parked her red Camaro under an oak tree. She slipped out of her sweat pants she'd worn and took off the light blouse. Those actions revealed a modest bathing suit that sheathed an athletically fit body that suited the young woman well. She pinned up her red hair before taking the sports bag from the back seat of her car. Close to the waterfront, she removed a large beach towel and laid it on the sand. Then she took out her disk player, but the ear phones into her ears and lay down on her back.

After ten minutes she turned over and gave the backside a toasting as well. She was lying there listening to her favorite band when she felt rather than heard a vehicle drive off of the road and onto the beach area. She reached down to her player and lowered the sound. The thud of a car door shutting quickened her heart a little. Maybe if she lay still, whoever it was would not bother her.

"I hear Daddy dearest arrested someone," came an all too familiar voice.

Ellie slowly raised her head and turned it to face the speaker.

"Kevin," she said.

"Hi there. Are you hungry? I think I can find some two day old Walleye in a container in my car," he said, obviously referring to their aborted dinner date.

"Look I'm sorry but…"

"Don't say anything, I really don't want to hear it. Besides it would probably be a lie anyway."

"What are you doing here?" Ellie said as she sat up, bringing the towel along the modestly.

"Ah, Ellie, you forget, I've seen it before," said the reporter. "And I really enjoy the view. Such lovely mountains and valleys…"

"That's enough."

"OK. No, I decided to stop by my folk's house after the funeral."

"Were you there as a friend or a reporter?" interrupted Ellie.

"Well, actually I was at my parents' as a son…"

"You know what I meant."

"I was at the funeral as a friend. But Ellie, I can't separate the two when it's my friends and acquaintances who are the news."

"Then we have nothing to talk about."

"Well, before you interrupted me I was going to tell you that mom came home from the funeral after I'd been there for a while.

She'd been helping in the kitchen. Ellie, she said that your dad arrested Shelley..."

"Kevin, I'm not going to say anything," broke in the redhead.

"I'm not asking. I'm telling you. Mom said that one of the ladies in the kitchen was talking about Shelley. They said they saw her in Cedar Grove on Monday morning about 9:30 and she was with a man other than her husband."

"Monday?"

"That's what she said. That would be good for Shelley, right? It would make it harder for her to have killed Mike, right?"

"NO, KEVIN! Don't you see your own story the other day reported that Shelley admitted taking her neighbor to Cedar Grove that morning. If anything it only confirms that she had something going on with him and that gives her a motive and an accomplice."

"Oh, yeah you're right. I need to go."

The reporter waved and then jumped into his car and took off.

"Now what was he in such a hurry for?" wondered Ellie. "Oh, crap!" she exclaimed when she realized she'd just given him a scoop.

Chapter Twenty-One

"Curds and No Way"

I caught myself singing on the tractor. Out loud. Very loud. And what did I sing? Well, I started off singing "Amazing Grace", remembering it from the funeral service earlier in the day. Then I went on to "Holy, Holy, Holy"; then one favorite hymn after the other. I admit that I got a little carried away, but who was there to hear me?

The first wagon had been just about full when I finished the first round so I decided to unhook it and hook up wagon number two. I looked wistfully down the field road at wagon number three and tried to mentally calculate how in the world I would extricate it from its position against a tree.

Wagon number two filled quickly, as it was about three feet shorter. I made it around the field but the last bale or two bounced off of their counterparts and flew off the back of the wagon onto the ground behind. I came rolling to a stop just as Ox came up the road, pulling an empty wagon.

"Hay goes in wagon," he commented as he pointed at the two piles of hay that had been bales before they collided with the ground.

He helped me unhook wagon two and attach wagon three to the baler. Then I helped him hook up wagon one. I headed back to the tractor to take off.

"Hey," he yelled. "Other wagon."

I watched in awe as he backed up the tractor and hayrack number one precisely to position it just above the tongue of wagon two. I crawled under and attached it, wondering all the time if I would ever get to be that good at backing a tractor.

"Be back in an hour," he said as he roared off with the tractor and two wagons. No first gear for Ox. He had to be in third gear at least.

I knew from Ox's previous explanation that he would head back to our place and unload the wagons himself. I'd remembered that when we baled hay at my grandfather's farm in Wisconsin, the two of us boys would be up in the barn trying to stack the bales as quickly as they rolled off the elevator. Grandpa would usually be the one taking the bales off of the wagon. Ox's plan was to run the bales up the elevator and let them drop into the haymow.

"We'll stack 'em later," he'd told me.

My third round went even better than the first two. I'd had no problems all afternoon and was really enjoying myself. The hay was just about perfect with its leaves still clinging to the stems. It had that fresh smell to it that could only be compared to the first mowing of grass in the spring of the year. No wonder cows liked it so much.

The afternoon proceeded with me baling and Ox chasing back and forth to our place to unload the hay. I admit to having the better of the tasks, but also knew that Ox would make sure things evened out. He did.

About 4:30 he rolled in with his tractor and the round baler behind it instead of empty racks. He explained that the barn was full and that the rest of the field could be round baled.

"OK," I said starting to walk to his tractor and the baler.

"No, you go home and milk."

I stopped in my tracks, turned to him and saw that big smile that told me he had just evened things up. There was no sense in arguing. I would have lost. So I mounted the 4020 and headed back to our place.

As I rolled through the farmyard, Shelley was putting away her horse and talking with a young man that I remembered seeing in the parking lot at church. He'd been talking with the attorney as Ox and I walked by. He had been dressed differently then he was now, but my gift for faces told me it was the same guy.

Shelley flagged me down and introduced the fellow as her brother James. I'm a pretty good judge of character and this was a character.

"James came to visit," she informed me.

"Nice to meet you," I lied.

"You, too," he lied back to me.

"I'm back here now," she informed me.

"You going to be all right?" I asked her.

"Yes, do you mind if I stop by to get some milk?" she asked.

My ignorance must have shown on my face because truly I could not think what she was talking about.

"Ah, OK," I said dumbly. "I don't know if Ox picked up any in town."

They both stared back at me, then started laughing. I half-heartedly laughed along with a joke I obviously didn't understand.

"Your milk," she said. "From the bulk tank."

"Oh. Of course. I knew what you meant," joining in their laughter.

"Ox lets me get a jug or so and I give him home made pickles," she said.

"I think we get the better end of that deal," I said remembering the pickles we'd had with our burgers the night before.

"I'll see you later," she said.

I could tell that her brother was not happy about that prediction.

Goat's stomach was really troubling him as he sped back to his office that afternoon. He was not one to be trifled with and several triflers had been trifling with him that afternoon, including his daughter and his chief deputy. When these kinds of things happened his tummy went on a rampage and evoked gas out of both ends, thus the open window.

He had called ahead and demanded a meeting with Wally Setten for 4:00. He was going to have to settle down by then so he could be at his best. He never liked matching wits with Setten and that held doubly true in recent weeks.

First off, he was going to have to go into the meeting hat in hand and let Setten know that he had attempted to take the Robison woman into custody that afternoon. He knew that he would then receive a lecture from Setten about communication with the County Attorney's office, about protocol, about ethics, about public relations, about jury nullification, and about showing your cards before you know what you've been dealt.

Then Goat would lay out his case regarding the preacher. He knew that would make Setten's day, because Setten was Catholic. It wasn't that he was prejudiced toward Lutherans; it was just that in the last year Setten had prosecuted two priests for child abuse and had gotten tired of the jokes about Catholics, priests, and sex. Goat knew that Wally would love nothing more than to have a go at a Lutheran preacher. The only thing better would be catching that Pentecostal minister doing something.

As he flew through the curves just before he got to Yellow Pine, his dispatcher called him on the radio.

"Sheriff, you have a call."

"What kind of a call?"

"Phone call."

"Can't it wait?"

"He says not."

"Who is it?"

"Says he's Pastor Brooks, from Harmony."

"Take his number and tell him I'll call him tomorrow."

"Ah, Sheriff, he says it's urgent."

"You tell him this - And I want you to use these precise words: 'We'll have a nice long conversation tomorrow.' Got it?"

The dispatcher repeated the statement back to the Sheriff. Goat smiled as he rolled into town and headed to his rendezvous with the county attorney.

Pastor B. and his wife sat on the steps for nearly an hour. He told her everything he could about the past four days including the time he had spent with Shelley. He didn't feel he could go into details with Mary about the specific conversations, but he also needed her to know that things might disintegrate rapidly if his new attorney was right. Her reaction had been better than he had expected, but then he should have known he'd married a bulldog.

"That Sheriff is being a bully, plain and simple. A bully," she said angrily.

"Let's put the best construction on, Mary. He's doing his job and it's tough. He has a murder on his hands, a drug ring through his nose, the media second guessing him, and an election coming up." They both laughed at his little joke.

"Bartholomew, you don't need to be nice about that man. I've heard you say more than once that you hoped Jim Barton would run against him. Now you're trying to make excuses for him?"

"No, I'm not. He absolutely scares me with what he might be thinking and planning, but I also have to trust that the Lord is laying this burden on me for a reason and Goat Carlson is a part of the burden."

"And you're sure there is nothing going on with Shelley?"

"I'm sure. She's a newly widowed woman who was kidnapped, has the mother-in-law of all mother-in-laws, has a murder charge hanging over her head, and has a brother who has been arrested any number of times on drug charges. She needs our help and our prayers. She's certainly not getting any help from anyone else."

"What about that Jack Forester and his friend?" his wife asked. "I've heard that they've been helping her with chores and putting up crops and such."

"I told you I went to talk with them that night you came looking for me…"

"I'm so sorry about that, Bart. I should have said something right away instead of letting it stew."

"You don't need to be sorry. Anyway, I've known Jack for nearly a year now and I still can't figure him out. And this new guy is even tougher to figure out."

The crisis was over for the couple, at least today's crisis. Pastor B. knew that what awaited them in the future could be even tougher. He gave his wife an extra hug and kissed the top of her head. Just then, they both heard the phone ring. Both scrambled to get it. Pastor B. won.

"Hello… Yes, this is Pastor…Oh, yes! My wife said someone had called…Who is this…I'm afraid I don't recognize the name…Oh! Well, yes I heard about the raid…I'm not sure what has happened to them…I'm sure I would have heard something if your wife or children had been hurt…Your sure you want to do that…Is there a number I can call you back at…All right… You want the County Attorney, Kevin Walters, and the lady deputy…Well, I'll have to call the Sheriff…No, really I know the Sheriff and if he isn't informed about…All right. 10:00 in the church. Yes, I'll leave it open."

"What was that all about," asked the pastor's wife.

"Lonny Jeffries wants to give himself up."

"Who is Lonny Jeffries?"

"I hope he is a murderer. I need to make some calls."

When I got back to our place, I pulled the tractor and wagon over by the outside hay shed as Ox had directed me. I unhooked the wagon and pulled the baler over to the machine shed. The baler backed into its assigned position and I was actually able to disassemble the power take-off and unhook the baler without mishap. I took the tractor over to the fuel tank and topped it off. Those tasks accomplished, I headed for the barn.

I decided to put off the milking as long as I could so as to increase the production. Even an extra half hour, I calculated, might produce an extra hundred pounds of milk. That being the case, I fed the calves, including the newest that had arrived during the night.

We'd taken number 81 and moved her into the barn after morning milking. Her milk had now come in nice and clear and she would be a welcome addition to our bulk tank. Another cow was due within the next few days so we needed the space in the maternity barn.

As I walked through the barn, I heard a dog barking. Since I knew that we didn't have one, I assumed we must have a visitor. Sure enough, standing outside the door into the tank room was my new friend Shelley. I opened the door and she came in, leaving Max outside guarding the entrance. She carried with her two half-gallon jugs.

"Help yourself," I said.

"I would, but there isn't any."

"Oh. You're right," I said as I opened the lid to see an empty tank. "How did you know?"

"The valve is open," she said pointing to the outlet through which the bulk truck sucked our milk into its tank.

"Now what?" I thought.

"You're not much of a dairy farmer, are you?" Shelley asked.

"I'm trying," I replied.

"Here, let me help," she said.

With that she expertly shut the valve and squirted some liquid from a reservoir hung on the wall into a container, which she emptied into the bulk tank. She then grabbed a hose hanging on the wall and attached it to the faucet hanging over the sink.

"Hold this," she commanded, placing my hands around the hose. She then turned on the hot water and we let it run for a few minutes.

"That's enough," she said. "See this dial. Then we turn it on and let her go. Ox usually goes out and pushes up the feed while it's washing."

"Um," I thought. "There is more to this lady and my good friend than what I had originally opined."

We walked out into the barn. I snatched up the broom, then moved up and down the feed aisle, pushing feed back up to the cows. Long tongues started snagging what feed there was, cleaning the cement feed bunk down to the bare essentials. That task completed, I decided to start up the manure chains to get that task out of the way.

"Ox always waits for the chains until he is milking," Shelley educated me.

I ignored her and went back into the milk room just as the rinse cycle was finishing up. Shelley opened up the valve again, cranked on the water, and then sprayed out the tank of its soapy residue.

"There," she said. "Clean as a whistle."

I smiled a thank you. I grabbed the first of the milkers and went out the door, ready to start my appointed rounds.

"I shut the valve again," Shelley informed me as she came out with the second milker.

I put that one on the next cow and returned to the milk room to bring out the third milker. We have four milkers, but Ox had told me to only use three when I was milking alone.

I had three milkers going and was really tempted to bring out the fourth, when I heard a screeching sound. The manure chains came to a screeching stop. Just then milker one started to suck air, indicating that it had sucked its customer dry. The screeching emanating from the chains continued and I was torn between the sounds hitting my senses. The chains started to buck in place, striving to complete their journey but held up by something.

"I'll get the milker," Shelley hollered above the din.

I ran down the aisle to the switchbox for the manure system and flipped the handle. It didn't take a genius to see that something had caused the chains to jump from their track.

I got back to the cows that were being milked, but by then I was out of breath and embarrassed, knowing what was coming. She didn't disappoint me.

"You know, Ox always waits to run the chains until he is done milking, but I think I told you that," she said it with good humor. I think I liked this lady. Obviously Ox did. I secretly hoped that our mutual respect for her would be uneventful.

"Wally," said the Sheriff.

"Sheriff," said the County Attorney.

That is how the previous hour had started. It had gone downhill from there. The Sheriff had come to the meeting thinking that it was his meeting. He had discovered quite quickly that he may have called the meeting, but Wally Setten had taken over the meeting with one question.

"I understand that a pastor over in Harmony tried to get a hold of you. He even indicated to you that it was an emergency. Can you tell me why you wouldn't talk to him?"

Goat had realized immediately that something was going down and the County Attorney knew what it was. Goat did not. And that made the Sheriff very uncomfortable.

"I was driving and trying to deal with something. I said I'd call back."

"You evidently said, and I quote, 'We'll have a nice long conversation tomorrow,' end quote. Is that correct?"

"It might have been something like that."

"Did you intend it as a threat?"

"Of course not."

"Well, Goat that is the way it was perceived. Now would you like to know what the good pastor was calling about?…Goat would you like to hear…"

"Yes, Yes, Yes. What was the guy calling about?" exclaimed a frustrated Sheriff.

It was then that the County Attorney sounded the death knell for the Sheriff's ambitions to run unopposed for re-election. For, from now on he would have a vulnerability unlike any he'd experienced in his previous elections.

The County Attorney laid out the scenario for tomorrow's surrender of one fugitive by the name of Lonny Jeffries, a.k.a. "Crank" Jeffries, a.k.a. Sonny Jackson, a.k.a. "Sweets" Jeffrey. He had made arrangements to surrender himself at Trinity Lutheran Church in Harmony at 10:00 in the morning.

To the Sheriff's blank expression to the name, the County Attorney had the distinct pleasure of informing Carlson that Lonny Jeffries was, in fact, the owner of a farm about six miles south and west of Milton.

Panic began to erupt in Goat's brain.

It was a farm that had been visited only recently by the Maplewood County Sheriff's department.

Wally Setten informed the Sheriff that the intended surrender would be orchestrated by the County Attorney's office.

"OK, I'll have my men waiting there for us to come out," piped in the Sheriff.

"No, Goat you will be conveniently at a meeting of the Joint Drug Task Force. I hope you understand the irony."

"Now hold on. You have to have peace officers there."

Goat was sure that Wally had already planned to have Jim Barton there and wanted to force him to show his cards.

"Oh we will Goat. As a matter of fact, Mr. Jeffries has made a special request. Our newest and prettiest deputy will be taking the prisoner into custody."

"Setten," yelled an almost apoplectic Sheriff, "you can't do this. I'm an elected official in this county and I will not have my power taken away by some damned attorney."

"Sheriff, my friend," replied a calm and collected County Attorney. "It is already done. Oh, by the way, there will be two other people present. Pastor Brooks will be there to provide spiritual guidance to us all and Kevin Walters will be there to document the events for posterity."

The Sheriff slammed the door on his way out.

Ellie liked to use metaphors and the only one she could think of right now was taking a big swig of what you were sure was nice cold milk and getting a mouthful of sour milk. The kind that had already starting turning to chunks. The kind of milk that when you drank it, a year would pass by before you could stomach the thought of another glass of the white liquid.

That's how she felt after getting off of the phone with the County Attorney. Mr. Setten had told her what was going to be happening on the morrow and it made her sick to think of what this whole thing must be doing to her father. She didn't know whether to call him or not. That afternoon's arrest debacle had already set father and daughter at odds; this might just push them over the edge. In the end she decided not to call.

She thought through the ramifications of the news that she had heard from the County Attorney. Positively, it just might help her friend Shelley if this fellow Jeffries confessed to murder. On the other hand, he might just affirm her father's assumption that Shelley had an accomplice and a motive.

Ellie walked out of her apartment and down the hall to Mrs. Ingvaldson's apartment to talk to Shelley.

"She's gone. Went home. I think she wanted to be by herself," came the reply from Shelley's mother to Ellie's inquiry.

Shelley's mother had been more than a little cool to Ellie.

Ellie stopped by Bob's Market and picked up one of their rotisserie chickens, a container of Cole Slaw salad, some dollar buns, and a 2 liter bottle of Coke. She threw it all in the back seat and headed out of town. She had the fixin's for a nice supper, but who would she share it with.

There was Kevin. But he was probably back at work. Frankly, he was about the last person she wanted to have supper with, even though she doubtless owed him a meal.

There was her Dad. If she were a loving daughter, she would head to his place and help him through what she knew had to be a crisis.

There was Shelley. She had experienced the burial of her husband, her own arrest, and then release. And certainly the next day might even be more difficult.

Then there were Jack and Paul. Both had helped her the night before when she'd been injured. They were big strong farm dudes who likely had nothing planned for supper.

Ellie estimated that she would have just about enough chicken and other food to feed the three of them if she held back her own appetite a little. She certainly had a reason to stop by to thank them for what they had done to help her the night before.

"Yes," Ellie decided, "those two boys are in for a nice evening."

Sheriff Carlson had cooled down, but only slightly, by the time that he arrived at his office. He greeted the dispatcher with a barely audible response to the man's warm welcome.

"I transferred a call to your voice mail," reported the department secretary as he walked by her. "It was that nice Mr. Setten."

The secretary would later tell her husband that the Sheriff had actually growled his reply just before he slammed the door, breaking the glass in it. That was how she was able to hear the voice mail.

"Goat my friend, I'm sure that you'll have cooled down by now," came the voice over the speakerphone. "I want you to give our friend Andy a call and tell him that we need to postpone Mrs. Robison's visit with us until late afternoon. I appreciate you taking care of that for me Goat and do you suppose you could arrange for some coffee for that meeting."

There were later reports that prisoners in the jail applauded and cheered upon hearing the Sheriff's language and diatribe against the County Attorney. It was that loud and vociferous.

Shelley actually was a big help with the milking. I had decided to leave the manure chains until Ox got back, even though I knew he would give me a difficult time about them. I figured it was more important to get the milking done. Shelley would wash the cows' udders and teats just ahead of me putting the milker on. It saved me time and steps, both of which allowed us to finish the milking on time despite several mishaps that had occurred.

Shelley offered to clean up in the milk room while I fed the cows. I was so surprised that she knew how to do things around our farm, but she informed me that she had often helped with the milking at our place over the last few months. She loved doing it and had covered for Ox several times when he had been away at auctions buying equipment, cattle, and feed.

We were laughing at a joke as we exited the milk room. Shelley was carrying her jugs of milk and I was carrying a three-pound brick of cheese slices and two pounds of butter that the milk truck driver had left us. Max had just started barking with what, Shelley informed me, was his "welcome" bark.

There standing in front of us was my now favorite deputy.

"Ms. Carlson," I greeted her.

"Shelley, Paul," she replied coolly. "I'm surprised to see you here."

"I live here," I said.

"Not you, her," she answered with a half-hearted chuckle.

"I could say the same thing to you," chimed in Shelley.

I felt like I was about to watch a cat fight. Both women eyed each other warily, trying to figure out what the other was up to. I knew they were friends, but friends who had, in the last three or four days, both gone up and down a roller coaster of emotions. The new Paul Banion Rule Book of Domestic Tranquility suggested that I intervene.

However, my intervention was unnecessary as the Ox-man arrived just at that moment. He drove his tractor with round baler into the yard and within a few feet of Ellie's Camaro.

"Too tough," referring to the hay that started taking on moisture in the early evening and made baling difficult.

Ox is a man of few words and those who are uninitiated to him think that is a negative reflection on his mental faculties. Not so. Ox is one of the most intellectually astute people I know. Within seconds he had scoped out what was transpiring between the two friends.

"You milking?" he asked Shelley, rightly giving her an opportunity to explain her presence.

"Just helping. I stopped by for some milk and Paul was running behind so I said I'd help out."

"Pickles?" Ox asked.

"Next time. Maybe even a fresh batch."

It dawned on me that Ox was proceeding with this conversation for my benefit as well as Ellie's so I chimed in.

"Shelley tells me that she helps out quite a bit around here," I said.

"Yep," replied Ox.

Ellie was surprised by the answer. It was obvious she had no idea that Shelley not only knew her neighbor, but also actually had worked with him.

"Well, Mike used to work the afternoon shift and Ox needed help and was willing to pay me to help with chores so I did," said Shelley.

Ox's strategy seemed to work as Ellie's countenance changed and she suggested that the four of us have supper together.

"I've got a chicken, some cabbage salad, buns, and pop," she offered.

"I've got cheese slices and butter," I countered, lifting the products I'd just brought from the milk house.

"I've got some leftovers from church," offered Shelley. "It'll just take me a few minutes to run home and get them."

Ox looked like he'd been left out of the party, as he had nothing to bring.

"Don't worry old friend," I teased. "We'll let you eat. But you have to help me with something first."

Ox looked at me and shook his head.

"The chains?" he asked. I just smiled.

Chapter Twenty-Two

"Goldie And The Three Bear Mystery"

Shelley hopped into her car, stored the milk jugs safely on the floor and hurried out of the drive. She'd left Max with Paul and Ox. She did that for two reasons. The first was that she didn't want to have to deal with getting Max in and out of the car. The second and real reason was that leaving Max would force her to come back. Because, truth be told, she had just wanted to run when Ellie showed up.

As Shelley approached her drive, she spied dust down the road a short distance. That seemed strange since normally a car just ahead of her would have been leaving a trail of dust from some distance. The only explanation would be that it was a car that had emanated from her own drive. Suddenly she wished she'd brought Max with her.

Shelley swung her car as close to the house as she could. She scooped the two milk jugs from the floor and hustled into the house. The first thing she noticed was how quiet the house was. She walked through the entryway and as she did, she saw Mike's jacket and his mud boots. Her own straw hat and light jacket were hanging there next to his clothes.

She went into the kitchen and opened the refrigerator to put the milk away. She spotted the plate of lemon bars covered by aluminum foil.

"Funny," she thought. "I knew that foil was on tight."

She saw that the hot dish leftovers had also been tampered with. She pulled that casserole out along with the plate of bars. She reattached their coverings. Shelley knew there was also a plate of sliced ham she'd slid in the meat drawer. She pulled it out and discovered it appeared untouched.

She found a box in the closet and was putting her bounty into it; along with a jar of last year's pickles when she realized that lying in the sink were a plate and glass. The sink had been empty when she left.

"What now?" thought the widow.

It was then that Shelley headed to her room, first grabbing an umbrella that was sitting in the corner of the entryway. She walked up the steps quietly, thinking how silly she was; yet not wanting to give up the little protection the umbrella provided.

She walked by the bathroom door and pushed it open. The hinge on the door creaked.

"I'll fix it tomorrow," Mike had said. But tomorrow was always a day or two away.

The bathroom was empty, the seat on the toilet up, providing another reminder of an existence that had ended. Then she remembered that she had, in fact, used the toilet after changing that afternoon.

"This is really getting weird," she said out loud.

The door to the second bedroom was wide open. Its previous occupant had not made the bed. Shelley realized the room and its contents would need to be fumigated because that person would not use it again.

Shelley came into the master bedroom and saw that it appeared undisturbed. She was about to leave the room and the house, when she remembered the memorial cards. She had placed them all, unopened, under the nightstand next to her bed. She had discovered the hollow hiding place when she was trying to find somewhere to hide her diaphragm from prying eyes and Mike.

She lifted the stand and placed it a few feet to the right. The pile of cards was still there. She placed the stand back over them.

Shelley left the umbrella on the bed where she had dropped it. She went down the stairs two at a time and grabbed the box on her way out of the kitchen. She went quickly down the sidewalk to her car, put the box on the hood, then opened the passenger door and put the box on the seat. As she rounded the front of the car, something she'd just seen needled her mind, but she couldn't think what it was.

She got in the car, turned the ignition and put the car into reverse. Just as she was about to put it into drive it hit her. There was a message on the telephone answering machine. Her eyes had seen the number "1" on the machine and it had registered in her brain. It was just now that she remembered that she had cleared the machine just before leaving to get the milk.

The brake lights went on the Grand Prix and Shelley slammed the car back into park.

Two minutes later Shelley was back in the car and heading out of her drive way. She had some news to share with her friends.

The phone calls were finished; maintenance had been called to fix his door, again; and Sheriff Carlson was just about at the end of his rope.

The call to Andy Ratcliff had been the worst, at least at first. Ratcliff would not leave well enough alone.

"If I'm going to have to rearrange my day for you Sheriff, the least you can do is tell me why."

The Sheriff was so fed up with the arrogance of attorneys whom he had to deal with; he was beginning to think it *was* time to retire.

In the end the Sheriff had told Ratcliff something unexpected was going on the next day. He hadn't given him details other than to say that the County Attorney was going to be busy at 10:00.

"Good, then I can meet with my other client in the morning. Oh, by the way Sheriff, my other client is Pastor Brooks. I wanted you to know, so you would be aware that you should not have contact with him unless I'm there."

"He's going to be busy tomorrow morning too," had come the Sheriff's reply. He had then hung up.

The phone had rung almost immediately, but by then the Sheriff was walking by the secretary's desk on his way out to his White Explorer.

"Sheriff, its Mr. Ratcliff on line one."

The Sheriff smiled, tipped his straw hat and said, "You have a good evening Sandra."

"What should I say to Mr. Ratcliff?"

"You tell him, and I want you to use these exact words: 'Elvis has left the building.'"

"Uh, 'Elvis has left the building'?"

"Yep."

"So much for that idea," thought Ellie as she saw her friend, Shelley walk out of the barn with Paul. Paul had even been formal with her calling her "Ms. Carlson."

"I wonder if they think I had something to do with what dad did to Shelley," thought the redhead at the cool treatment she received.

The three of them had been standing uncomfortably, each trying to figure a way to get out of an obviously delicate situation. That was when Jack had come riding in on his tractor, like a white night to the rescue. Jack had talked more in the intervening ten minutes then she had heard him say during either of the other two or three times that they had talked.

It had been obvious to Ellie that Jack and Shelley knew each other well. They had an ease about them that told her they had spent time together. Ellie could see that it had surprised Paul as well.

In the end, Shelley had gone home to get some more food, the guys had gone to the barn to deal with something, and Ellie had offered to go into the house and start preparations for supper. It had been a long time since Ellie had felt so domestic.

Ellie decided that it was such a nice evening that they would have their meal outside. She found enough dishes, glasses and even a serving dish or two. She wondered what Shelley would be bringing from home and hoped that she would have her own dishes, as the selection here was limited.

Like her father the night before, Ellie couldn't resist the temptation to look around the house quickly. She peeked into the bathroom and saw, not the clutter she expected from two bachelors, but a bathroom where cleanliness and order seemed to rule. The two bedrooms she looked into also showed the same immaculate tidiness. The third bedroom wasn't a bedroom but an obvious office, but it was unlike any office she'd ever seen.

She heard the door open and scooted into the bathroom, closing the door silently behind her. She quickly flushed the toilet and came out to find Shelley sitting at the table.

"What you doing?" asked Shelley.

"Bathroom," came the one word reply.

"How is it?"

"Surprisingly clean."

They both laughed then Shelley walked down the hall.

"You're right," she said, then shut the door.

Ellie looked over the commodities that Shelley had brought in. She took a nice looking casserole out of the box and put it in the microwave oven. She then took the aluminum foil off of the lemon bars. She opened the pickle jar and stuck a fork in it, expecting that she would not find a pickle plate in the cupboards. The ham could be served cold, she decided.

"Not bad," she commented out loud as she served the spread of food.

Shelley walked into the room, put her arm around her friend and said, "Unless you physiology has changed, next time you say you were 'going to the bathroom', put the seat down."

Ellie looked at her friend, realized she'd been found out, and laughed. The two then compared notes on their surveys of the farmhouse.

Ox was actually pretty good about the mess with the manure chains. I couldn't help but think that his good nature might be related to the fact I'd just discovered the secret of who had been helping him with chores for the last year. Of course that discovery also brought with it some concern for my good friend. You see, I know how ladies are attracted to his quiet, good looks. I hoped that recent events would not come back to bite us in the rear any more than they had.

It only took Ox a couple of whacks with his sledgehammer to get the wayward chains back in line. He had me flip on the switch and stand right by it just in case. But "just in case" did not happen. The manure all found its way into the slurry pit and was pumped the 60 yards out to the holding pond.

As we waited for the chains to make their rounds, Ox came over to where I was standing by the switch. We shared a few pleasantries, quite unlike Ox to do; talked about how good the hay had looked and discussed some tasks that he had planned for the morrow. After twenty minutes, we walked through the maternity pen, where number 53 was getting close, but still no cigar, then wended our way up to the house where our company awaited us.

"Damn gophers," growled Ox, pointing at a little critter that scurried across our driveway.

I knew from my days on gramps' farm that there were two types of gophers that drove farmers crazy. The worst were pocket gophers that actually bored deep into the soil, pushing the excavated dirt into mounds that raised havoc with equipment, especially haying equipment. Pocket gophers could destroy a field.

The other kind, which we had just seen, is a striped gopher. That's what "Goldie the Golden Gopher", University of Minnesota sports mascot, is. They just dig holes, chew on roots, eat grain, and generally make a nuisance of themselves.

We went into the house and Ox went to his room. He came out of the room with a .22 rifle.

"What are you doing with that," I asked.

"Gopher," he replied.

The two women in our kitchen were startled when Ox came in with the rifle, but quickly changed their attitude when I explained what the Ox-meister was going to do.

"I'll do it," they both offered.

Ox and I looked at each other. He handed the rifle over to Shelley and started to explain how to use it.

"I know, I know," she interrupted.

"Come on Ellie. I bet we find more than one."

Ox and I started to lug the food out onto the patio while the hunters stalked their prey. I had a whole new appreciation for the two ladies who would be sharing our supper. Ox and I waited a few minutes, but both of us had been shorted a good old-fashioned potluck lunch by certain actions that had happened. Our nibbling soon turned to full-fledged stuffing of as much food down our gullets as we could.

We heard a couple of shots and assumed our hunters would come back empty handed. Not so. Within ten minutes they were back with two of the striped critters in hand.

"Where do you want them?" asked Ellie.

"Well, I know this spot over at Shelley's…"

"Don't even go there," interrupted Shelley.

Ox walked over to the shed and got a shovel. Ellie plopped the carcasses on the shovel, then Ox disappeared for a few minutes. I invited the ladies to sit down to our repast, but they both excused themselves to go wash their hands. Therein, I speculated, lay the difference between men and women rodent hunters. I doubt that Ox or I would have even thought of washing up after the executions.

Ellie had to admit that the evening had been relaxing and fun. Much more than the evening before when she had ended up on

Paul's couch with a near concussion. Shelley was back to her old self and many of the worries of her own day had been lost in the company of the evening.

She and Shelley had been so excited about the .22 that Jack brought out and had immediately confiscated it from him and offered to do the hunting for gophers. Shelley especially hated the little varmints having lost her favorite mare to a gopher hole that she had hit at full tilt. Truth be told, it probably had been a hole dug up by a wolverine or fox after a gopher, but from Shelley's perspective it had been a gopher.

Shelley had taken the gun and from over 100 yards had dropped the first gopher they saw dead in its tracks. Ellie had been really impressed with her marksmanship.

"Daddy taught me," Shelley had said to Ellie's inquiry.

"Wow! My dad taught me too, but I sure couldn't have made that shot," replied Ellie.

There was a moment of awkwardness as both women thought back to events earlier in the week.

"Here, you try the next one," offered Shelley. Then she took a couple of steps back and was out of Ellie's line of sight.

Ellie moved stealthily forward. Just then, 50 yards ahead, one of the critters popped its head out of a hole. Ellie quickly raised the rifle and pulled the trigger, all in one fell swoop. The gopher jumped six inches into the air, flopped around a couple of times and came to rest.

"Now we each have one," said Shelley. Ellie couldn't help but think she might not be referring to the gophers they were carrying.

They got back to the patio and Ox took care of the bodies. The girls then went in to wash up.

"Are we OK?" asked Ellie of her friend.

"What do you mean?"

"Well, I don't know how you must feel right now, with Mike, and what Dad did and…"

"Ell, how long have we been friends? Are we going to let a little thing like kidnapping, murder, my arrest, my brother's arrest, and certain accusations your dad made come between us?"

"Well, now that you put it that way, I guess not." Both women laughed and continued as they came out to the patio.

The two gentlemen waiting for them looked at them curiously, and then smiled at what must have been a private joke.

"Come on dig in," said Paul.

It had been a lovely evening between new friends who had been drawn together through a strange set of circumstances. That's how Shelley saw the evening of the day she buried her husband. If she thought of it in any other way, she would only feel guilt.

The four new friends had laughed the night away, not talking about the past, for that seemed to be of no interest to the men. Not talking about the distant times of yore, even though the two guys professed to be cousins and friends for nearly all their lives. And certainly not talking about the past four days, for each seemed bound and determined to forget how much each had been forced to cram into such a short time.

As the evening was winding down, the very near future did rear its ugly head. Paul had been the one to broach the subject of the coming day and had been surprised though not shocked to find out that the appointment with destiny or at least the County Attorney had been postponed. Ellie said little other than to confirm that she knew about the change. It had been Shelley who had been able to share more information about what may have transpired.

"I had a message on my machine when I got home," reported the merry widow. "It was from Andy. He said we would be meeting with the County Attorney and your dad," the latter directed at Ellie, "tomorrow at 4:00 instead of 10:00."

"I was told to be at Trinity in Harmony at 9:30," conveyed Ellie. "I'm not sure what is happening."

"It sounded like Pastor might be in some trouble," suggested Paul.

"No," said both women simultaneously.

"Andy said that he thought pastor had something to do with it, but wouldn't or couldn't say what," said Shelley.

"Yeah, the sense I got from Mr. Setten was that he was going to be there too. He's the one that called me."

"Why would he call you?" asked Paul.

"Yeah, I hinted around trying to find out, but he didn't say much. Said something about Dad being out of town, but I usually know his schedule and he wasn't going to be anywhere but his office waiting for Shelley to turn herself in."

"You know, Pastor said something weird when he and I were meeting with Andy. He said his wife had gotten a call from someone wanting to surrender. Pastor seemed to think that would clear everything up, but when Andy questioned him, he really didn't know anything. But he referred to it in the message."

"So, what was your message from this Andy fellow?" asked Paul.

"He said 'the County Attorney had something come up that would cause him to be elsewhere at 10:00. It sounds like Brooks may have been right about the surrender.'"

"What time did you say you had to be at the church?" asked Shelley.

"9:30 in the morning," replied Ellie.

"Sounds like your friend Mr. Setten has a date," offered Ox.

That was when Shelley remembered what it was that had been needling her mind all evening.

"The light wasn't flashing," she said quietly.

"What light?" asked Ellie.

"On the message machine."

Shelley then shared her version of "Goldilocks and the three bears", detailing the food, the room, and now the message machine. All had been used by someone, a visitor, but likely not a young maiden with golden locks of hair.

With over six years of undercover work in my past, I knew enough to control my emotions. Yet, strangely, I found myself more and more attracted to the blonde woman sitting across from me at the table on our patio.

Perhaps it was empathy. I had known what life was like when, if you let it control you instead of you controlling it, every breath felt like it was your last, every sound was someone about to destroy you, and every event had more than one meaning.

As Shelley relayed her brief story, I could see that she became more concerned as each individual experience joined with other evidence of someone being in her house.

"Is there a simple explanation?" I had asked. "Could it just be someone who knows you well enough that they wouldn't feel ill at ease coming in and helping themselves?"

Shelley thought on that a minute, then smiled.

"It could have been my brother James," she said. "He was out at the farm late this afternoon. Yes, it was probably him. Oh, thanks. I'll sleep so much better tonight."

"Speaking of sleep," Ellie suggested, "I need to get some. It's almost mid-night."

It was shortly after that when Ox and I walked the two friends to their cars and said our "Good Nights."

Ox headed over to the barn while I went into the house and finished cleaning up. I took the last pickle out of the jar and was just about to pop it in my mouth, when Ox walked in.

"Good?" he asked unnecessarily since he had eaten almost the entire jar over the course of the previous hours.

"Yes, Ox, the pickles are good." I replied. Then I realized he was not talking about the pickles and felt pretty stupid.

Changing the subject, I suggested to Ox that it would be very interesting if we were to get done with chores early enough in the morning that we could get into town by 9:30 or 10:00 to get some supplies.

"Might want to do some praying right about then," he had suggested.

That's my Ox; sharp as a tack.

Chapter Twenty-Three

"Sleep the Sleep of the Dead"

Ellie slept soundly for the first night in five. It had been nearly 12:30 in the morning by the time she had parked her Camaro and quietly entered her apartment building.

Over the past six months she had developed the practice of bringing home a file or two to review before falling asleep. She had calculated that if she fed her mind with information just before drifting of to sleep, then while she was sleeping, the computer in her brain would organize and arrange the information in the most logical manner. Each morning when she woke up, she expected that a new insight into the case would emerge.

Ellie knew that it was unusual that a probationary officer would be bringing home case information, but that had been one of the advantages of having the Sheriff as your father. "Yes," she thought, "there are advantages and disadvantages."

One of the disadvantages had been apparent the afternoon before when the County Attorney had called and told her that she had a special assignment for today. As she lay awake, staring at the ceiling of her apartment bedroom, she couldn't help but wonder what lay ahead for her. She had an instant of foreboding that rolled through her body from head to toes

It was that same sense that one gets when about to embark on a journey and you simply get this sense that you will not be returning. You wished you could roll over and go back to sleep;

which is what Ellie must have done, because the next thing she knew her phone was ringing.

"Hello," she rather tiredly answered.

"Ellie, Ellie, is that you?"

"Yes, Kevin it's me. Who else did you expect to answer my phone?"

"Well, I tried all night last night to get hold of you."

"You didn't leave a message."

"Well, I did try."

"What is it Kevin, that prompts you to call me at," Ellie looked at the clock and realized it was 8:30, " um this morning?"

"Well, I had wanted to stop by for coffee. I have to be there in Harmony at 9:30 and thought we could have coffee before my appointment."

The time he mentioned caught Ellie's attention. It could not be coincidence. It was the same time she was supposed to arrive at Trinity.

"OK, I can have coffee with you. Where do you want to meet?"

"How about your place?"

"Whoa, my place. Why my place?"

"Because you just woke up and won't have time to get anywhere else."

"How did you...never mind. OK, my place. What time?"

"How about now? I'm right outside your door."

There was something about the manner that Andy Ratcliff had spoken to Pastor B. the previous evening that had relaxed the cleric enough so that he was able to get a good sleep. When he woke up his wife was out of bed and he could smell good things emanating from the kitchen.

Their previous evening had been filled with conversation and much, much more. Mary had become the tigress of old, a woman filled with desire that he had not seen in months if not years. As a matter of fact, she had tired the poor preacher out. This morning, Pastor B's prayers would include one of thanksgiving. It would, however, not go into great detail over what he was giving thanks for. Just the thought of his bride had made him hunger for more.

"Bart, don't. At least not now. Wait until after breakfast," his wife had warned him when he came up behind her standing at the stove.

"You make me warm all over," the minister said.

"That's the oven."

"No, Luv, it is you."

Breakfast had included dessert for the first time in recent memory. The second helping of that dessert had caused a nice smile on his wife's face, but also had caused Pastor B. to get to the church later than he had planned. He opened the doors and went into his office, calculating that he had at least twenty minutes before anyone else would show up.

He'd been in the office when his door rattled ever so slightly. That usually meant someone had opened the outside door. That action usually caused enough air movement, that his door emanated a tiny warning. A trustee had offered to tighten it, but the pastor had deferred as he liked to take advantage of the early warning system it provided when someone came in.

Pastor B. decided to get up and greet whoever had entered. He was a bit surprised to find no one there.

"Probably someone dropping something off," he surmised.

Just then a stranger in a suit walked in the door. He came forward with arm outstretched and introduced himself as Wally Setten, County Attorney.

"Bart, I appreciate you helping us out here. We'll try to make this as quick and painless as possible. I told Deputy Carlson to be here at 9:30 and the same for Mr. Walters. Have you heard anything more from this Jeffries fellow?"

"No," replied an unhappy Pastor B. His wife was the only one who called him "Bart" and he made a strict practice of having parishioners address him as Pastor Brooks or Pastor B.

"Hi, Pastor B." came a greeting from a lovely redhead in uniform.

"Hi there Ellie"

"Deputy," came the greeting from the County Attorney, somewhat miffed at the obvious relationship between deputy and pastor.

Friday morning was different for Shelley. It was the first morning that she woke in her own bed and knew that Mike was not there, would not be there, would never be there again.

She had gotten home a little after mid-night. Ellie had followed her home and stayed just long enough to check that she had no unwanted visitors. Shelley had then gone up to the master bedroom and stripped it clean of sheets, pillowcases, bedspread, and mattress pad. She had taken them all down to the laundry room and put them in water, the hottest water she could get to come out of her washer and she didn't care if the sheets bled or if the spread shrunk or if everything turned a dull gray. She wanted to sleep, alone, on clean sheets.

As that load was washing, she ran back upstairs and took everything off of the bed in the guest room as well.

"I'm done with you too," she exclaimed to herself.

She took clean bedding for both beds out of the hall closet and completed making the beds up.

She got the vacuum cleaner out of the hall closet and vacuumed the hall and both bedrooms.

Next, she took all of Mike's hanging clothes down from the closet rod. She filled up a garbage bag with his underwear, t-shirts, and socks and put everything out in the hall to be taken downstairs in the morning.

Finally, she cleaned the bathroom about as clean as it had ever been. She took Mike's toothbrush, his floss, which he never used, his shaving cream, his razor, his deodorant, his toe nail clippers, his comb and brush, his butt cream, his athletes' foot cream, and his shampoo and threw them all into another garbage bag. She took down the moldy, rust laden shower curtain that she had begged him to change and put up the new one that had sat on the counter top for three weeks.

By 1:30 in the morning she was exhausted but feeling fulfilled. She took a quick shower, smelling the new plastic of the curtain. She enjoyed not having to work around his Irish Spring soap, which she had tossed. She used her own Oil of Olay, soaping herself thoroughly with it and then enjoyed the rinse job.

She slept naked for no other reason then that she wanted to feel the clean sheets on her clean body.

When the alarm went off at 6:30, she turned it off and went back to sleep. It wasn't until the phone rang at 9:45 that she woke up again. She didn't answer the phone, assuming the answering machine downstairs would pick it up. It did, but there was no message left.

At 10:00 she went downstairs and made herself a quick breakfast of toast and jam with instant coffee.

By 10:25 she had saddled Mocca and was out enjoying the first morning ride that she had taken in years. Instead of the usual route, Shelley headed out the drive and down into the ditch where she followed a trail made by 4-wheelers that her neighbors were constantly running. She figured she would be safe since those neighbors were either in jail or on the lam.

The dreams returned to Goat that night. They were dreams of happier times with his wife and daughter. They were dreams that had never been reality, but always dreams. No one could tell Goat that his dreams weren't real. He had always been convinced that he had been a good husband and a good father. Of course work had always come first. That was as it should be in Goat's world. Law enforcement is what he had been born to. It was what he had wanted from the time he was six years old and riding around on a stick horse on his grandfather's farm.

A wife and kid were things that provided him with a haven to come to whenever the real world got to be too much. It was just that his wife and daughter had always wanted so much more than what was left after a day tracking down the bad guys. No, the dreams were welcome old friends to the shamus.

He had decided to skip breakfast at the Crystal Lake Café, a place he had avoided the last few days since his run in with some local riffraff. Instead he swung through McDonalds and grabbed a number 3 with a medium orange juice. He had been to the office and had swung into the drive thru just before he headed out onto Highway 94 as it touched the city limits of the county seat. Goat had almost finished the hash browns when his radio crackled to life.

"Officer involved in shooting, please stand by."

The Sheriff switched over to a different frequency and called the dispatcher directly, all the while praying that it wasn't one of his men.

"Sheriff, we just got the report in."

"Was it one of ours?"

"The report came from a local."

"Which one?"

"John Sweeter."

"Harmony?"

"Yes."

"I'm on my way."

"This is like throwing a surprise party for someone who doesn't show up," thought Pastor B. as he studied the other people waiting in the entryway of the church. The County Attorney was studiously looking at the bulletin boxes, reading names from the tags that identified each. Ellie Carlson was trying to avoid conversation with Kevin Walters who was following her around like a lovesick puppy. And, Pastor B. was at a loss as to whether or not he should invite people to come around him for a moment of prayer.

The Attorney had taken time at 9:30 to explain to them all exactly what Pastor B. had arranged; namely the surrender of Lonny Jeffries.

"Who is Lonny Jeffries?" had been the question from Walters. The Attorney and Ms. Carlson had both seemed to know.

"He is the one that got away on Monday," reported Wally Setten while looking directly at Ellie.

"The one the Robison woman took to Cedar Grove?" asked the reporter.

"We think so," replied Setten.

"So what am I doing here?" asked the journalist.

"Damned if I know," came Ellie's interjection.

"When he called me, Mr. Jeffries requested that you be here," offered the pastor.

"Well I've got a few questions."

The questions had to wait, for at just that time, 9:38 AM, Jesus and all His disciples were destroyed. Pastor B. began his petition time with the small group, all of whom had found their way to the tight weave carpet to join him in prayer.

Reaction time is usually better among the young, but Ellie was genuinely surprised to see that Pastor B. had made it to the floor a millisecond before either she or Kevin Walters had. The sudden burst of brilliant light as the beautiful stained glass windows along the entryway to the church shattered into a million and one pieces was so totally unexpected that it took all of their brains time to take in what was happening.

Ellie saw rather than heard the barrage of gunfire. The burst of broken glass blowing at them in what seemed to be slow motion was like watching a rainbow shatter. One instant there were lines and boundaries and form, the next there was a hail of brilliant, but totally disjointed color in total and complete disarray. It was like looking into one of those toy kaleidoscopes that changed shape and color as you turned it.

The four horizontal bodies were covered with glass and debris. They all lay there momentarily. Ellie was the first to push herself up, cutting her hands in the process. She shook her head and an avalanche of colored glass fragments came out. The deputy reached out to her former boyfriend and touched him on the shoulder to see if he was alive. She heard him moan, which was a good sign.

"Pastor B., you all right? Pastor B?" No answer emanated from the prone man.

Sirens began to disrupt the silence that had followed the salvo. The third man in the floored quartet began to stir.

"What the hell?" he started, then perhaps realized where he was or perhaps lost the words to describe what he was feeling, especially in the groin area which had become noticeably moist.

Ellie struggled to her feet and then helped both Setten and Walters to theirs. They all turned their ministrations to the Pastor.

"I'm all right. Just let me finish." For indeed, the pastor had been praying. "Amen," he said to no one or to Him. "I am finished."

The screech of brakes and the slamming of a car door heralded the arrival of reinforcements.

More sirens could be heard joining in the cacophony of emergency sounds as volunteer ambulance and volunteer fire department personnel threw down their aprons, saws, dental equipment, wrenches, and paintbrushes to rush to the aid of those in peril.

"Deputy, may I speak to you," requested the local police officer.

"Sure, John. What's going on?"

"Well, sir.. I mean ma'am, we've got one down outside. The ambulance crew is working on him, but it…ah…it doesn't look good."

"Oh, my. Do you know who it is?"

"No, ma'am. He's not familiar to me. But one of the ambulance guys says he knows him from the bank."

"A bank employee?" asked the deputy thinking the shooting was a robbery.

"No, a customer."

"Have you called it in?"

"Yes, ma'am. I actually called the county and MHP and reported it as an "officer involved shooting" because I saw your car sitting right by the man."

"Let's go look, shall we?"

"Yes ma'am."

As Ellie walked out the door, she pulled her cell phone from its holster on her side and rang her friend Shelley's number. There was no answer. She was about to leave a message when she came upon her second dead body of the week. This one was pretty fresh and bore a striking resemblance in death to the young man who on Monday had opened the gate for her to drive the truck and trailer onto the farmyard. The ambulance staff was just getting ready to put the man's body on a stretcher when Ellie suggested they wait.

"John," she said to the local cop, "do you have some tape in your car?"

"Yep. I'll go get it."

Then Ellie turned her attention to one of the ambulance crew.

"Bob, are you the one that said you knew the guy."

"I didn't know him other then to say 'hi' as he drove through the drive thru. Name was Jeffers or Jeffries, something like that."

Chapter Twenty-Four

"Three Blind Mice"

Ox and I finished off chores and, truth be told, would have liked to return to our respective easy chairs for a morning nap. Neither of us was used to staying up as late as we had the night before. But it had been an enjoyable evening. I had laid awake for more than a few minutes thinking through the week and in particular events involving my neighbor and new friend Shelley Robison.

Being familiar with the contents of the Sheriff's file on the murder investigation, or at least the contents that had been available to me through the file folder I'd found in Ellie's car, I was more and more concerned about the direction things might be going for her. That was especially true if our speculation of the previous evening was correct and the person Shelley said had kidnapped her was turning himself in.

I wanted to believe her, but friendship had blinded me before and I wasn't about to let it happen again.

"Town?" asked Ox in his ebullient way.

"I'd much rather take a nap."

"Humph," was his reply.

We both took quick showers and changed our clothes. I grabbed a cup of coffee on the way out the door and let the Ox drive our vintage green Chevy truck.

"Nice shirt," I commented to Ox as he appeared from his room wearing a pink, western style shirt.

"Thanks," he said ignoring my sarcasm.

The decision to go to town had little to do with any need we had for supplies, but rather was based on our curiosity about what might be transpiring at the church at 10:30. We had timed our journey to arrive just prior to the appointed time, but as we drove into the small berg we now called home, we surmised that we were going to be too late. Flashing lights from fire, police and ambulance were radiating from vehicles located in front and around the church.

As we drew closer, we spotted medical personnel administering aid and comfort to several people, including one officer who had unmistakable red hair. Ox pulled over half a block before the scene and we walked up to join a small crowd that had gathered. The crowd was held back by yellow tape.

I pointed at the tape and in particular one spot that seemed to be covered in blood. Obviously the dispatcher of the tape had been injured. That conclusion caused me to search out our friend and sure enough we could see that the attendant was wrapping her hands in gauze.

It was about that time that Ellie caught site of us. She called over a police officer standing just to her right and spoke briefly to him, pointing her white-mitted hands toward us. He walked toward us with a question mark countenancing his face.

"You Paul and Jack?" he asked us.

"Yep," was Ox's reply.

"Deputy over there wants to talk to you. Nice shirt," the deputy offered.

The latter comment directed at Ox in his pink shirt.

We both ducked under the tape to a murmur of questions from other members of the crowd who were wondering why these strangers were being invited where they were not welcome. We walked behind the ambulance, which is when we saw a yellow sheet of plastic covering what could only be a body. My heart picked up a beat or two when I saw the yellow covered mound.

We greeted Ellie with perfunctory smiles, waiting for news that would lead our emotions down one path or another.

"Shelley," she started and my heart skipped a beat. "I can't get hold of Shelley, and I'm worried about her."

"Is she at home?" I asked.

"Yes, at least that's what she told me."

"When was the last time you tried?"

"Just now."

"Do you want us to go look for her?"

"Would you?"

"Sure, I'll have her call you when we find her."

"Paul, Jack, be careful. I don't like what's going on here."

Neither did Ox and I. We turned and walked away just as the fellow we'd seen on television the last couple of nights came limping up, his pants leg torn open to reveal bandages.

"Who can't you find?" asked the reporter having just overheard the last fragment of conversation that passed between his favorite deputy and two men. One of whom he vaguely recognized as someone he'd seen just recently, but then the guy had been almost toothless.

"Yeah, who can't you find?" asked the Sheriff as he arrived two seconds later, missing out on the original conversation.

"Ummm, I can't find Pastor B," lied Ellie.

"I just saw him over there talking to John Sweeter, so don't feed me that line again young lady," said the Sheriff. "You may be my daughter, but you are also a deputy in my department and I have about had it with not being kept in the loop with what is going on."

"Oh Dad," started the redhead.

"Ellie, I mean it. You were talking about Shelley Robison weren't you? You think she may have had something to do with this. You know darn well that had we gotten Jeffries into custody he would have confirmed my suspicions."

"No, Dad I don't think that. I'm worried about Shelley. Who ever did this could be after Shelley too."

"Well, she had better show up in Setten's office at 4:00 this afternoon or I'll issue an "armed and dangerous" on her."

"Dad, please stop…Your anger at Shelley has made you blind to the facts…I know Shelley…and I knew Mike and his brother and believe me when I tell you that they knew some characters who would not think twice about shooting someone in broad daylight right here on the streets of Harmony."

"Four o'clock," restated the Sheriff then walked away.

Mary Brooks came running down the street and threw herself into her husband's outstretched arms.

"Thank God you're alright!" she exclaimed. "I heard the sirens while I was out in the garden."

"I'm OK, just a little shaken up. I'm afraid the trustees are going to have a busy weekend trying to put the windows back together." But the pastor's attempt at humor fell on deaf ears.

"Bartholomew Brooks, how could you get involved in this? This is that Robison woman's doing."

"That's what I think too, Preacher," came a remark from the Sheriff who had walked up behind them.

"Sheriff, leave her out of this. You too, Mary. Shelley has gone through enough this week without you continuing to act as judge, jury, and executor."

"Preacher, her youth and beauty have blinded your common sense... Ma'am," he said as he tipped his hat.

"Bart, you know he could be right."

"Mary, I don't want to talk about it right now."

Ox and I tried to get back across the crime scene tape and out of town without being observed by anyone. It was a fruitless attempt at anonymity, especially when one of us was wearing a pink shirt.

We had just about made it back to our truck when an unfamiliar voice stopped us.

"Hold on there a minute," the man we had learned was the County Attorney said. "I don't think I know you two gentlemen."

Both Ox and I stopped and hesitated momentarily before turning to the man.

"You may be right about that," I said.

We both turned again to get into the truck, the man kept coming toward us.

"I said to hold it," he repeated.

Neither of us did.

I had shut the passenger door just before he reached for it. I pushed the lock button down. He started to pound on the window.

"Look mister," I said as I rolled the window down. "I don't know who you are or what you want so unless you have a badge, a warrant, and a gun, I suggest you step back. Oh, by the way, did you know that your pants are wet?"

The man looked down at his suit pants and in that instant, Ox pushed the starter on the floor, popped the clutch and away we went. I looked into the rearview mirror and actually saw a grown man waving his fists at us. I had seen everything. With my knowledge of what the Sheriff was trying to do and now what the County Attorney was attempting, it was an obvious case of the blind leading the blind.

I knew Shelley was innocent and I thought I knew how to prove it. I just hoped Ox and I could get to Shelley before the sheriff arrested her or the killer or killers made an unholy Trinity of murders in my new hometown.

Chapter Twenty-Five

The Black Widow

It had been a long time since Shelley had taken a ride in the morning of a weekday. It was a fine late July morning. The humidity was starting to build, but it was still pleasant as she rode through the ditches along the dirt roads that were starting to disappear in Maplewood County. At one point she came out of the ditch and started to ride on the road itself.

Mocca, Shelley's Palomino gelding, was feeling his oats and wanted to run so Shelley let him have his head. She'd bought Mocca from a car dealer in Hawks Hill who'd used him for calf penning. Mocca could run flat out, stop on a dime, reverse direction, chase down a frisky calf and the rider could be drinking a cup of coffee and never spill a drop.

They had galloped nearly half a mile when Shelley reined Mocca in to a canter. He was starting to lather up a bit and Shelley did not want him to overdo even though he seemed anxious to keep going at full tilt. They continued on that way until they came to a field road that led into a clean field of alfalfa stubble. Shelley had ridden a few times through the field last fall. She knew that a series of paths and field roads would eventually lead her up to Paul and Jack's farmyard.

Twenty minutes later, Shelley rode into the farmyard from the backside of the farm. She was surprised to find that the green pick-up was gone and neither of the young farmers was around.

Mocca's ears pricked up when she heard the plaintive whinnies of several horses penned up to the left of the barn. Shelley had heard the story of how the animals had arrived, uninvited at Jack's place.

The blonde dismounted and led Mocca over to the corral where the horses and some feeder cattle were penned up. She wrapped the reins from the bridle around the top wooden plank of the fence. The corral was just out of the line of sight from the rest of the yard, so Shelley heard rather than saw a vehicle come into the yard at a rather high rate of speed. She heard two car doors slam, so assumed it was Jack and Paul. She took the time to pull the saddle off of Mocca, then walked around the hay shed and out into the yard just as the two men came running out of their house, one in a pink shirt that nearly matched her own blouse.

Surprisingly, Paul dropped to his knee and Jack took a sideways position at his full height. Both were holding rather large pistols and they were directed right at Shelley.

"What are you doing here?" demanded Paul as he stood and dropped the gun to his side.

Ox and I both wanted to laugh at the ridiculous spectacle of the County Attorney waving his fist at us, while looking at his obviously wet pants. We wanted to, but didn't as we moved as rapidly as our old green truck could take us.

We pulled into our driveway, and as we did, Ox's pager went off. Ox checked the signal and saw that the pager had started to go off nearly twenty minutes earlier, but the system he had installed only covers a mile or so. It keeps going off until it is deactivated. What that all meant is that some twenty minutes previous, something had triggered an alarm out on the north hay field. Now we were faced, not only with trying to find Shelley, but also establishing what had invaded our little spot in the world.

We swung right up to the house and went in as quickly and quietly as possible, not knowing if someone might have made it into the house. I did a quick look through while Ox grabbed our weapons from the hiding place in the vent in the wall.

"House is clear," I informed Ox.

"Barn?" he asked.

"Let's go," I replied.

We went out of the house carrying our weapons at our sides and were just about to split up, with Ox taking the north side and me coming in from the east when a blur caught my eye. I immediately dropped to one knee to give Ox a clear shot. He swung his body forward so that he offered a minimal target. Both of us raised our weapons and aimed at the intruder. Thankfully we recognized the face under the western hat as belonging to Shelley Robison, the very person we were sent to find. She was wearing a pink blouse, and blue jeans.

"What are you doing here?" I asked as nicely as I could.

"What do you mean 'What am I doing here'? What the hell are you two doing with those...those things," she said pointing at our side arms.

She was obviously shaken up and I wasn't sure what had caused it although I hoped that it had been us, since the alternative might actually be worse.

"All right, let's all catch our breaths and settle down," I said. "We were actually coming to look for you."

"Why?" she interrupted. "And why did you need those guns?"

I tried as best as I could to explain that Ellie had tried in vain to call her and had not gotten an answer.

"So she sent the cavalry? And when did you see her?"

"Town," was Ox's reply.

"So, were you at the church too?" complained Shelley. "What is this, did everybody get an invitation except for me?"

"Believe me, it was a party you did not want to attend," I said. "There was a shooting."

"OMG! Was it Ellie?" exclaimed the now distraught blonde.

"No, it was evidently your neighbor – that Jeffries fellow we were talking about last night. He's ahh... He's dead."

It was obvious to me that Shelley's legs began to wobble and she was about to swoon. So I grabbed her and picked her up to carry her into the house.

"What are you doing?" she said. "Let me down. What were you thinking?"

Ox almost broke out laughing himself as I put the woman back down on her feet.

So I was wrong. She wasn't about to swoon.

"Guns," Shelley thought. "They have guns."

She knew she shouldn't have been surprised. After all, Jack had told her that both he and his cousin Paul had been in law enforcement. It was just that in the almost year that she had known Jack; she had never seen him use a pistol. And these were such big guns and it looked like they really knew how to use them.

More important and more critical had been the news about Jeffries. She'd only seen him two times, once when she stopped by to introduce herself when they had first moved in and the second time had been earlier this week when he had escorted her to Cedar Grove.

"Why him?" Shelley asked herself. "Why would someone want him dead? First Mike, now our neighbor. What are people going to think?"

She had been genuinely upset when Paul had grabbed her and begun carrying her to the house. It wasn't his actions that had upset her, but rather the fact that he had assumed she was about to faint. It was going to take a lot more than that to cause her to faint.

"Ellie is worried about you. They don't know why this guy was shot or who did it. If it was the same person or persons who did Mike, she was concerned someone might be after you next. That's all."

"Well, I'm just fine as you can see."

"Yes you are," said the shorter of the two men standing there.

"I'll put them away," said the taller as he took both guns and walked to the house.

"So, how did you get here?" asked Paul, looking around for a vehicle.

"Mocca,"

"Mocca's here?" asked Ox as he returned. "Where is he?"

"Over by the corral. When did you get horses?"

Paul replied, "Ellie thinks they came from the place they raided, your neighbors. They came wandering in Monday, late morning. The County asked us to take care of them until other arrangements can be made."

"There are a couple of nice Appaloosa mares in there," observed the horsewoman.

"Yeah, I noticed," replied Paul.

"Well, I guess I should get going. I still have to have lunch and then head to Hawks Hill for my appointment with Mr. Setten."

"How about I drive you home?" suggested Paul.

"No, I've got Mocca here."

"I'll ride him home," offered Ox.

"We told Ellie that we'd keep an eye on you," proffered Paul to allay any further concerns.

"All right, but I'll make you both lunch when we get there. Let me help Jack get Mocca saddled, then we can go. Here, Jack. You can wear my hat, since you're already wearing my blouse."

Paul had gotten a good laugh out of that one.

It took nearly two hours for crime scene investigators to complete their work at the church. They had been able to recover only two casings and those had come from the road, laying out in the open. The men had also recovered 10 of an estimated 25-30 bullets, but most of those they had collected had been damaged beyond any use. They had made a preliminary determination that it had been an automatic weapon, which didn't surprise Ellie since she had heard the barrage of bullets as they sprayed the front of the church.

One of the investigators thought that the first two shots had taken out the victim and the rest had been for effect. They certainly had an effect.

Once the body was removed, Ellie felt she could leave as well. Other deputies would complete the questioning of any witnesses, although it appeared that there were none that could be of help. She walked over to her car and radioed in that she was available.

"Sheriff wants to talk to you," she was told by the dispatcher. "Says to call him on his cell phone."

"Over," replied the deputy.

She waited a few minutes to place the call, but when she got her father on the phone, he was surprisingly contrite.

"Ellie, once I saw that you were alright I needed to leave"

"Dad, are you OK?"

"Yeah, I'm OK. I'm just starting to think some of these things through and ..."

"Dad, Dad are you still there?"

"Yeah, maybe it is time for me to hang up the spurs."

"Dad, don't say that. We've all had a rough week. It's brought the best and the worst out in all of us."

"Ellie, I think that there is more to this week than what we thought. I'm starting to think that friend of yours…"

"Shelley?"

"Yeah, Shelley. I'm thinking she might just know more than…"

"Dad, don't start…"

"No, hear me out. I'm thinking she might know more than she thinks or someone may think she knows more than she actually does."

"Well, I asked Paul and Jack to go find her. I couldn't get a hold of her this morning."

"Maybe you better go too. It seems like anyone around that woman gets in trouble or dead."

"Jeez, Dad. You just don't let up on her do you?" ended Ellie.

It only took a few minutes for Shelley to saddle up Mocca. She adjusted the stirrups for Ox, then held Mocca as Ox climbed aboard. Mocca let out a sigh when he realized that Shelley's one hundred and ten pounds had been replaced by two hundred and twenty. Mocca fidgeted a bit, but Ox was able to settle him down and get him moving in the right direction. The horses left behind let out whinnies of protest and followed along the fence line, begging the Palomino to return to them.

Shelley and Paul watched as Ox road the reverse path that Shelley had ridden an hour or so previous. When they no longer could see horse and rider, Paul escorted the widow to the green truck.

"Your carriage awaits," Paul said gallantly as he opened the door.

"Nice," Shelley replied. "No seat belts. It smells old."

"It is. 1951 vintage Chevrolet pickup."

Paul pulled out a lever, turned the key, then used his left foot to push the starter located on the floor. The truck fired right up. Paul tried to put it in gear, but ground the gears before finding the right one. He turned to Shelley and smiled sheepishly.

"Ox usually drives," he said.

"What would you do without Jack?"

"I do not know. He is one in a million."

"I'm beginning to think both of you are pretty unique."

"No, No. Just a couple of farm boys trying to make a living."

"Uh Huh."

Paul wheeled the vehicle out the driveway, took a left onto the tar road in front of their farm, then took another left onto the dirt road that eventually led to several more farms. The second of which belonged to Shelley.

As the two drove down the dirt road, Paul kept looking off to the left. Every once in a while he would catch a glimpse of pink and gold through the woods that bordered the road.

"He's still riding," Paul said pointing his head toward the woods.

"Mocca's the best, Ox will enjoy his ride. I've got some of that ham left for sandwiches."

"Sounds great. Any of your pickles?"

"I think I can find some."

Paul put the truck into third and hit the accelerator, demonstrating one of his many appetites, this one for Shelley's pickles. The truck rumbled down the road, warm summer air invading the cab through the open windows. As Paul accelerated the noise of the truck and the dirt road made conversation nearly impossible, but the two passengers enjoyed the trip. They were welcomed into the yard by Mad Max who came bounding up to the truck and jumped up on the passenger door to welcome his master.

"Down Max, down!"

"That's alright," grumbled Paul.

They were nearly through the open screen door when they heard the clip-clop of a horse approaching.

"He made good time," suggested Paul.

Shelley and Paul paused to watch Ox ride into the yard. Instead of pink and gold, they saw only gold. They looked at each other and did a quick turnaround, letting the door slam behind them. Both ran down the grass to the barn where Mocca now stood shaking his head at the reins that were dangling. The saddle was slightly askew and the horse kept lifting his left, front leg in pain. Paul tried to approach the horse, but the animal shied away. Even Shelley had a difficult time getting the horse to stand still long enough to catch the reins.

"Paul, there's blood on his neck!" exclaimed Shelley.

"Get him to hold still."

"I'm trying. Let me get his bridle off and this halter on."

"Don't fiddle with that now. Where's Ox?"

Shelley looked at Paul, who realized she had no more of an answer than he did.

"Get in the truck."

"Shouldn't we call someone?"

"You can if you want; I'm going to go find Ox."

"Am I losing it?" thought the Sheriff as he drove off.

He had been on the verge of tears by the time he had gotten away from the crime scene. His nose was plugged, his eyes red and on the brink of dumping a flood. He hadn't felt this way since the day his wife had died all those years ago.

The Sheriff arrived back in his office and gently shut the door to his office. He went in and sat at his desk and contemplated. He thought of his little farm just twenty minutes away. He saw the photo of himself and the Governor that dated back to the early 70's when he was a rising star with the Bureau of Criminal Apprehension. Nothing stopped him back then. He glanced at the framed newspaper article detailing his first election win some twelve years previous. There was a photo of him testifying before the legislature two or three years ago, when his good friend and local legislator had carried a bill that allowed local law enforcement to confiscate property of criminal enterprises. He'd been a hero with all the cops in the State that year.

Now, he was a joke, not even allowed to show up at the surrender of the first murderer this county had seen in 9 years. And, even that fiasco would get blamed on him.

"If Deputy Carlson calls in, tell her to call my cell phone," the Sheriff told the dispatcher. "I'm heading over to Harmony again."

"Yes, sir."

The call had come nearly twenty-five minutes later. While it had begun better than the last few conversations they had had, it had ended badly. It seemed no matter what he said; his daughter was going to defend Shelley. It was time for him to sit down with Shelley Robison and have a heart to heart conversation without attorneys, friends, or pastors present.

The Sheriff came down the county road past the Mueller place then took a left. A dark blue or green Mercury Sable nearly clobbered the Sheriff's Explorer as the Sable slid through the stop sign and sped off in the direction the Sheriff had just come. The lawman was tempted to take off after the lawbreaker, but thought better of it when he saw the emblem on the trunk that indicated a prominent dealer in the Twin Cities had sold it.

"Tourists," he said out loud. "Drive around here like they own the roads."

He jotted down the license number, thinking he'd find out who they were and send them a warning. He continued down the road, passing the farm that had been raided five days previously. He noticed that the gate was now standing open, which surprised him since he'd ordered it padlocked shut.

"Must be family," he thought but decided to check it out after his visit to Ms. Robison.

He approached the driveway of the widow Robison's farm and turned into the driveway, nearly crashing head-on into a classic Chevrolet pickup that was coming at a good clip down the drive. The driver skidded to a stop and tooted the trucks melancholy horn. The Sheriff returned the toot with a blast of his own horn and a flip of his siren switch on and off. He turned his flashing lights on and stepped from his car.

"Sheriff, get back in your car and move it," yelled the driver from the door of the pickup.

"You just hold on Banion. I want to talk to that woman."

"Sheriff, we haven't got time. Now please move!"

Just then another County vehicle pulled in behind the Sheriff's car and turned its flashers on as well. Ellie Carlson stepped from that vehicle and marched up to her father, who by then had been joined by the occupants of the pickup.

"Tell your damn father to get out of the way, NOW!"

"Dad, Paul, what's going on."

The two men got into a shouting contest. Shelley pulled Ellie off to the side and quickly explained what was going on. Ellie pulled out her side arm, aimed it in the air, and fired. Silence ensued with both men dropping into a crouch, ready to spring on each other.

"Dad, they were going out to find Jack. He's missing. The horse he was riding came back injured and with blood on it," said the deputy. "Shelley, you come with me. We'll head over to Paul's place and see if Jack is there, if not we'll follow the trail as far as we can. Dad, you take Paul. He will show you the back way to their farm. Stay on your radio."

G. T. had a mixture of pride and resentment over how his daughter, the youngest and most inexperienced officer had taken over the situation. The two police vehicles backed up and took off, Ellie's rapidly going down the dirt road and the Sheriff's going a half mile then turning into a field road.

"That gate wasn't open when we came over," reported Paul upon observing the same gate the Sheriff had seen ten minutes before.

"Probably family. I'll check it out later. Let's find your friend."

The two men were quiet as they drove into the alfalfa stubble. They both rolled their windows down to hear better. As they drove, they were both acutely aware of the lack of sound that surrounded them. Once a car drove by up on the dirt road. They could hear it, but didn't see anything but dust.

"Tourists," said the Sheriff. "One of them dang near killed me when he went right through the stop sign."

Paul got out of the Explorer a couple of times to see if he could see any kind of trail or tracks, but only saw what must have been Shelley's from in the morning. The two men had been traveling silently over, first the alfalfa field, then along a fence line, and finally approached the large wooded area that surrounded Paul's farmyard. The trail was really rough and only someone on horseback or in a 4-wheel drive could make it. They had gone about one hundred fifty yards into the woods when Paul spotted something.

"There, off to the left. I see pink."

The Sheriff looked at Paul strangely."

"Pink?"

"Ox was wearing a pink shirt."

"Pink?"

"On him it looked good."

They moved forward as far as they could go, then got out of the Explorer and started hiking through the dense underbrush toward the splash of color Paul had seen.

"Ox," Paul hollered. "Is that you?"

"No," came back a faint, female voice in reply. "It's us."

It took a few minutes for the two pairs to join up.

Ellie was still shaking as she and Shelley sped over to Jack and Paul's farm. She was upset about treating her father in the manner she had. She was upset that her good father was with Paul and she wasn't. She was upset that Jack seemed to be missing. And, she was upset because she had just come from seeing her second dead body in a week. Of course those were just a few of the things that had caused her blood pressure to go off the charts in the past week.

"Ellie, are you OK?"

"Let's just focus on finding Jack," came Ellie's reply.

They had gotten to the farm and Ellie had directed Shelley to go to the house while she checked the barn. Three minutes later they had met in the farmyard and starting their hike along the trail Shelley had followed to get to Paul's place that morning.

"Mocca is so gentle, I just can't imagine that he threw Jack unless something really spooked her."

"You said Mocca was hurt. Where?"

"She was limping and she had blood on her neck and on the saddle horn."

The two women followed the trail for a hundred yards, and then it veered off to the right on another path that was not the one Shelley had come over on. They had just started down that trail when they heard Paul calling them.

The four searchers joined up and considered the possibilities. As scarce as the trail was to the right, it did appear that Ox had taken that direction.

"Sheriff, why don't you and Ellie go back to your vehicles and head back to Shelley's? Shelley and I will keep walking this trail. It's bound to come out by the road somewhere. If you are waiting on either end of the road, you'll see us when we come out."

The two Carlson's eyed each other, and then took to their appointed rounds. Ellie felt more than a bit of consternation as she turned back and saw Paul reach out his hand to help Shelley step over a log in the path.

The deputy got to her car and radioed in to the dispatcher what was going on.

"The Sheriff and I are involved in a lost horseback rider over here north of Harmony. Keep us posted if there are any 911 runs out here, especially if they involve ambulances."

"10-4. Deputy Chief Barton wants to talk to you."

"Tell him to call my cell phone, but give me a couple of minutes."

Ellie swung her car into place. She had a good view of at least ¾ of a mile of the road. She assumed that her dad would have as much or more from Shelley's drive way.

Her cell phone rang.

" Carlson," she answered.

"Ellie, its Jim. You left before we had a chance to talk about that murder vic in Harmony. Does your dad want you to be the principle on it?"

"I don't know Jim. I doubt it since I was kind of involved in it. Why?"

"Well, we just got an anonymous 911 call. It was from a pay phone in Parkers Prairie. The caller said we should look at Jeffries' barn for evidence of the killer."

"That's what they said?"

"Notes say and I quote 'Male voice - Exact words: Look in Jeffries barn.'"

"Thanks Jim. Dad and I are out by there right now. When we're done we'll go look."

Ellie sat for a few more minutes, then saw her bedraggled friends emerge from the ditch on the left nearly out of her line of site. She hit her siren once, then turned it off again. She put her car in gear and drove down to where the two were standing.

"You guys look rough," she greeted them.

"We went through some low areas and some pretty heavy thistles, but this is where he seems to have come out. His trail heads down there to the west."

"Get in. I think I can follow it from here."

Ellie flipped her radio to the channel father and daughter had agreed on using for more private conversation.

"Dad, we have a trail. Paul and Shelley just came out of the woods. It's pretty faint, but I can see it …just a second it crosses the road and goes into the ditch on the other side. Why don't you head this way and see if you see anything."

Paul jumped out of the car and went down into the ditch.

"I've got it. There's a trail of a small vehicle here too."

"What does he mean 'too'?" Ellie asked Shelley.

"We spotted a trail in Paul's woods. Looked like a 4-wheeler had been there. We thought maybe Jack had gone after it."

"Oh," said Ellie. Then she put two and two together.

"Paul, come back up here. I have an idea where Jack might be. No, don't argue."

Paul climbed back up from the ditch. His shoes and pants were covered with mud and muck. He was out of breath and sweating profusely. Ellie thought he was on the verge of a melt down, both physically and emotionally.

"Hang in there Paul," Ellie said to the man who had just climbed into the passenger seat.

Shelley tried to put her hand on Paul's shoulder, but the wire cage that separated the back seat, which was used for prisoner transfer, from the front kept her from reaching her goal. Ellie smiled to herself, but only briefly.

Ellie accelerated her car down the road at the same time she clicked on her radio and told her father to meet them at the Jeffries place.

When they arrived, she swung into the driveway for the second time that week. This time it was without the big truck and cattle trailer. This time the gate was not an impediment and she drove right on through. She advanced rapidly to the barn on the right side of the yard. As she arrived at the destination, she jumped from the car, pulled her weapon, and hollered at Paul to take the shotgun from the front seat holder. In the background she could hear

Shelley's futile attempt to extricate herself from the back seat. She was unsuccessful, since the doors were inoperable from the interior.

"Stay put Shelley," the deputy demanded. She ignored the pounding on the glass.

Ellie and Paul moved forward. Ellie was surprised at the professional manner that Paul took on as they invaded the barn. He covered her, then she covered him as they advanced forward into the semi-darkness of the barn.

"Over here," Paul shouted.

Ellie responded quickly, holstering her weapon. She took one look and ran out of the barn. She popped open her trunk and grabbed the first aid kit stowed there. Then she opened the back door, handed the kit to Shelley and told her where to go. Literally.

"In the barn, last stall on the right. It's Jack. He needs help. I'm calling for an ambulance."

Just then the Sheriff rolled up to Ellie's car.

"Dad, its Jack. He's in the barn." Ellie said, nearly on the verge of tears. "He's hurt bad."

Foreboding. That's the emotion I had as it became apparent that Mocca had deposited his rider somewhere along the trail back to Shelley's. We searched carefully and in vain, then decided that Ox must have taken a different path back than the one that Shelley had suggested.

As Shelley and I followed the scant trail through the woods I became more and more concerned. The cause of my concern was another trail that I caught about thirty yards into our search.

"Look at that Shelley," I said to my search partner. "Those are off-road tracks and there are horse tracks over them."

"So," she replied.

"Ox was following someone."

"How do you know that? Those other trails could have been done anytime."

"No, we would have known."

"How?"

"Let's keep going," I replied in non answer to her question.

I wasn't ready to let her know about the perimeter monitoring system we had in place. My guess was that the pager had gone off as Ox was starting his journey and instead of playing it safe and coming back to get a weapon and assistance, he had decided to check it out.

As we traveled through the woods, the going was tough in places, but usually because a vehicle had torn up the path or run down undergrowth, which made it difficult to traverse.

We talked little, but what we visited about cleared up much of the mystery of the past week. Without knowing that she was doing so, Shelley filled in many of the blanks that had existed for me since we had first met. The new knowledge did little to alleviate my gross concern for my friend, for unknown to him, I was convinced he was now pursuing a person who had already killed at least two people and ruined the lives of many more. I dared not share this information with my current compatriot for fear that, in her loyalty, she would turn on me.

As we exited the woods, we were forced to go deep into a ditch laden with water and muck. It was obvious to us both that the vehicle Ox had been pursuing had gotten stuck. Whether its own driver had extricated it or if Ox had helped, it was difficult to discern.

We broached the road and waved at our personal deputy who was ensconced at the end of the road. She hit her siren and came on the run. We turned the other direction but could not see the deputy's father.

I shared my concerns with Ellie. She agreed and we moved off following the trail. At one point I got out of the car to follow the trail in the opposite ditch. It was just then that Ellie called me back. She made great haste for a little short of a mile, then swung into a drive that she was familiar with.

I'd only recently heard the story from Ellie of the raid earlier that week. I had thought it an excellent piece of lawmanship and was surprised that she said both she and her father had been the subject of some ridicule. I also reflected that she and her fellow officers were lucky to have had the results they did. I had known a number of people directly and indirectly involved in the sale and distribution of illicit pharmaceuticals and knew for a fact that they often possessed some serious weapons and had a penchant for using them.

This also began to cause me concern for my friend and ally, Ox. He would have entered this situation without the knowledge that I had gleaned in the last hour.

We arrived next to the barn; the location the deputy said had been specified by the anonymous caller. We both exited the vehicle, she with her side arm, and me with the standard issue shotgun. We moved forward using strict hostile house procedures. We found my friend in the last stall on the right.

The reader will excuse me as I struggle to adequately express to you the sense of passion I experienced as I saw my dear friend laying in great disarray and obvious distress. I could tell by his color that he was alive, although totally unconscious. The cause of his unconsciousness was not readily obvious. What was obvious was that he had experienced excruciating pain before losing his faculties. My first inclination was to destroy, to annihilate, and to cause great bodily pain and harm to anyone directly or indirectly involved with what had happened to my friend. Instead I cried out to Ellie to get help.

All too soon, yet not nearly soon enough, I was joined by the object of my current loathing. I turned to the sound of footsteps and exclamation to see Shelley.

"You, you did this," I angrily spit out. "Get out of here."

"I think she did it too," came the unfriendly voice of the Sheriff.

Shelley left the barn totally devastated by what Paul had just said. It was true that she felt responsible for so much of what had happened this past week. Two deaths and one person critically injured. If there was anything in the world she could do to change any of it. She would.

"It's about time someone else sees this whole scheme the same way I do," thought Goat Carlson as he looked over the shoulder of his new partner in crime solution. He didn't say it out loud, for he saw in the eyes of this man kneeling by his friend, a fire that shook even him.

"Looks pretty bad there, young man," suggested the Sheriff.

The man turned to him without speaking, and then turned back to his friend.

It took fifteen minutes for the volunteers to gather together, grab their gear, and race their ambulance to the farm. The crew immobilized the victim, inserted an I.V. and prepared to transport him.

"Hawks Hill," said the man Paul had seen at the scene of the shooting just a few hours before. "They have the best Triage. They can transport him to Fargo if need be."

"Any idea why he is unconscious?" asked Paul.

"Doesn't seem to be any head trauma, but he obviously has a very badly broken leg and probably some ribs. His shoulder might be separated and...ah, I don't know if you noticed, but he's missing a finger. His pinky on the right hand. All in all, it's probably a good thing he's unconscious."

"Can I ride with him?"

"No, sorry."

Paul looked around, bewildered. The Sheriff stepped forward and offered him a ride. Paul accepted gratefully and the two men walked quickly to the Sheriff's Explorer.

Ellie came forward to talk to Paul, but thought better of it when her father shook his head.

Ellie was nearly numb emotionally. She had overheard the exchange between Paul and Shelley and had gone after the distraught woman as she left the barn.

"Just take me home," Shelley had said.

"I'm sure he didn't mean it," Ellie replied.

"Oh yes he did. He's been questioning me for the last hour. He even told me just before we came onto the road that he had finally figured it all out. And to think I was happy about that. I had no idea he had joined your father."

Ellie couldn't say much more to her friend. She didn't know what had transpired between the two as they had walked through the woods. But she was still convinced that Shelley was innocent, and she was going to prove it.

Ellie drove Shelley the short distance to her own home. She walked her to the door, but declined Shelley's offer for coffee.

"I need to get back. I'll stop and see how Jack is doing. I'll call you when I know."

"Thanks Ellie. Tell Paul I'll get chores started."

"Ah, Shelley. Don't you have an appointment this afternoon?"

"OMG. I forgot. I'd better get going. I won't be able to do chores, I'll be in jail. LOL"

"You let Andy handle things," replied Ellie.

"I know. I know."

Chapter Twenty-Six
"And the Answer is"

Mary came running down the street to meet her husband who had finally gotten rid of the last of the media, who had arrived, drawn like flies to a carcass, to question the preacher about the events that had led to the destruction of Jesus and the disciples and the demise of one Lonnie Jeffries, desperado who had planned to use the good offices of Pastor B. to turn his life around. Or so was the explanation that the cleric had used with the media.

Strangely, he had been the only one of those directly involved in the massacre of the windows and the criminal who had stayed around for reporters to interview. Kevin had taken off with his film crew, presumably to scoop everyone else. The County Attorney had left almost immediately after visiting the men's room for a considerable time. The deputy had stayed with the body and dealt with whatever witnesses she could find, but she too, had left. Pastor had seen Jack Forester and his nice friend Paul talking to the deputy and then leaving quickly, but they hadn't really been involved.

Now here was Mary, quiet, patient Mary coming running down the street again. The pastor wondered what news she might have that would prompt her energy.

"Bart," said a winded Mrs. Brooks. "I just talked to Sue Arndt, who talked with Libby Schwarz, who said that the ambulance went out about an hour ago to the Jeffries place. Libby said that when they got there a man was very badly injured. Bart, Mickey Schwarz says it was Jack Forester who was the one hurt. He's being taken to Hawks Hill Hospital."

"Oh, my," said the preacher. "Does the car have gas?"

"What?"

"Well, I told you to get gas in the car yesterday. Did you?"

"No, I'm sorry. I forgot with the funeral and everything."

"Never mind. I'll get it."

"Where are you going?"

"Well, to Hawks Hill, of course."

I was really worried. My friend had not even moaned when they had put him on the sled to keep him immobile. They had tried to straighten out Ox's leg, but it was obvious that they were only going to be able to get it so it would ride on the stretcher. It was really damaged.

The Sheriff was moving at a good clip, eighty or better and still hadn't put on his lights or sirens. I was impressed with his driving ability. Actually, the Sheriff impressed me with a lot of his skills and insight that I had seen over the last few days. I just knew that he was wrong about Shelley and now he was wrong about me thinking Shelley was guilty of anything other than having worn a pink blouse that morning.

I had guessed that the slight injury on Mocca had come either from something very sharp or from the grazing blow of a bullet. After seeing Ox's finger was missing, it didn't take much to surmise that the same thing that had caused the horse's injury had likely caused Ox's finger amputation.

The other thing that I knew that no one else did was that someone having tripped our alarm system had likely drawn Ox off trail. I had no doubt that it could very well have been someone who had spied Shelley riding over to our place not that much earlier in the day. Conclusion: It wasn't Ox that they, whoever 'they' is, were after. It was a blonde wearing a western hat and pink blouse, out for a ride on a Palomino.

The Sheriff concentrated on his driving and passing of cars, a few of whom honked the horns at us. We blew through Crystal Lake at over 80 miles an hour. We rounded the curves before Yellow Pine at only slightly less. We discovered the width of the shoulder of the road by using it to pass a semi. A motorcycle had attempted to stay ahead of us, but the Sheriff bumped its rear end going 73 and the cycle decided to pull over.

"Here," the Sheriff said as he handed me a scrap of paper, "write that guy's number down. There was another guy, dang near killed me over by your place. Damned tourists."

He read of the number. I looked at the piece of paper. It had what appeared to be another license number on it. I jotted down the numbers he gave me, then adeptly put it in my shirt pocket, thinking by doing so I might save a fellow "tourist" a ticket.

I know that in retrospect it seems silly now, but the last 10 minutes of the trip, I worried about what insurance Ox had to cover his medical treatment. I knew that was one of those things that, despite all of my planning over the last two years, I had not thought of. Certainly paying cash for an extended stay in the hospital would raise flags.

We arrived at the hospital just as the ambulance was pulling into the emergency garage doors. I was actually there to greet my friend as the ambulance crew wheeled him through. My friend was breathing through an oxygen mask while lying on the stretcher.

"Ox, can you hear me?" I asked, but got no reply.

A nurse came walking briskly down the hall and directed the crew to exam room one. That same nurse stopped me from entering.

"Are you family?" she asked.

"No, I mean yes."

"Which is it?"

"I'm his cousin and friend. We farm together."

By now the Sheriff had arrived and I knew that he was listening with interest to my answers.

"Well, who is his next of kin? Does he have a wife? Parents? Someone who can sign documents, guarantee payment?"

"I'll do that…the guarantee payment."

"Then please step up to the front counter and complete the admission papers."

"Yes, ma'am."

"Oh, is he allergic to anything?"

"Ahhh. I really don't know. He's never told me about anything."

"Is there anyone we could call?"

"I'll, mmm, I'll see what I can do."

I went quickly to the admissions desk and completed the information as best I could. I explained that I would try to get additional information as soon as possible. I had given them my banking information, which Ox had prepared and given to me on a sheet of paper when I had first arrived, and that seemed to satisfy them for the moment.

I looked around and saw that the Sheriff was sitting in the front row. He tipped his head to me and convinced me that he wasn't about to disappear anytime soon. I decided to confront him head long and use his natural inquisitiveness to my advantage.

"Sheriff, I have to make some phone calls…Do you mind sticking around here in case Ox wakes up?"

"Who's Ox? Oh, I get it Paul Banion," he said pointing to me, "and his friend Ox. Pretty clever."

"Perhaps too clever," I said to myself as I walked to a pay phone.

Ox and I had set up a system for calling our parents in the event of an emergency. I dialed a phone number that was unlisted in Chicago; it forwarded my call to another unlisted number in Phoenix, which forwarded the call to a number in New York City, which then forwarded my call to Ox's uncle in California. If all went well, he would call either my parents or Ox's and have them available within 10 minutes. This time the system worked, but I could see that there might be bugs in it.

The Sheriff came strolling up to where I was attempting to work my magic on the phones.

"Any problems," he asked.

"Well, I'm having a tough time getting someone to do chores. I tried Shelley and got no answer."

"Why would you try her?" he asked suspiciously.

"She's done chores for Ox in the past."

"She's probably on her way to Hawks Hill. She's meeting with the County Attorney and me in forty-five minutes."

I waited him out and he finally left to go back to check on our patient.

I quickly dialed the special number and with a series of rings, clicks, and more rings, I received an answer.

"E.Z. is that you?"

"Yes, Aunt Norma," I said in case anyone was listening.

"It's Jack, isn't it?"

"Yes, I need you to listen and to give me information. Jack's been hurt and we don't know how bad…No, you just need to let me get this information from you."

I rattled off a series of questions that the admissions clerk had given me and within eight minutes, had all the information I thought necessary. I promised Norma and Edward that I would call back as soon as I had any information.

I dropped the answers off with the clerk and headed to Ox's emergency room. He wasn't there and neither was the Sheriff.

The Sheriff was pretty impressed with the "Banion kid", as he referred to him in his thoughts on the rapid trip over to the hospital. He hadn't even squirmed once on the trip over and it had been one heck of a trip.

Goat had made several attempts to glean information from Banion, but to no avail. He was about as close mouthed as they came. About the only reaction he had gotten was when the nurse suggested Banion should call someone for medical information. He had used the name "Ox' instead of Jack and Goat had realized that the nickname had to be a play on words. That was when he decided he would try to listen in on the conversations Banion had.

But Banion had smelled out his ulterior motives and attempted to get rid of him. Of course he hadn't succeeded. Goat had been listening behind the corner as Banion talked with his "Aunt Norma."

Goat had gotten back to the room just as a surgeon was completing his exam.

"If we've got the permission slips signed, let's go. That leg needs to be worked on immediately. We may have to bring in a thoracic surgeon as well, depending on what the X-Rays show in his lungs," the doctor had said.

"He's pretty bad, Doc.?" asked the Sheriff.

"Yes."

Goat had gone to the admissions counter and told the clerk that he had to leave. He asked her to inform the young man, who would be bringing the information on Mr. Forester, of his departure. The clerk had agreed.

Goat still had a few minutes left before he had to be at the County Attorney's office. He stopped in the hospital coffee shop for a quick cup of coffee. He sat there contemplating the day's events and what might still be coming.

"What's she doing here?" he asked himself as he glimpsed his daughter entering the hospital lobby. "Doesn't she work anymore?"

His daughter hesitated a moment and was met by the preacher from Harmony. They walked forward together to the reception desk. They were there only for a brief time when a volunteer came up to them and seemed to lead them somewhere.

"Curiouser and curiouser," the Sheriff said.

He swilled the last of the coffee and headed out to his Explorer, still parked illegally in the entrance ramp to the hospital.

After spending a few minutes with her friend and reminding her of her appointment later that afternoon, Ellie had gotten to her own car and driven off. As she got to the end of the driveway, a thought crossed her mind. She stopped her car, then put it into reverse and backed it up into the yard.

She walked up to the house and knocked. Shelley came to the door.

"Where's your horse?"

"In the barn."

"Can I see him?"

"What for?"

"Come on, Shelley. Let me take a look at him."

The two women walked to the barn where Shelley hooked a lead rope to the halter of her gelding and brought him out of the stall. He was still limping, but not as bad.

Ellie looked over the horse and found a slight tear in its hide just a little front of where the saddle would have been.

"Let me see the saddle."

"It's right over here. I was going to try to wash the blood off."

Ellie looked the saddle over carefully, and then found what she was looking for. She pulled out her pocketknife and sliced through some of the rawhide braiding on the horn.

"Hey, that's a $600 saddle."

"There's a hole here. This is flesh," Ellie said as she used her knife to scrape some material off of the saddle horn

She dug some more.

"You see this slug?" Ellie asked, "I think it's from a rifle, probably a thirty caliber and its only half there."

"So?"

"So, if my hunch is right somebody was taking a shot at a target that they really couldn't see. They were shooting at form and color. The color was pink and gold."

Shelley looked down at her blouse, then at her horse and felt faint.

"They weren't after Jack. It was me."

"That's right," said the deputy. "And I think the bullet hit Jack's hand, and then slammed into the horn right here. When it hit the metal it split. One piece embedded itself right here and the other piece hit Mocca in the neck."

"I don't care. Ellie, they were trying to kill me. That's why Paul was so angry. He figured it out. He was mad because they killed Jack instead of me," said the now sobbing widow.

"Shelley," comforted her friend, "Paul was just upset, and he's worried about Jack.

"I've got to go," said Shelley as she ran to the house.

Ellie returned the horse to her stall, but put the saddle into her trunk. She wanted to take it back to the office to have someone else look it over and confirm her hypothesis. As she carried the saddle, she noticed that it was really loose. There was scuffing on the saddle horn and on the rear of the saddle. She looked at it closely and saw green stains along one side of it. There was a buckle missing from the same side.

After loading the saddle in the trunk, Ellie turned back to the house and wanted to go in.

"No," she thought. "She's going to have to deal with this herself."

Ellie drove out of the drive way and turned left. When she got to the Jeffries driveway she pulled in and parked her car. She walked around in ever widening circles with her car as the focal point of each loop. On the fifth sojourn around her car she was nearly 30 feet out from the car, when she spied a shiny doodad in the grass. She picked it up and walked back to her car, opened the trunk and compared it to the ones still attached to the saddle.

An inkling of an idea started to foment in her brain. It was time to get some answers. Ellie jumped into her squad car and headed to Hawks Hill and the hospital. She needed to try to get some answers from Jack.

Chapter Twenty-Seven

Oh Brothers, Where Art Thou"

Pastor B. swung into the Super America station, used his credit card, and filled up his car. He had quickly changed clothes before leaving the house, but the slacks and shirt were already clinging to his body from the sweat that was profusely emanating from his body.

He pushed his six-year-old car, while staying within the speed limit plus five or six miles an hour. The trip from Harmony to Hawks Hill was uneventful, although frustrating at times. The two-lane highway can be challenging when the farm traffic of tractors, grain trucks, etc. clog up the roadway. He did pass one young man who was on the side of the road working on a motorcycle. It appeared the front wheel was akimbo. On a different day the cleric may have stopped to offer assistance, but not today.

The preacher arrived in the parking lot and turned his vehicle into one of the clergy parking spots reserved for the pastors and priests of the area. It was one of the few perks that the hospital provided.

As he got out of his car he saw Deputy Carlson walking through the doors into the hospital lobby. He increased his speed and got through the doors himself just as she was crossing the carpeted reception area.

"Deputy," he said loudly. "Ellie."

The deputy turned around and then came back to greet the reverend with a hug.

"Pastor B., what are you doing here?"

"I got word that Jack Forester was injured in an accident and had been transported here. You too?"

"Yes. Pastor, I was there. It didn't look good. He was unconscious."

"Oh my."

"Let's go see if we can find Paul or my dad. They came over together."

"They did?"

"Yeah. Will wonders never cease?!"

The two had gone up to the information desk and were told that Mr. Forester was in surgery.

"Are you family?" asked the receptionist.

"No, just friends," replied Ellie.

"I'm his pastor," said Pastor B.

"Well, if you'll just wait a minute, I'll have a volunteer escort you to the family waiting room. Just check in with the volunteer there at the desk."

"Thank you," they both said simultaneously.

The volunteer showed up a few minutes later and took them both to the waiting room. The room was empty except for the volunteer at the desk.

"And who are you here for?"

"Forester, Jack Forester."

"Oh, yes. They've just started. You can have a seat over there. Would you like coffee?"

Both had declined and then sat down.

"I wonder where Paul is?" remarked the deputy. "I don't see Dad either."

"Which Paul are you looking for?" asked a friendly voice coming from the young man himself as he entered the room.

"Oh, Paul. How is he?" asked the deputy.

"Don't know. I had to make some phone calls and when I got back to the emergency room he was gone and so was the Sheriff. The clerk said they'd taken Ox up to surgery and that your dad had to leave to get to some meeting with the County Attorney."

"Did he regain consciousness?" asked the pastor.

"No, pastor, not while I was there."

The three sat quietly for nearly forty-five minutes before a nurse in scrubs came in.

"We've got the leg set and pinned. I'm afraid there's not much we can do with his hand."

"What about his ribs, were they broken?"

"Well, the X-rays look pretty good and they decided not to do surgery. Can you tell me, did he have a fall or was he hit on the head somehow?"

"We're really not sure. We found him unconscious? Why?"

"Doctor is thinking that he's had a concussion. Most likely from a fall. There doesn't appear to be any one point of contact."

"He may have been thrown from a horse," explained Ellie.

Paul looked at her sharply.

"That would explain things," said the nurse. "I'll let the doctor know."

After the nurse left, Paul looked questioningly at the deputy.

"Do you know something?"

The deputy explained to the farmer and pastor about the bullet fragments, the blood, and the grass on the saddle. Then she went on.

"There's no doubt in my mind that someone took a long rifle shot at what they thought was Shelley. I think Jack saw them and took out after them on the horse, even though he had been wounded in the hand. Somehow he ended up at the Jeffries place and somehow the horse went over on him. That's when his leg was broken and he got the concussion."

"How did he end up in the barn?" asked Paul.

"I don't know. He must have been dragged in."

"But by whom?"

"I had guessed there was gunplay involved. I'm afraid I also assumed they were after Shelley."

"Yeah, she told me you were pretty rough on her."

"Oh, you're right. I said some nasty things to her," replied Paul.

Pastor B. reached out and touched the farmer on the knee.

"Paul, we've all had a rough week. Don't be hard on yourself. I'll give Shelley a call and talk to her."

"Can't, Pastor B.," informed Ellie as she looked at her watch. "She's at the County Attorney's office right now. She's 'surrendering' to my dad and Mr. Setten."

"But she didn't do anything," argued Paul.

"I realize that," replied the deputy. "I think I know who did."

"So do I," replied Banion.

"Who?" asked the pastor.

"It was the brother," they replied simultaneously.

"Which brother?" asked Pastor B.

That is when the simultaneity stopped.

After Ellie had left for the second time, Shelley went up to her room and went to the closet.

"What do you wear to an arrest?" she asked out loud, then broke into hysterical laughter.

She was tempted to call Andy and ask him, but realized the fact that she was on the verge of total and complete mental collapse might cause her to become hysterical with him.

She opted for a light, summer green blouse with khaki slacks and her brown pumps. The clothes were laid out along with her under garments. She took down her robe from the hook in the closet that it hung on and crossed to the bathroom in just her bra and panties.

It was as she opened the door to the bathroom, that she thought she heard Max bark. She slipped her robe on and walked back to her bedroom to look out the window at the yard.

"Now what does he want?" she said to herself as she tied the sash on her robe. "I don't have time for this."

"Hi, sis," said a voice from the kitchen as Shelley descended the stairs. It was not the voice she had expected.

Pastor B was totally confused when Paul and Ellie both agreed that the person behind the events of the past week was "the brother". What confused him was that each of the two sleuths had come to the same conclusion, but about a different brother.

The deputy was convinced that it was Shelley's brother James who, as an informant, had enough information that he could have easily impeded the raid. He likely knew where Lonny Jeffries was hiding out and had ready access to Shelley's house and could have easily played the message on her answering machine and deduced that Jeffries was going to be at the church. He had the same experience with guns that Shelley had and was likely just as good a shot. They certainly knew that he was connected with the drug trade and would have access to weapons, both automatic and rifles.

Paul on the other hand was convinced that it was Mike's own brother Rob who was the culprit. He'd first become suspicious when he saw him walk into church with a pronounced limp, thinking that Ellie's errant shot had actually found a mark. He also had seen the cuts on his hands, which certainly indicated that he had likely been in a cornfield recently. His hesitancy to shake hands could be inferred to mean his hand was still hurting from the blow he had bestowed on Ellie.

What Paul hadn't been able to figure out was how someone from the Twin Cities could have been involved in activities in Maplewood County. It was only after his questioning of Shelley that he became aware that Rob often visited his brother on weekends and actually had more of a drug problem than Mike ever did. Shelley had assumed that Rob had left early Monday morning to go back to his job in Minneapolis like he did most Mondays, but it was certainly feasible that he had stuck around long enough to have shot Mike.

Ellie countered with James' disappearing act at the funeral and his unwillingness to provide additional information after he was arrested in the raid. He knew where Mike and Shelley kept their twenty-two and was familiar enough with the corn fields and the irritation of tiny cuts that he would have worn gloves. And the clincher for her was that he had been found during the raid with only his underwear on and no other clothes that fit him.

"Obviously he had gotten rid of the pants and shirt because they had blood on them."

Ellie also pointed to him knowing that Shelley often rode her horse over to help Jack with chores and that James' whereabouts were unknown for both murders.

"That's what you call "MOM', Ellie explained.

"What the heck is 'MOM'?" questioned Paul.

"Means, Opportunity, Motive," she replied.

"Well, at least we all agree it wasn't Shelley," stated Pastor B., still confused as to who really did it.

The other two looked at each other.

"Shelley," they said with renewed simultaneity.

It was 4:15 in the afternoon. The Sheriff was in Wally Setten's office. Andy Ratcliff was in Wally Setten's Office. Wally Setten was in Wally Setten's office. Shelley Robison was not in Wally Setten's office. There had been no message, no phone call, no telegram, no e-mail, no smoke signals, no pony express, and special delivery indicating that Shelley would not be present.

"OK Setten, now what?" asked the Sheriff. "I had her in custody yesterday. Now she's probably long gone."

"Oh, Goat quit being some melodramatic," said the defense attorney. "She probably had something come up and is delayed. Give her another ten minutes."

"Alright by me," quipped the County Attorney, knowing that his acquiescence would drive the Sheriff mad.

"You damned attorneys are…"

"Now, now, Sheriff, watch your language. There's a lady present," lightheartedly said the County Attorney. "Oh, that's right, she's not here."

Goat walked out the door and slammed it. He heard laughter behind the door he'd just shut.

"They just don't get it," spewed the Sheriff.

The Sheriff walked down the hall, took the elevator to the first floor, and then meandered through some offices to get to his own office, just off the jail.

"Hi, Dad," said the redheaded deputy who had just walk in from the other entrance.

She had Paul Banion with her.

"Why aren't you at Mr. Setten's office?" she asked. "Have you already brought Shelley over for booking?"

"She never showed up. Those two monkeys up there are laughing about it."

"She didn't show up? Dad, she was getting ready to come when I left. She was going to take a shower and drive over to see if she could see Jack at the hospital. She never came there either."

"I'm going to put out a bulletin on her," said the Sheriff.

The Sheriff saw the two young people in front of him look at each other and obviously make some kind of decision.

"Dad, we can prove it wasn't Shelley."

"It was the brother," interjected Paul.

"Which brother?" asked the Sheriff. "Mike's or Shelley's"

"Yes," they both replied.

"Rob, what are you doing here?" asked Shelley. "I don't want you here anymore."

"Sis," said Shelley's brother James, who was sitting in the chair across from Rob. "He's Mike's brother. He's family."

"James, that part of my life is over. He is not part of my family anymore. Now please, both of you leave. I have to get ready to go and surrender myself."

"Actually you don't," said Rob.

"Rob…"

"Keep quiet baby brother or you'll end up with her."

Shelley's heart skipped a beat.

"What do you mean?" she asked Rob, who was suddenly holding a pistol he'd taken from behind his back.

"James, what does he mean?" directing the question this time to her own brother.

Rob told James to go upstairs and get some clothes for Shelley. Rob returned with the outfit she had just gotten out of.

"You do look nice in pink," commented Rob. "Of course so does that friend of yours."

Shelley looked first at her brother then at Rob.

"It was you that hurt Jack."

"I'm not the shot your little brother is. Of course he was at closer range when he shot Mike. Now me… my choice of weapon is a Mac 10. It sprays bullets so nicely, it's hard to miss."

Pastor B. stayed at the hospital while Paul and Ellie raced over to the county offices to try to forestall any action against Shelley. Since he was directly involved and had been perceived by the Sheriff to be just as guilty as Shelley, it was decided he should remain with Jack in case he woke up.

At a little after five o'clock the nurse came in to say that Jack's surgery was complete and that he was in recovery and would be there for about 45 more minutes. Pastor B. decided to take the opportunity to call his wife and let her know what was happening.

"Hi, Honey," he started. "How are you?"

"Just fine, Luv," he replied, "How are you? How is Mr. Forester?"

"He just got out of surgery and will be in recovery for another 30 minutes or so."

"Is anyone else there?"

"Mr. Banion and Ellie were here, but they ran over to the County offices."

"And they left you there alone?"

"Yep. It was pretty important. Between the two of them, they think they've solved the two murders. They wanted to get over to where Shelley was supposed to be meeting with the County Attorney and Sheriff to answer questions."

"Shelley Robison?"

"Yes," replied the pastor.

"I didn't know she was still being questioned."

"Uh, well…I… uh…thought I told you."

"Well, she wasn't being questioned this afternoon; I just saw her driving through town about an hour ago. She was with her brother James. I just assumed they were going to the cemetery. Rob Robison was in the back seat with them."

"Oh, my!" said the pastor as he hung up. "Now what?"

I'm not one to panic, but if I were, it would probably have happened as Ellie and I left her father's office. The fact that Shelley had not shown up for her little get-together with the authorities was troubling from many different points of view. While Ellie and I disagreed on who had done the murders, we were certainly in agreement that Shelley had not and that right now she might be in trouble.

As we walked by the dispatcher's office, the woman behind the desk called Ellie over.

"There's some pastor trying to get hold of you. Says it's an emergency. Should I take a message?"

"No, I'll take it."

Ellie was on the phone for a minute or two at most, but each second seemed to drain more color from her face. I was despondent at the thought that my friend and comrade of so many years had met his end, for I was positive that it was the gregarious cleric informing us of Ox's demise.

Ellie turned to me, her lips quivering.

"They've got Shelley."

Chapter Twenty-Eight

"Planes, Trains, Automobiles, and Trucks"

Ellie sat down at the nearest desk and grabbed the phone. She directed Paul to do the same.

"Get a hold of the preacher's wife. Here's the number." Ellie rattled off the number from memory.

Paul pulled out a piece of paper from his shirt pocket and wrote it down. He picked up the call and got through right away. Mrs. Brooks was helpful only in that she was able to give the time she had seen the trio and the general direction they were headed.

Banion hung up the phone and looked again at the sheet of paper. He remembered that the Sheriff had given it to him to write down the number of the motorcycle that had been persuaded to yield to the Sheriff's car. Banion got up and walked over to the dispatcher.

"Can you get me the owner of this car? The license number is right here."

He handed the woman the slip of paper. The woman looked over to the redhead, who shook her head in the affirmative. Ellie remained on the phone in a heated conversation that did not seem to be going her way.

A couple of minutes later the dispatcher reported to Paul that the license came back on a rental from Econocar in Minneapolis. She had looked the number up and handed it over to Paul.

Paul jumped back to the desk he'd been using and made a call to the rental company. He used his official tone, explained that he was calling from the Maplewood County Sheriff's office, which he was, and that he needed to know who had rented the car.

When Paul got off the phone, he was smiling a small grin of satisfaction.

"Your dad just about clipped our suspect," Paul said to Ellie who was just hanging up her phone.

"Who?"

"Robert J. Robison was the licensed driver who rented the car that was seen, by your father, speeding and going through a stop sign about the time that Ox was probably injured."

"OK, but I still think James did it."

I was really impressed with Deputy Carlson. She took control of the situation and directed those around her, mostly me, to get things done in an orderly and organized fashion. I had made a couple of phone calls and had gotten information on the general direction the three people had gone. I'd also found out that the Sheriff had nearly arrested my suspect for reckless driving.

I was especially impressed to find out that the good Deputy had been on the phone with someone she knew at the local TV station. She had been able to finally negotiate the use of their corporate plane. I wasn't sure what Ellie had been forced to agree to, but it noticeably had not been something she had wanted to agree to.

The set up was that the plane would take off as soon as possible and try to bisect the probable path of the desperadoes. We assumed that they were heading south to get onto Highway 94 which ran the width of the state and would lead them most quickly to the Minneapolis-St. Paul area, where they would easily get lost and could then do away with their safety net, Shelley.

We alerted the Highway Patrol of the impending chase. Ellie did that in a very professional manner while going 60 miles an hour through downtown Hawks Hill. It was an improvement over her father.

We spoke little as we headed south and east on the major highway. We topped speeds of 110 miles an hour and zipped by trucks and cars as though they were standing still. At Alexandria we picked up a Minnesota Highway Patrolman. He swung in just behind us and radioed that he had not seen the vehicle in question.

The timing was such that we began to question whether our assumptions had been correct. We were able to connect with the plane that was coming north and which by that time had nearly reached St. Cloud. They too, had seen nothing.

Ellie quickly changed strategy and asked that the plane come back up Highway 71, which ran nearly parallel to 94 but went through every little town along the way. Less than ten minutes later we had them, or at least we had their car.

"Car 54, we have the vehicle in question on visual. They appear to have been in an accident."

"10-4. What kind of accident?" I asked as Ellie continued to drive, heading for the first exit that would get us over to 71.

"Car and train. The train looks like it won. Location is approximately 3 miles south of Oakley. There appear to be emergency vehicles in route."

"10-4, Please remain on scene until we get there," I asked the pilot.

We arrived on the scene of the accident about two minutes after the local emergency crews.

"One fatality," reported the police officer who met us as we got out of the car. "We've been following you guys on the radio for the last half hour. Not surprised it ended this way. It's one way to get your perp."

Ellie and I moved forward with dread, assuming the fatality was our friend. The car was a mangled mess, although the passenger compartment was relatively undamaged. The paramedic lifted the yellow oilcloth to reveal a blonde head. Both of us took a deep breath as he did so. Both of us let the breath out as we saw that the body was that of Shelley's brother, James.

Shelley couldn't quit crying even after Rob had slapped her a couple of times. Her brother had been decent enough to turn his back when Ellie took off the robe to put on her clothes. Not so Rob. He'd even made a move to touch her breasts, but she slapped his hand away.

After she was dressed, they had forced her to reveal where she had hidden the memorial cards. They took time to rip them open and absconded with about $300 in cash that good folks had given to help defray costs of the funeral. Rob had called it "Going Away Money" and had gotten a good laugh out of it. James had been quiet.

Long-term plans did not seem to be in strong supply.

"You drive," Rob had demanded of the weeping woman. "Jimmy-boy, you sit up there in front with her."

The ensuing hours had been ones of sheer terror for the woman, ending only when, in a moment of desperation she drove headlong into the side of a train standing on a rail spur. Her hope had been that Rob, who was sitting in back without a seatbelt, would be hurdled through the windshield to his death. But it had been her brother, with both lap and shoulder belt in place who had died immediately upon impact.

"You stupid, stupid bitch," yelled Rob as he extricated himself from the rear seat of the car. He broke the remaining glass out of the driver's side window and pull Shelley out by the hair, raking her back over the remnants of glass.

"Get moving," he had demanded.

They had walked a couple of blocks, when they heard sirens.

"In there," Rob directed her into a small yard completely enclosed by shrubs that were six feet high. He kept his gun on her.

"Shut up," he said to her whimpers, pleading that she be let go. "I need you now more than ever."

Just then a man drove up with a pickup truck just like Jack's. He parked the vehicle next to the yard the two were hiding in, walked into the enclosure and headed for the house. Rob quickly sprung up behind him and clobbered him on the head. As he did so, Shelley ran through the gate and took a sharp left. She kept running and running and running.

She ran past a police officer, she ran past two children watching as the demolished car was pulled from the train, she ran past Ellie and she ran past Paul. She ran until she could run no more. Then she heard a gunshot and her nightmare ended.

Both Ellie and I realized immediately that the remaining two passengers of the car had likely not gone far. We informed the local constabulary that there were indeed two more passengers including a blonde woman, likely a hostage. They fanned out, as did we.

We had been looking a few minutes when the twin of my vintage Chevrolet pickup pulled up in front of a house not more than a hundred yards down. I half expected to see Ox jump out and greet me. But, alas the driver was a little old man who probably had bought the truck new. As I watched the man walk into his yard, I was shocked to see a blonde phantom come flying out of the same gate and come running right at us.

Shelley ran past the officer who was just a little ahead of us. He yelled at her but to no avail. The crazed woman ran past her friend as though she was not there and totally ignored my outstretched arms. I turned to see her stagger another hundred yards and then stumble and fall just as a shot rang out.

The Deputy's weapon had been at the ready as she walked along the road. Shelley had blown by her just like she wasn't there. Ellie resisted the urge to go after her friend and instead was watching the gate as Rob Robison came out and jumped into the cab of the pickup.

"Hold it right there, Rob." She had shouted, pulling out her weapon.

A police officer just ahead of her had pulled his weapon as well.

The two officers moved ahead on the suspect. Ellie looked in and saw that the man was attempting to turn the key, but to no affect.

"Rob, give it up," the Deputy shouted.

The man took his hand from the inoperable key.

"It won't start. It won't start!" he shouted.

Then his hand reached for the gun on the seat. Both officers again shouted warnings. But Rob Robison would not be warned.

Chapter Twenty-Nine

"Alone"

Christmas was Pastor B.'s favorite time of year. It was a time of renewal, of peace, of forgiveness, and gift giving and gift receiving. It was also a time of reflection for the cleric; a time for him to use the life events of the previous years as fodder for his sermons. This year he was especially blessed with provisions for his sermon fare.

In the past five months there had been a lot of healing. Shelley had finally started coming back to church after being absent for nearly three months.

"Yes, it had been her brother's funeral," reflected the pastor. "That was the last time she was here."

The good pastor had received a Christmas card from his delinquent member Jack Forester. It was a beach scene with a message saying, "I'm on the mend. See you soon."

Jack had been hospitalized for nearly ten days. Despite Pastor B's offers to find medical and nursing help, Jack had decided to head back to his native California for his recuperation.

Pastor and Mary Brooks had taken Paul Banion under their wing, introducing him to people in town, inviting him to supper, trying to find him a mate, and finally welcoming him into membership in their church. Pastor had gone out to visit Paul several times and was always surprised that Paul would show up within seconds of his arrival. It was like he had a built in fifth sense. If only the pastor had known that his very presence immediately set off all sorts of alarms.

Despite his voting for Jim Barton, Pastor B had congratulated Goat Carlson when he won his re-election. Pastor had heard that Jim had offered to resign when he lost the election. Goat had been magnanimous in victory, promoting Jim to Chief Deputy.

"But I am Chief Deputy," Jim had said upon hearing the news.

"Well, I demoted you yesterday about noon," said the Sheriff referring to Election Day.

Ellie Carlson received a citation for her work on the Trojan Horse case, by which name it became known. Her idea to use the truck and trailer to gain access to the nearly invasion proof drug factory has been used in five states and Ellie has become a folk hero for the way she had handled it.

Meanwhile:

"Hey boss, did you see this story from Minnesota? Don't that guy look like E.Z."

"He sure does. He damn sure does."

The End

The Farmer Stands Alone
Bill E. Schultz

www.ingramcontent.com/pod-product-compliance
Lightning Source LLC
Chambersburg PA
CBHW071246170626
46809CB00001B/83